WHEN DOVES LAUGHED

BERYL CARPENTER

"A longing fulfilled is a tree of life." Proverbs 13:12 (NIV)

authorHOUSE®

AuthorHouse™
1663 Liberty Drive
Bloomington, IN 47403
www.authorhouse.com
Phone: 1 (800) 839-8640

Published by AuthorHouse   10/05/2017

ISBN: 978-1-5462-1072-6 (sc)
ISBN: 978-1-5462-1073-3 (e)

To Rhoda and Janice,
great encouragers and best of friends

ACKNOWLEDGMENTS

— • —

I started this journey to produce one book about Sara Elena and the expulsion of the Jews from Spain in 1492. Somehow, the saga has grown as Sara exerted her desire and determination to overcome a caravel-sized boatload of obstacles. Along the way, I learned to love the research, plotting, building characters and discovering the ending that would satisfy me and my readers.

My husband, Robert, provided untold hours of editing and timeline checking. The Saturday Panera bunch, my invaluable critique group, gave good counsel and their unique perspectives. Joy provided a thorough final check.

Readers kept asking, "When's the next book going to be ready?"

To all of you, thanks.

Beryl Carpenter
August 2017

SARA

Chapter 1

Naples, 29 March 1494

"Fire!"

Sara's scream woke Juanito. He joined in with wails of his own. She stumbled to his cradle and picked up her little boy. She patted his back.

"Be still, Juanito. If you waken Raul and Beata again, they won't let us stay here. I'll sing to you." Sara patted and jostled her little one as she hummed a lullaby. She sat on the edge of the bed in her brother Raul's guest room and rocked back and forth. A whiff of air whispered above her. The motion and sound calmed both of them. Finally, Juanito took a deep breath. His body relaxed as he fell asleep again. On tiptoe, Sara made her way back to the cradle Raul had fashioned for her baby. Juanito didn't wake as she slipped him back into his bed.

Sara returned to her own bed and sat on top of the covers, legs bent.

"When will I be free of this menace?" The darkened room made no reply.

It's been a week since the fire that destroyed my restaurant and apartment above. I need to put the horror behind me. But, what a fire! It began in the dark hours before sunrise, with a crimson moon hanging in the sky. Church bells raised the whole neighborhood to come douse the flames. I escaped with little time to spare.

At the time, I could only grab Juanito and stuff a few essentials into a bag. Smoke stung my eyes. Juanito startled and sucked in the foul air. Church bells called the town to pass buckets of water, but in the end my home and restaurant were destroyed. The moon, yes—I remember the reddish glow of the moon. Sara shuddered.

Later, Captain Ferlandini found me and helped me out of danger.

"What's the news about Juan and my brother Luis? Did Columbus find them at La Navidad and bring them back on his second voyage? I have to know," I said.

"I'm sorry," said Ferlandini. "It seems the whole crew of the wrecked Santa Maria was destroyed by a fire in the fortress. We didn't find many bodies."

Is Juan really gone? And Luis, too? I always hoped they would return.

Sara shivered at the distressing images. She slipped back under the pale coverlet and closed her eyes.

* * * *

Sara awoke late after sleeping fitfully the rest of the night. She sat up and saw Juanito sitting in the cradle, eyes on her.

"Hi, little one. Why is your mother still in bed? Why won't she come and take care of you? Is that what you think?"

Juanito's eye dilated. He sat still for a moment considering, then opened his mouth in a pink-gummed, four-tooth grin.

"Blub."

Sara's laughter bubbled out like a fountain. She jumped up and reached for Juanito.

"Funny boy. You say the wisest things." She tickled him under the soft folds of his chin. "You're getting plump. Well done." Juanito struggled through the diaper changing. Sara pressed one elbow on the squirming child to keep him in place.

"You are an adventure, little boy." She tapped a finger on his nose. "Now, let's get you dressed."

By the time she tended to herself and got down the stairs, the church bells pealed the time. Nine o'clock.

"No wonder you're wiggly. You must be hungry." She hurried to get to the kitchen, her skirts swishing as she walked down Beata's well-scrubbed tile hall. "Hello, Beata. Sorry I'm late. Another night of tortured sleep."

"You need your rest, after what you've endured." Beata patted her on her shoulder. "Have something to eat." She swirled out of the room, chasing little Angela.

Sara tore a piece of bread off the loaf she bought yesterday and cut some bits of cooked carrots she saved overnight for Juanito. She sat him on her lap and let him eat from her hands. The bench creaked.

"I don't even have a table. All I do is sit on my brother's bench and fight off my terrors in the night. And my home is a charred mess!" Her voice rose.

"Goo."

"What did you say?"

"Goo."

"You're right. I should 'go' and do something about it. No more moping!" She punctuated her words with a fist on one leg. Juanito made a fist and hit her on the leg, too. He laughed.

"Let's go right out and find a carpenter to make some furniture. And rebuild our home. Should we do it, Juanito?"

Juanito bobbed his head.

Sara smiled as she cleaned Juanito's face and wrapped him onto her back.

"You are too heavy to carry like a baby anymore, Juanito. You're a big boy."

"Bi—"

"Is that a first word?" Sara cocked her head and listened. No answer from Juanito. "Just a coincidence, I think." She grabbed a straw bag and stepped out the door. "Let's find that carpenter Raul told me about. I want the best one in Naples."

Sara strode forward as fast as she could in the shoes Fortunata had lent her. The sky hung blue overhead, draped with white swaths of clouds. The air smelled fragrant, like sprigs of rosemary and lavender tucked into a clean bed. Sara stopped to inhale. A gray cat sidled up to her and twirled around one foot as she started walking again.

She stubbed her toe. "Ow, these shoes are too big and too worn. I can feel every cobblestone." She stopped to swat the cat away and massage her toe, and then wrinkled her nose. "Guess I need some shoes, and a dress that doesn't smell like smoke." Sara continued on her way with a smile. People passed her on the street with a wave and "*Buon giorno.*" She nodded but kept going. At the third corner, she turned onto a side street.

"Almost there. I know there's a carpenter shop or two on this block." Sara walked along the tree-lined street. Tiny finches flitted from branch to branch gathering their daily rations. Sara pointed to a dog yawning and stretching in a shaft of sunlight. "Do you see the dog, Juanito?"

She felt Juanito wave his hands and wiggle his legs.

"Gog!"

"That's right—dog. Clever boy!" Sara felt Juanito wave his arms. Sara moved along looking for just the right place. "Raul told me there's a shop here that makes the most beautiful chairs, with carved acanthus leaves and scrollwork. I don't suppose I can afford that, Juanito. Well, maybe just one. The others should be practical and functional." She sniffed the air. "I smell newly cut wood." She stopped. "Here it is."

'Carlo the Carpenter,' the sign said. Stacks of wood lined both sides of the wide doorway. Some boards were thick and rough. Sara ran her hand along those and got a speck in her finger. "Ouch." A sudden gust of wind lifted sawdust into the air. Sara inhaled the most delicious piney smell, like stepping into a forest glen, fresh and prickly to the nose. She ran her hand along a stack of smooth boards and detected a faint, earthy aroma. She remembered her mother making a creamy white candy and stirring in a handful of nuts shaped like butterflies that smelled just like that.

"A smell can take you back to your childhood. Ha, this is your childhood. Right, Juanito?" Juanito squirmed.

A man bent over a plank of wood jerked his head up.

"*Signora*. How can I help you?" The man pulled a rag from his pocket and wiped dust off his face. "Excuse my manners. This is a dirty place. Please sit down." He pulled out a chair for Sara and wiped it off. She unstrapped Juanito and held him in her lap.

"Hello, my name is Carlo." He bowed and rubbed a hand through his salt and pepper hair. Bits of sawdust cascaded onto the floor.

"*Signor* Carlo, I had a fire in my place last week. I need some new furniture."

"Was that the fire during the night a couple of weeks ago?" He scratched his ear with a callused hand.

"Just a week ago, but yes. That's the one. I need furniture for my apartment and also for the restaurant below. So, I need to get a fair deal from you. Good quality but not fancy. If I give you a lot of work, I need a reasonable price from you."

"I can help you, *signora*. Let's start with the apartment. Tell me what you need built. First your home, no?"

"That's right." Sara bounced Juanito. "First, the stairs need to be rebuilt. Then, I need a bed for this little one. He's growing fast. Then a bed frame for me, and two dressers, a small table and two chairs." She fingered the carved work on the chair she sat on. "Could the two chairs for the apartment be like this one?"

"A good choice. You need something a little finer after your ordeal. What's next—for the restaurant?"

"Well, I need lots of tables and chairs, at least six tables and maybe benches or chairs to go with them. I need a counter built in the kitchen and new doors throughout. And shutters. And new stairs."

"That is a large order."

"It all depends on the price. I have some money, but will it cover all that? I don't know." She shrugged her shoulders. "I did this once before, and not long ago, when I first bought the restaurant."

"Let's just start with the apartment furniture. We can make arrangements about the stairs. Now, look through my workshop and see if you can use any of the things I already have made."

Sara picked her way through the workshop. Several bed frames leaned against one wall. Next to it, several chests of drawers gleamed with coats of varnish. A few small writing tables perched along the wall next to the chest. "Here's another chair with carved leaves." She stroked it like a beloved child. "I'll take this bed frame, this chest and two of the chairs with carved leaves." She ran her hand over the smooth wooden surfaces. "And this writing desk. That's all for now." Sara swirled around and looked the man in the eye. "Oh, and a small bed for a child. I didn't see one."

"I will give you a good price for the whole order. Let me write it for you." Carlo limped to a desk in one corner and brushed dust off of it. He took a quill and parchment and made a list. "Here you are. See the price. Do you agree to that?"

"I suppose so, but I'd like to ask my brother for advice about the rest." Sara accepted the parchment and folded it. She stuffed it in her bag.

"I'm sure I have a small bed in my shop, *signora*. What's your name?"

"Sara Sánchez."

"*Signora* Sánchez. Why didn't your husband come with you?"

"He's— he's gone on a long voyage." She looked away, her voice strained. Juanito pulled her hair. "Stop it, little one."

"Very well, *Signora* Sánchez, Please consult with your brother. You have much to consider." He bowed low.

"I admit I'm dazed. I want the furniture for the apartment, Signor Carlo, and will have to think about the rest of it. I'll come back tomorrow." She handed him some coins. "This is all I can pay today as a deposit."

"There's no need for that now." Carlo gave the coins back. "This afternoon I'll have my apprentice load the child's bed and the other bed in a cart and bring it to you. You will need that, at least. And I'll send someone to build new stairs whenever you decide. Best wishes, *signora*." He smiled and bowed several times.

"Bless you, Carlo." Sara left, one burden lifted. She stubbed her toe as she walked up the street. "I know what I need to do next, Juanito."

"Goo."

"No, shoes!" She laughed.

Sara's next stop at a cobbler's shop produced a flurry of measuring and showing of soft leathers and sole-making materials, 'for the lady's inspection.' She chose black leather with buttons and decorative stitching. The cobbler nodded his approval and measured her foot.

"When will they be ready?" said Sara. "I need them quickly, as I'm wearing borrowed shoes."

"Two days should be enough for me to have them ready, *signora.*"

"I'll pay you this much now and the rest when I get them, signor." He dipped his head in acknowledgment as she placed some coins in his hand.

Sara exited the shop and returned to Raul and Beata's. She fed a fidgety Juanito and put him to bed for a nap. "Beata, could you watch Juanito while I shop for a dress?"

"Go, Sara. I'm here with Angela already. She's sleeping, too. Take your time. Did you decide on furniture?"

"It's too confusing and too much. I need to consult Raul tonight." Sara shouldered her bag and opened the heavy door. "The shopping shouldn't take long."

"And get two," said Beata.

"What?" Sara paused.

"Get two dresses. You need them." Beata smiled and waved her out the door.

Outside, the sun beamed down on chattering robins and revealed all manner of green tendrils pushing up between cobblestones, along the wall, in the corners and even in roof gutters. Weeds pushed through boldly, yellow wildflowers twirled their new skirts, warming oregano and woodsy rosemary exuded their fragrances. Ferns unfurled and fiery geraniums flaunted their spring finery. The bouquet of smells, colors and shapes from these intrepid plants overpowered her senses as she stepped quickly along the streets. *Spring is here!*

Where's that dressmaker's shop? On this block or the next? Sara quickened her pace and not just because of anticipation. For the last block she sensed someone following her. Two people were matching her steps, keeping a few paces behind her. *If I can just make it around the next corner—I can dash into the shop. I know it's there.* Sara panted for air. Her heart raced.

"*Signora* Sánchez?" A hand caught her shoulder. "You need to come with us."

"Who are you?" She spun and stared at the thin one. "Did Morales send you?"

"How did you know that?" The short one clamped his hand down tighter.

"I remember you both. You helped Morales chase me across Spain." Sara struggled to free herself from the one holding her. "I'll never go with you." She dodged to one side, but too late.

One of them knocked her on the head. The world spun.

Chapter 2

✳

Sara's eyelids fluttered and opened. She rolled on her side. *It's getting dark! Where am I? How did I get here?* She touched the tender spot on the back of her head, a lump that throbbed with intensity. *Oh, I remember. Morales! His servants came to get me and I refused to be taken.* She winced. *I have a grand headache because of it.*

Sara looked around at her surroundings. It was a good-sized room furnished with a bed, which she was lying on. In another part of the room sat a heavy table with dark wood and an ornate pedestal supporting it, a new design she'd only heard of. The chairs matched in careful detail and dimension. A brocaded cloth was thrown over it, and a silver candelabrum displayed itself in the center. Wrought iron barred the one window, but a brocade drape softened the prison-like effect. A large copper bowl with glowing coals burned in another corner.

Sara slid her legs over the edge of the bed and got up. She tried the door handle. Locked! *A few bangs should rouse someone.* She hit the solid door as hard as she could. She shook her sore hand and then kicked with her foot. "Let me out, let me out! Come here and let me out!" The sound echoed throughout the silent house. Soon, Sara heard footsteps and a key in the door. Creak! The door swung open.

"At last. You need to let me—" She rushed the door trying to get past whoever was coming in. A strong hand stopped her. "You again!" shouted Sara. "Why are you holding me?" She looked eye to eye with the thin one.

"My name is Alexo, and I'm Padre Morales' steward. Paco, grab her arms and set her in the chair." Paco, though a bull of a man, quickly fulfilled the command. "It would go much easier for everyone if you cooperated," said Alexo. "Will you do that?" Sara shrugged her shoulders. Paco guarded the door.

Alexo ducked out the door and returned with arms full. "Now, señora, first some light." He produced a candle and lit the silver candlestick." Next, I've brought a basin and hot water, soap, toweling and a fresh dress. And a mirror."

He set these on one end of the table and crossed his arms. "You put up a struggle when we came to escort you here. Didn't she, Paco?"

"Ay, what a fight," said Paco. "I have scratches on both arms!" He displayed his wounds.

"All I remember is a knock on the head. I don't trust you and I certainly don't trust Don Antonio." Sara's sharp words sliced the air. "After his attack on me, he disappeared. We all thought he was dead. Even a body floated in the harbor. Now, here he is alive—and again stalking me."

"You must realize." Alexo spoke as if instructing a child, "This will be your permanent home beginning today. Your outbursts will gain you nothing."

"But I have a baby, Juanito! He needs me." Sara responded by running toward the door again and pounding both fists on Paco's ample middle. He grabbed her wrists and twisted them behind her back quick as a seaman tying a knot. "Ow!" Sara stamped her feet, but Paco evaded her heels with a few dancelike steps.

"Your baby will be cared for by your brother and his wife. That's where you were presently staying, no?"

"Yes, but—"

"You have a new life now. You promised yourself to Padre Morales, so you must keep that pledge."

"I didn't mean it. I never wanted it." Sara let her arms fall to her sides and returned to sit on the chair. "What happens now?"

"You need to wash your face and prepare to meet Don Antonio. He's eager to see you when you are properly readied. Do that now." Alexo turned to go. "You have one hour to look your best. Use the time wisely." Paco followed Alexo out the door. A key turned in the lock.

I'm alone. What are my options? None. Sara touched the dress on the table. It was fern green and had long full sleeves with leaves embroidered along the edges. *This is a beautiful gown—a houppelande. And I need one. If I can find a way to escape, then I'll have at least one new dress. But what a way to earn it! And it's so fancy.* Sara took the scented soap and began washing her face. *My only way out of here is through that door, so I'd better play along with the game as long as I can.*

Sara took a good long time to clean and improve her appearance. The soap smelled of olive oil and lemon verbena, she noticed, as she scrubbed her hands and face. *I'll use it to shampoo my hair, too.* But when she finished toweling her hair, she gasped. *Isn't there a brush? Just like a man to forget that essential! I'll have to braid and coil my hair and find a brush when I escape. That will be a tangle.*

Sara slipped the green *houppelande* over her head with care not to disturb the arrangement of hair she'd just improvised. The gown full in the skirts but fitted in the torso, had laces in front, which made it possible for her to complete the dressing herself. *Maybe I can talk to Don Antonio and convince him I must return to care for my baby.* She looked in the mirror. *At least I look decent.* She slipped on Fortunata's borrowed shoes and spread the gown's skirts out as she sat down on a chair.

Soon a key clicked in the door lock and the person she never wanted to see stepped into the room. Don Antonio Morales turned the key on the inside and fastened it to a chain on his belt. Sara watched every move of the dreadful man, all senses heightened.

"Good evening, Sara." He bowed with a flourish. Her jaw dropped. Morales noticed and giggled.

"You're not wearing your clerical garments," said Sara.

"No. I had this men's *houppelande* made to be just like yours, long and flowing with draping sleeves."

"And it's green! I've never seen you wear green." Sara covered her mouth with one hand.

Morales swept farther into the room, promenading back and forth. "I really enjoy having a rich garment for a change. It's only to wear at home, of course, but I indulged because you have finally come to live here." He gazed at her and smiled with gray teeth and lips. Morales coughed and spit into his handkerchief. "Well, what do you think?"

"It certainly brings out the color in your face, *señor*." Sara stifled a shudder. *He's not well. He looks terrible. Green like his robe.*

"Thank you, Sara." A slimy smile oozed over his face. Don Antonio pulled at his sleeves and smoothed back his silver-streaked hair. On his hand he wore a ring with a large red stone. It shone in the candlelight and its facets bounced red fireflies all around the room. "I have great hopes for tonight." He glanced at her a little too long.

Sara felt her face color. She looked down at her folded hands.

"Would you like to know my plans?" Don Antonio asked.

"Very well—yes."

"We'll have something to eat first. You must be hungry."

"I'm sure I couldn't eat a thing."

"Don't be so modest. We'll have a good meal while we exchange pleasantries. We'll get to know each other better. Would you like that?"

"That sounds horrible." Sara spoke under her breath.

"What?"

"If you want to." She lifted her chin.

"Good." Morales rang a bell and within seconds servants appeared with dishes, cutlery and goblets. After the table was set, a servant presented the two of them with a first plate—cold asparagus with olive oil, and a loaf of crusty bread. Morales picked up the bread and tore off a piece. Its crust broke into a score of pieces. A stray sunbeam caught the flaky snowstorm. "Ah, *crujiente,* crunchy. And for you, my dear?" He handed Sara the loaf and she broke off a small piece.

Sara picked at her food, although she loved asparagus. Morales tore into his bread and devoured the asparagus spears whole. "Not hungry, my dear?" He leaned over the table. With his beaky nose and green robe he was a strange tropical bird. Sara frowned and shrank back. *How can I get away with that key so out of reach on his belt?*

A key turned in the lock. Wonderful smells preceded the servants through the doors—rich and savory aromas. Sara's stomach growled. "Mm." She offered a smile as she gazed at the offerings: beef stew with chickpeas and carrots, and a plate of sizzling mushrooms cooked in garlic butter.

"Getting an appetite now, Sara?" Don Antonio filled her goblet with red wine and re-filled his own. "Surely your passionate nature includes enjoyment of food." He raised his goblet. "To your health—*salud*—and to our new beginnings together." He arched his black eyebrows and curled one side of his upper lip. Sara choked and nearly spit out the wine.

"I don't know what you mean, sir." She chewed on a bite of tender beef, letting the taste and seasonings lull her into serenity again.

"You are mine now, finally my own, and I won't let you go. No pleading, no excuses will make me change my mind. I've waited too long. Besides, your husband is dead. Just accept that fact." He took a large spoonful of chickpeas and shoved them in his mouth, while continuing to talk. "You may as well decide to submit to me. This arrangement is permanent." He took a breath and choked on his food. Gasps and heaves followed and then real, ragged coughs as his illness asserted itself. He spat a blot of bright blood and chickpeas onto his plate and wiped his mouth with a napkin.

"You are not well. You won't live long enough to have a relationship with me." Sara threw down her napkin and stood up. "That suits me well."

"Be seated," hissed Don Antonio. "Now, a dessert for your pleasure and then—"

The servants brought in a lemon sponge *torta*, a tangy cake with raisins and whipped cream, and removed the dinner plates. Sara ate in spite of the way Don Antonio was acting. "I have plans," he said. "Couldn't you love me just a little—*un poco*?" Sara gave him a faint suggestion of a smile. *He really is a pathetic creature—and evil itself.*

Finally, the servants cleared all the dishes and cutlery, closed the drape at the window and bowed out. The key turned and clicked behind them. Don Antonio looked at Sara, then, his chin high, and eyebrows arched. His lips parted in an sliding smile. "At last, we are alone."

I don't like what's happening! Sara jumped up and began pacing around the room. "Thank you for the wonderful dinner, Don Antonio. I was hungry, after all." Sara clenched her hands as she walked.

"Anything for you, Sara." Don Antonio pushed the heavy chair away from the table and unfolded his angular body. Sara heard one knee pop into place. Then he cracked his knuckles and gave a polite cough. "I'll join you on your *paseo,* your evening walk around the room, my dear." He drew closer to Sara and tried to take her hand. She stiffened and clasped her hands behind her. He took her elbow.

Sara stopped near the table and turned toward Morales. "Nothing has changed, Don Antonio. I never intended to be your companion. And I don't want that now. I have a baby, and I'm hoping my husband is alive." The flames of the candles glowed in Don Antonio's dark eyes. *Almost like anger.*

"That is unfortunate," he said with measured words. "But, it's irrelevant." His hand sliced the air, dismissing Sara's words with a gesture. "You made a promise and now you will keep it." Morales grabbed at Sara's arm and moved closer, lips puckered. "Kiss me now, Sara. I will give you what you desire." She dodged his mouth. "I hope that's me." He gripped harder and tried again. His lips brushed hers, thin, dry and insistent. She wrenched free, leaned over the table and blew out the candles of the great shiny candlestick. The room compressed into blackness.

Sara stubbed her toes, but got herself to the other side of the table. She listened in the darkness to the slow, dragging steps of Morales. And his coughs. He couldn't conceal those. She tiptoed to the far side of the room near the bed. She hid behind the drape that separated the sleeping quarters from the great table.

"You can't hide from me, Sara. I will find you." Morales hissed under his breath. Sara imagined a slithering snake, forked tongue sensing her location in the shadows. She cringed. She edged out from around the bed toward the table again. Morales followed her slowly.

"I have excellent hearing. I know where you are, Sara. I told the servants not to disturb us. Any noises they hear they will think of as our courting games." His quiet voice penetrated the air. Then a spasm and coughing engulfed him. "Ack." He spat.

Give me strength! Sara reached for the candlestick. *It's too heavy!* She pulled at the heavy cloth it sat on. Morales came closer, dragging his shoes across the tiles. She heard another round of retching coughs and spitting. Sara felt hot breath on her neck.

"There you are, my dear." Don Antonio's bony fingers clamped on her shoulder. Sara's hands finally closed around the candlestick's base. She lifted it and turned a little too quickly, bringing the candlestick around and down onto his arm. "Ay!" He bellowed, and grabbed her again with both hands. Sara raised the candlestick between them. In their struggle, she pulled away and swung the heavy candle stand up and then around in an arc with all her might. She heard a crunching of bone, a moan and silence. She heard Morales fall backward.

What have I done? Sara moved away. She slipped on a sticky puddle on the floor and dropped the candlestick. Stumbling around in the dark, she edged closer to where she thought Morales lay. She bent down, found him and felt for a pulse in his neck. *Nothing.* She put her hand to his mouth. *No breath.*

He's dead!

At last. The thought came all too quickly. Her shoulders felt heavy. *I've desired this for a long time, but not by my hand.* Sara shuddered. A terrible coldness gripped her.

Beryl Carpenter

Sara searched Morales' body for the chain on his belt. She fumbled at its knot till it came off. *Wait! I should grab my bag and old dress.* Using her hands, she reached out into darkness and felt around the room till her fingers found the desired items. On tiptoe, she grabbed her things and slipped the key in the door. Click. She peeked out. Empty hall. She saw a light down the hall and heard talking from what looked like the kitchen area.

"Don't you think we should investigate? Something has happened." Alexo's voice sounded a note of alarm.

Sara sprinted the other direction on silent feet, found the door and escaped out to the street.

Chapter 3

❋

Sara's mind raced even faster than her legs. As she reached the first corner, she glanced back. A bright light shone through the open door. And she heard noises—voices—coming from Don Antonio's abode.

Sara kept to the shadows and rounded the corner. She paused to take a couple of ragged breaths, and then stretched her legs out. A painful muscle cramp gripped her right calf. She bit her lip and trotted down the street again limping, disappearing around the second corner.

Will they follow me? I'm sure they know where I live. What can I do? Sara turned an ear toward the street she had just taken. *It's quiet. I guess I'm safe enough for now—if I don't waste any time.* Her struggle with Don Antonio had drained her and now this run—Sara groaned. *I'm exhausted!*

Sara tried the latch on Raul's door. *It's stuck—no, locked!*

"Raul! Beata! It's me, Sara. Open the door!" Sara screamed as loudly as she could and banged on the heavy oaken door. A couple of heads popped out of neighboring windows.

"What's the matter? Are you crazy? It's late!" Sara ducked her head and listened at the door.

"Who's that? Sara? I'm coming!" Sounds of running feet, a crying baby, a creaking door—

Raul's face peeked out. "Sara, is that really you? Where have you been? Do you know what time it is?"

Sara pushed her way past all of Raul's questions. She got inside and Raul closed the door. "I was captured by Don Antonio's men. Knocked on the head and taken to his house.

I just escaped and I need to hide." Sara dropped her bag and leaned over, hands on her thighs, chest heaving. Sweat beads found a trail along her nose and cascaded from the end of it.

Raul hugged her. "We have been worried about you. You didn't come back after shopping. It's been hours." He held her out at arm's length. His eyes glowed.

Beata came into the light, her hair a golden cascade falling over her shoulders. She carried a sleepy Angela and a sniffling Juanito. Sara reached out for Juanito.

"Raul, calm yourself," said Beata. "Tell us what happened, Sara. And where did you get that lovely gown? Surely not from the dressmaker?"

"I didn't mean to be gone this long, but Morales held me prisoner."

"What?"

"It's true. Two men followed me as I went to the dressmaker's shop. Morales' servants. When I refused to go with them, they knocked me on the head. Next thing I knew, I woke up in Morales' residence."

"Again? Another abduction?" Raul's shout startled Angela, who let out a cry.

"Yes. Since I wouldn't go willingly, they—his servants-- kidnapped me and told me I would now live with Morales as I promised."

"No!"

"You know I never intended to do that. Just made a bargain to get Margarita out of prison. Since then, or even before that, I guess, he's been obsessed with having me for himself." Sara shuddered.

"How did you get the new gown?"

"Morales gave it to me. Wanted me to dress in my finest and dine with him. A celebration— 'a new beginning,' he said. Ugh!" Sara stuck out her tongue.

"How did you get free?" Raul's forehead creased as his eyebrows shot up.

"I don't have much time to tell you all this. They could have followed me here." Sara stared at the door.

"Please."

"The servants left us alone while we dined. I pretended to take a *paseo* around the room after dinner. Don Antonio followed and tried to kiss me. I panicked and ran to blow the candles out. In the darkness, we stumbled around the room. I tried to be quiet, but he heard me. Just when he grabbed me, I found the table, pulled the candlestick to where I could reach it and swung it around to keep him away from me. Unfortunately, it hit him—in the head—and he fell to the ground."

Beata gasped.

"It was then I got the keys off his belt and unlocked the door. Nobody was in the hall then, so I ran and got out the door before I heard noises behind." Sara let out a sigh.

"Is he dead? Did you—?" Beata sucked in her breath.

"I think so, though I didn't mean to kill him. Just keep him away. So, his servants may come after me at any moment." Sara nodded.

On cue, someone banged on the door.

"Hide!" Raul whispered. Sara ran to the guest bedroom carrying Juanito. She climbed into the wardrobe and folded the clothing in front of her. Juanito sneezed.

"Quiet, little one." She patted her young son on the back. She heard the heavy front door creak.

"Where's Sara Elena Sánchez?" She heard the muffled words through many folds of fabric.

"Do you know where she is? She's been gone for hours." Raul's voice powered over the others'.

"Señor Torres, there's no need to lie. I know she's here. And I have something to tell her." *That's Paco's voice,* thought Sara.

"Are you here to arrest her? She has a baby to raise."

"I know all about her. Don Antonio talked about her every day. Thought of nobody else. Please." Sara made her way through the hanging clothing and exited the wardrobe. She dragged herself slowly up the hall and faced a breathless Paco.

"I didn't mean to kill him. Truly, I didn't. Will you arrest me?" She hugged Juanito closer.

"I have no authority to do that. Señora Sara—and I have no heart to cause you pain. I'm just a humble servant." Paco looked at her with a steady gaze. "I came to tell you I'm sorry. Sorry for all the trouble you've had. Don Antonio has persecuted you. Followed you for many months. I just wanted to say that we understand that."

"Where's Alexo?"

"He's preparing the body for burial."

"I need to leave now, don't I? But, I didn't try to kill Don Antonio." Sara's words spilled out in a stream. She paused. "You have to believe me."

"We will bury Don Antonio here and then leave Naples," said Paco. "We will return to Spain and will have to report our master's death to the Inquisition. You will be safe here for a while. But, I think the Inquisition will send an investigator here to dig into the details of his death. Our master, Don Antonio Morales was powerful, you know, so it will be looked into."

"I'm very sorry." Sara bit her lip.

"He was sick, of course," said Paco. "Consumption would have taken him in a few months." He turned to go. "Don't blame yourself."

"However, the Inquisition may not see it the same way." Paco bobbed his head.

Sara stood there with open mouth. She watched Morales' servant leave.

"I think you're safe for a few hours." Raul shoved her toward the bedroom. "Go lie down. When the sun comes up, we'll make a plan for you." Sara shuffled down the hall, her green gown swishing with every step.

"To bed, Juanito. Are you as tired as I am?" Juanito gurgled a reply and Sara eased him back into his bed. Then she unlaced and unbound herself from the volumes of green brocade and laid it over a chair. Sara slipped into her sleep shift and unwound her braided hair. She slid herself under the covers and laid her head on the snowy pillow.

I sought the Lord and he answered me; he delivered me from all my fears. The familiar psalm tiptoed into her mind. *Lord, help me once again. I have many fears.* She closed her eyes and drifted into sleep.

* * * *

The next morning came too soon.

"Do you realize you came home last night about one o'clock in the morning?" Raul greeted her with a question and a hug as Sara walked into the kitchen, Juanito on one hip.

"I never heard the church bells, then or this morning." She sat down and plopped Juanito on her lap. He reached his hands out and caught a piece of bread on the table. "Good job little one. Let's get started eating."

"What's will you do?"

"I think I'll eat first."

"Very funny." Raul raked a hand through his unkempt brown hair. "You need to get away soon, to be sure of your escape."

"Why do I have to go again? I don't want to. I just started to rebuild my restaurant and home."

"Nevertheless, inquisitors will come after you sooner or later. How can you gauge when they'll find you?"

"I have no idea. But, later would be better," said Sara. "Besides, I want to wait for Juan. He still might come back."

"Sara, no. Don't torture yourself with false hopes." Beata gave Sara's shoulder a squeeze.

Tears welled up in Sara's eyes. "But I want to hope. I can't think Juan is dead just yet. It's too soon." She covered her face with both hands. Juanito squirmed and slid through Sara's hands to the floor. He looked up at Sara and then took a few halting steps, then sat down hard on his bottom.

"Sara, I'm sorry. But you must make realistic plans. And you need to leave here to avoid being arrested."

"If Juan comes, you'll tell him where I went, won't you?" Sara sniffed and wiped her eyes.

"Yes, dear sister," said Raul. "We'll do all we can to help you reunite, too."

"From the first, I wanted to go to the Holy Land. My friend Margarita is there now, and Rodrigo, her husband. How can I get there?"

"We'll have to go to the harbor and speak to the different agents of the vessels. We can find out quickly where the ships are heading, and when."

"Could you help me with that, Raul?"

"Of course, *mi hermana*. I will go right after I finish my toasted bread and cherry *mermelada*." Raul smeared a scoop of the sticky jam on a thick piece of yesterday's bread.

"Thanks. I need to go find Leonardo and see if he can manage, or maybe even buy, the restaurant. I need to pick up the shoes I ordered and maybe order one or two dresses. I didn't get there yesterday." She made a lopsided grin.

"Well, you have one good dress for meeting royalty," said Beata. "It's beautiful, but get two dresses you can wear everyday, one to wear and one to wash."

"So practical, Beata. Thanks. I'll just clean up Juanito and start my errands. I have a list of furniture I need made. Raul, should I go ahead with it or just leave it to someone else?"

"By the way, Sara, Juanito's new bed came this afternoon." Beata smiled. "Juanito slept in it already. We set it up this evening."

Raul interrupted. "You asked me if you should order furniture. I'd like to see the list." Sara went to her bag and retrieved the folded paper. Raul studied it a long time, stroking the whiskers on his chin.

"It's a huge order, for sure. But if you don't want everyone to know you are leaving—maybe just your friends—I think you should buy some of the restaurant furniture, at least." Raul circled some of the items on the paper. "These ones."

"I might need furniture while I'm making all the arrangements." Sara set her chin. "I'd like to get back to my own place. I need to pay Carlo, too, for the apartment furniture." She patted her cheek. "I wonder if I have enough money to purchase a passage on a ship." Sara's brow pleated like a woman's neck ruff.

"Raul, find out what a ticket will cost and which vessels are going to the Holy Land. I'll go back with you tomorrow to make the purchase."

Raul nodded, wiped his mouth with the back of his hand and leaped to his feet.

"Count your money, Sara, but don't worry. I'll go make inquiries." Raul kissed Beata, patted Angela on the back and was gone.

"Sara, what about the repairs to your restaurant? Can't you go ahead with at least some of that? You know, repair the brick oven and replace counters and the stairs to the upper level." Beata cocked her head, like a patient dog expecting a reply.

"I can't do that until I find out the price of a ticket to the Holy Land."

"Surely you can stay in Naples for a week or so, till things are decided."

"I hope so. I'll try. And I need to get more clothing for Juanito. He's growing so fast." Sara stood up and reached for Juanito. "There's not a moment to waste."

By the time Sara scrubbed food off Juanito's face and hands and changed his wet pants, the church bell tolled ten o'clock.

Sara stepped outside into another beautiful spring day. The colors of spring looked even more vivid and the flowers smelled more fragrant than yesterday. The flaming geranium arched over a window grate and the scent of rosemary tickled her nose. "I can't stop to enjoy the day as I'd like to, Juanito. We have to go shopping!" Sara put on a big smile and took long strides. She reached the dressmaker's store in just a few minutes. But she did notice the new green growth on the skinny cypress, the heavy scent of the lemon tree's blossoms and the fuzzy white texture on the olive leaves.

Sara turned away from the delights of spring and looked at the shop she stood in front of. *It looks different in the daylight—and when I'm not trying to evade my pursuers.* A sign over the door said "Marta's Designs: Clothing and Furnishings." Sara stepped inside. A bell tinkled and presently a woman emerged from a doorway.

"May I be of service, *signora*?" The woman presented herself well, with upswept hair, a finely tailored dress and an intelligent face. "My name is Marta."

"Oh, I hope you can help me. My name is Sara Sánchez. I recently had a fire in my home and all my clothing is either full of smoke or burned. I need to order two new dresses."

Juanito gurgled and waved his hands. "Da. Da."

"Oh, and my little son needs some new clothes, as well. He's growing. Most of his clothes were damaged by fire, also." Marta looked at Juanito with lips and eyes wide.

'What a wonderful son," said Marta. "You must be relieved he sustained no injury in the fire."

"Yes, I'm very grateful."

"Now, then, come with me to my workshop. I have rolls of fabric and a few sketches of what I can make for you and your son."

"Do you have dresses already made up? Perhaps I could buy one today, if you do. I really am desperate to have something to wear." She looked down at the dress she had borrowed from Beata, or was it Fortunata? Marta shook her head.

"Unfortunately, no, but our seamstresses are very quick. Come this way, please." Sara followed the middle-aged woman into the next room. Three walls held rolls and rolls of fabric leaning against them. Finely woven linen, soft cotton and patterned wool— "Something for every woman's taste and need," said Marta. "As you see, we have luxury fabrics for formal occasions, and linen for everyday wear. We also have wool for capes and outerwear." Marta waved her hand at a few rolls of soft colored cloth. "These are suitable for children."

Sara stretched out her hand and felt a number of rolls, those that caught her eye because of color or texture. "I hope you don't mind if I touch them," she said.

Marta pulled out the rolls Sara had fingered. "Of course not. I like to see a person who enjoys the feel of fabrics as much as I do. And it helps you know how they feel when you wear them next to your skin." She draped a length of pale rose over Sara's shoulder. Sara shook her head. A length of pale blue-green met with approval, however. And another of caramel color. Marta pulled out a chair. "Look at these sketches."

Sara sat, adjusting Juanito in front of her. After studying the five or six drawings for some time, she chose two. "I like the dress with a scoop neck, high waist and decorated sleeves and neckline, and also the frock with square neck and fitted through the torso. You'll make it the usual way, won't you?"

"Yes, with simple piecing and belts, hooks and lacing to shape it to your figure." Sara nodded when Marta mentioned prices.

"Wonderful. I'd like both dresses made to order, and now how about some things for Juanito? And can you finish these things in a week? Or sooner?"

"Very good, *signora*. I have two daughters who can help me get everything sewed in no time. Now, we'll measure you and your little son. We need a good estimation of the amount of fabric needed."

Chapter 4

❋

That afternoon, Raul exploded through the door. "I have some news!" His eyes glowed below his arching eyebrows.

"What is it?" Sara leaned forward in her seat at the table. Beata gave Raul a peck on the cheek and turned her attention to him.

"Two vessels in the harbor right now are preparing to make the voyage to the Holy Land." Raul tweaked his nose so it wouldn't whistle. It did, anyway.

"Wonderful!" Sara clapped her hands. "When do they sail? And what's the cost?"

"Just a minute. Let me tell you." Beata and Sara looked at him and waited. "Well, first of all, I made excuses at my job saying I needed to purchase additional parchments for the shop. Then, I strolled down to the harbor. The tide was low, so the smell of salt water and creosote made me sick. I could never be a sailor!"

"Yes?" The women leaned forward.

"Talked to a couple of mates. I quickly found out who was going to the Holy Land, and you'll be surprised. One of them is the *Veronica*."

"Captain Ferlandini?" Sara smiled.

"Yes, but he leaves in two days. Can you be ready?" Raul scowled, his overgrown eyebrows forming a thatch above his brown eyes.

"I don't know! It's not much time." Sara clenched her teeth. "What about the other ship?"

"I wish you'd go with Ferlandini," said Raul. "I trust him."

"Go talk to your dressmaker and shoemaker," said Beata. "You need shoes and clothes if you're traveling."

"Did you talk to Leonardo yet?" said Raul, "And the furniture maker? What's his name?"

"Carlo. No, I haven't done that. I just placed my orders with the dressmaker and shoemaker. I thought I had some time. It's only been four hours since you left for work." Juanito tried some tentative sidestepping along the benches, moving his hands along the top to steady his steps. He stopped and cooed his delight.

"What's the next possible voyage after that?"

"I think they said two weeks. There's no time to waste," said Raul, shuffling his feet, his nose whistling softly.

"Is it that urgent?" Raul shrugged his shoulders. "If you say so, then I'll do it right away," said Sara. She jumped up and grabbed Juanito under the arms. "What time is it?"

"Sara, wait," said Beata. It'll soon be time for midday meal and rest time. Nobody will be working then." Beata gave her skirt a pull. "Sit down."

"I can at least go to the carpenter and place my order. I did count my money." Sara went into the bedroom she was using and opened the wardrobe. Extending her arm to the back, she pulled out a pouch and counted out a handful of coins. She folded a handkerchief around the coins and returned to the kitchen. Sara put the money in her bag. Juanito grabbed for her purse as he edged along the bench. Beata caught Sara's eye.

"I'll prepare lunch while you're gone. Leave Juanito if you want." Beata took Juanito while Sara grabbed her bag. Beata waved goodbye and acknowledged the grin Sara gave her.

Out on the street, Sara threw her bag strap over one shoulder and set off with arms swinging. She walked along the street that took her right past the shoemaker's door. *I wonder—* She turned in at the open door.

"*Buon giorno, signor.*"

"Good day to you." He stopped what he was doing and stood up.

"I was hoping my shoes might be ready." Sara gave him her best smile.

"*Signora* Sánchez, isn't it? Your shoes are almost ready. I knew you needed them, so it's the first project I worked on today, after you left. It has been only a few hours." He coughed and folded his hands.

"I know, sir. I'm just anxious."

"I understand. I'll have the work done by this evening. I can have them delivered to you first thing in the morning. Will that be satisfactory?"

"Yes. *Molte grazie.* Many thanks." Sara reached for her coin purse. Something was wrong. *It's too light. Where are the coins?* She reached her hand all the way to the bottom of the cloth pouch. Only two coins fell into her hands. She rummaged through her larger bag, looking for the stray coins. *Nothing.*

"What is the cost, *signor*?"

"Two more coins. See what I have done. Just a bit more work to do." He placed the shoes on the counter. The black leather gleamed. Sara noticed the pleats and buttons on each shoe. She gulped and brought out the two coins.

"These will be handsome shoes and will last a long time. I hope you like them."

"Thank you, *signor.* I like them very much. I'll expect them tomorrow." She walked out of the shop and turned toward the dressmaker shop.

Where are all the other ten coins I placed in my purse?

At the dressmaker shop, Marta greeted Sara and said indeed it was a good day. "I came to inquire about my order and see what progress you have made."

"My daughter and I have started one of your dresses and cut out the pieces for your young son's outfits." She looked at Sara. "I hope that's satisfactory. Didn't I just talk to you this morning?" A wisp of a question passed over her face.

"Please excuse me. I just need the clothes so desperately. Could you finish it all in two days?"

"That may be difficult, but we could finish the one dress, I think, and your son's set of clothes. It will mean extra hours of work, of course."

"I could give you something extra for the trouble." Sara clenched her hands.

"Yes, that should be all right. Just let me know when you will come for it all. Oh, and someone brought back a dress they didn't like. I can offer that to you. It'll fit you well. I'll see to it." Sara tried it on and clapped her hands. "Thank you, Marta. That will be fine. The best that can be expected. I will come back with the money." Marta wrapped the dress and gave it to Sara.

"I trust you."

Sara hurried to Carlo the carpenter and placed the order Raul suggested. "Signor, to start with, could you make the table and chairs, a bedframe for me, a chest, and could you send someone to see about repairing the stairs and making a new door?"

"I see you conferred with your brother and have made a wise decision. It's always best to take your time and do something well."

"Perhaps that is a good principle for living your life, too," said Sara.

"I have always found it so." Carlo bowed and Sara nodded and smiled.

"Since we talked about it already, I have talked to a carpenter who can come to you to build stairs and a door. Did you receive the child's bedframe?" Carlo folded his callused hands.

"Yes, thank you. It's very nice. And Juanito has already settled into it." Carlo smiled and waved as she left.

Sara returned to Raul and Beata's house and the smell of roasting chicken and fresh sautéed vegetables. "You're just in time, Sara. Come, sit down," said Beata, wiping her moist forehead with the back of her hand. Beata took the chicken off the spit and set it on a platter. With a sharp knife, she sliced it in half at the breastbone and then quickly severed the legs and thighs. She basted it with butter and squeezed a plump lemon until juice splashed over it all. A sprinkle of chopped tarragon and the masterpiece was ready.

"Beata, you're a wonderful cook. This looks and smells delicious." Sara complimented her sister-in-law with a smile.

"Taste it and then tell me you like it," Beata laughed.

"I can't wait while you talk about food. I want to eat food." Raul thrust out a fork and removed a large piece of chicken to his plate. He took a scoop of vegetables and passed them on. "Delicious."

All conversation stopped while everyone, including Juanito, enjoyed his or her food. Gradually, the conversation grew louder and more animated. "I'll get my new shoes tomorrow, and in two days can pick up one dress and Juanito's clothes. Also, I have a problem. I seem to have lost ten coins."

"What? How?" Raul's nose whistled.

"I don't know. I only know I had twelve coins in my purse when I first went to the dressmaker, but today I could pay only two to the shoemaker—ten are missing."

"Did you look carefully in every corner of your bag? Did you retrace your steps from yesterday?"

"Yes, and no. What good would it do to retrace my steps over the cobblestones where everyone walks? If anyone had found them in the street, they wouldn't know where to return them."

"Did anyone at Don Antonio's place have access to your bag?" Beata's mouth pinched tight as she spoke.

"No. Only Don Antonio was with me in the room. The point is, I'm worried."

"You recounted your money this morning, right. You got a big bag from Montenegro, and you still have what Juan gave you, right?" Beata's voice rose.

"I'll go with you tomorrow and help you purchase a ticket," said Raul. "Captain Ferlandini will treat you fairly."

Sara cocked her head and unclenched her white fists. "You're both right. I am panicking. Surely it will be several weeks before Spain sends a inquisitor."

"It may never happen if Morales' servants keep their mouths shut."

Sara blew kisses to both of them. "You are right, of course. But, just in case, what other vessel is bound for the Holy Land?"

"The *Star of the East.* And yes, I think it will be less costly. But that's because it's an older vessel and a bit tired and worn," said Raul. "The captain looked tired and worn, too." He chuckled. "It may be his last voyage."

"When does it leave?"

"In three days."

"I could use some extra time. There's much to arrange here."

"I don't advise it, Sara. The crew looks surly and the ship needs maintenance. The captain has an odd look, too. I don't trust him."

"I guess it's the *Veronica* for me, and the voyage that's two days from now," said Sara. "Now, to work out the restaurant repairs and talk to Leonardo. I think he'd make a good manager till I return."

"Or, sell it to him and then you'd have more than enough money," said Raul.

"All right," said Sara. She pushed away from the table and grabbed Juanito. A wadded handkerchief fell from his hands. Something else caught her eye. She examined the bench more closely. "Look! Between the slats—someone has inserted something shiny. Could it be my coins, Juanito?" She tickled her little boy and he giggled. She worked one out with a knifepoint. "It is! I imagine I'll find all ten of them there, won't I?" She worked until all ten were freed.

"The mystery is solved." She strolled to her room and walked around it in circles, her little boy over her shoulder, till Juanito's eyes get heavy. "Now, time for a rest, you rascal," she whispered. She laid Juanito down gently. Sara leaned back in a chair and took a deep breath. *Why do I worry so much? What's wrong with me?*

* * * *

Sara visited the carpenter shop after siesta was over. Carlo greeted her with courtesy and a sprinkling of sawdust in his hair.

"*Signor* Carlo, when can I expect to have my new furniture?"

"Well, my dear, I think you need new floors and stairs, counters and doors first. Isn't that right? It will take time."

"Yes. But I must travel soon and don't know when I can return."

"Do you have an overseer that could be trusted to take care of your property?"

"I have someone in mind who can oversee the project, but I need to ask him first. I'll return shortly." Sara walked to her charred restaurant and apartment. *Would Leonardo be here? I don't know how to reach him otherwise.* Sara heard *plop* and *scrape, scrape* and walked into the restaurant. "Hello, Leonardo," she said. "I'm so glad to see you."

The silvery head looked up from his bricklaying job. "Sara, I hoped I'd see you today. I have something to tell you." He dusted off his hands and wiped mortar on his work pants.

"Yes?"

"I'm repairing the brick oven, so we will soon be able to make bread."

"That's wonderful, Leonardo. That will mean a good income right away. That is, if everyone comes back."

"I'm sure they will. You developed some regular customers at your restaurant before the fire."

"I'm afraid I have some bad news, Leonardo. I have to leave town for a while. In fact, I may never return. I don't know." Sara's voice quavered.

"What happened? Something to do with Morales again?"

"I'd rather not say anything." Sara wrung her hands. "But, I could really use an overseer for the restaurant while I'm away."

"Are you asking me to do that?"

"Yes, or you could buy it. I may never come back."

"Your problem is really serious, isn't it?"

"Ask my brother sometime about it after I'm gone. I don't want to tell you now."

"*Signora* Sara, I can't buy the restaurant, I'm sure. I'm not a rich man. And it takes time to amass enough money. I'm sure you wouldn't want to wait that long." He reached in his pockets. "I have ten silver coins I was going to use for the oven repairs and some other repairs. I can offer that to you. But I will faithfully take care of your restaurant. I'll bake bread. And, I'll make your restaurant a success again."

Sara's eyes filled with tears. "Thank you, dear Leonardo. You are a true friend. Keep the coins and use them to buy bricks and pay for the furniture. I put the restaurant in your hands." She took his calloused hand and squeezed it. His cheeks colored. "I have a few details I need to work out with you today and tomorrow," said Sara, "including repairs and new furniture. I will accept the new carved chairs and a few other pieces."

"Oh, and let me make a list of what you can expect for the restaurant." She bought a slate board at a market stall and wrote down her instructions for Leonardo.

Juanito woke up feverish and irritable the day Sara was supposed to sail. "Raul," she said. "Could you get my money back for the passage I booked on the *Veronica*? I just can't leave today."

"Do you want to get caught?" Raul raised an eyebrow. "I heard today that Giuseppe Fiorito was arrested by the Inquisition. Yes, in Naples. Dragged from his home and locked up."

Sara looked him in the eye. "Juanito is sick."

"Get on board. I'll get you some medicine from the doctor."

"No, Raul," said Sara. "I've decided to stay in Naples. If trouble comes, I intend to face it here." She clenched her fists and narrowed her eyes. "No more running."

"If that's your decision, I'll help you all I can," said Raul. "I'll go get that medicine now, and your ticket money."

Sara nodded and hurried to tend Juanito. When Raul returned, she prepared a small amount of the herbs for her one-year-old and gave it to him, one spoonful at a time.

"Mama," said Juanito, his face glistening and eyes mirroring fear. *His or mine?*

"Juanito, you rest now and soon you will feel better, not hot." She patted him and smoothed the coverlet around him in his bed.

"Hot, hot," said Juanito, or something like that in his baby words. His arms hung limp beside him. Sara tiptoed out.

"How's your little boy?" said Raul.

"Not his usual self. He's too quiet." They both chuckled together.

"I'll leave you now, and try to get your money back, now that you're staying. Be sure to let Leonardo know." Raul embraced Sara. "I'm glad you're staying. We would have missed you terribly and worried every minute about you."

"Thank you, *mi hermano.* But, there may be problems here in Naples. Who knows? This life we've been dealt is full of uncertainty."

"It calls for wisdom and courage every day, right?" Raul patted Sara on the back and left for home. Sara went back to watch Juanito for a while. She sat in the corner of the room on one of the new carved chairs. She ran a finger through the smooth grooves and flourishes of the acanthus leaf design and let her thoughts float.

My hope is in You all day long. Her eyelids closed.

Chapter 5

Sara wrung her hands. *What kind of person am I? Did I kill Don Antonio? I don't know. Am I really sorry he's dead? No. Morales tried over and over to ruin me, to possess me as a religious man is pledged never to do! He was a horrible man! He deserved to die!*

Will the Inquisition bother to hunt me down? It's a long way from Spain to Naples. But, the recent arrest of Signor Fiorito chills me. That's the local arm of the Inquisition, surely. Perhaps Alexo and Paco will not report me—make up a story that Don Antonio died of consumption. All that coughing and blood from his insides onto his handkerchief. Disgusting! I should feel pity for him, though, and forgive him. I can't! I won't. He wronged me.

So, I'm free, but my husband is dead. I should be mad at you, God. Do you care about me, and my fatherless son? How will we live?

Sara opened her eyes and saw Juanito's face up close. He squealed. "What are you doing, little one? You must be feeling better." She picked Juanito up and hugged him to herself. "You make me happy and hopeful, dear one." She put her nose close to his little ear. "And you smell like my sweet baby." She nudged him. Juanito giggled. She poked him again. Another giggle, and then a laugh. "Let's go outside and enjoy the sunshine. Would you like that?"

"Da."

"It won't be long until you're talking and making sense. Let's go." Sara kissed Juanito on the cheek and then slung him on one hip. She went to the stairs and down to the main floor. The Saturday sun greeted them, hot and demanding in the cobalt sky. A few clouds dotted the deep blue expanse like puffy *trapunto* embroidery on a dress.

Sara scanned the sky. In the distance, a dark spot appeared.

"Signora, that's a storm cloud over there you're seeing. It's far off, probably down by the end of the peninsula—the boot. But, we could have rain today." The man nodded and continued on his way past the restaurant, closed for repairs. She acknowledged his warning and looked again.

"See the dark cloud, Juanito?" She pointed. "There's a storm coming on the sea." Juanito shook his head up and down. A cloud scurried to block the sun.

Sara turned on her heels. "Back we go, Juanito." Sara swung Juanito up in the air and over her shoulder. He squealed. "I wonder how the *Veronica* will weather the storm?" They went back inside and up the steps to the living quarters.

"I'll hold onto you. Don't worry." She sat down hard on the bed and rolled Juanito back and forth as if it was a game. "Feel the waves?" Juanito gurgled. "Let's stay here, Juanito. Your bed is the safest place now. But, ooh, my insides are rolling like the waves. I hope I don't get sick." She gave Juanito a silly grin. Bile rose in the back of her throat, but she swallowed it down. "This pretending is becoming real--I will not get sick." Instead, Juanito started crying and did get sick. Sara sighed. "That was not a good idea."

* * * *

Two weeks later, someone knocked on the door--a bold tattoo that rattled it.

"Who's there?" Sara ran down the stairs. "It's so early in the morning."

"First Mate Moretti, Signora Sánchez."

Sara flung the door open and came face to face with a neat uniform, a three-cornered hat with a long feather and a black brush of a mustache. She took a step back.

"Why have you come?"

"Then you are Signora Sánchez?" The brushy mustache twitched with each word.

"Yes."

"There's been an incident with the *Veronica*, and Captain Ferlandini's been injured. He asked me to inform you." Moretti clicked his heels together and straightened his posture even more.

"Oh, no!"

"The captain hoped you would come to him. We've just returned to Naples. He's been set up in his own abode again, with extra nursing help. The housekeeper and cook have enough to do just managing the extra cooking and washing that an invalid needs." Moretti shifted his feet.

"What has happened? Did it involve that storm we saw even from here? Please, tell me more. Come in and let me offer you some refreshment." Moretti nodded his head and doffed his hat. Sara led him into the restaurant to the nearest table. She shifted Juanito to her hip and walked into the kitchen.

"Thank you, signora. We've come back in a hurry and meals have been meager."

"Tell me all that happened and I'll fix you something. Here's some bread." She set a plate of day-old bread and slices of sheep's cheese in front of the ship's mate and went for some limonada.

"You're right, signora," said Moretti. "The *Veronica* got caught in a tempest two weeks ago. It came up without warning. Lightning flashed and thunder crashed overhead. The passengers held onto their seats or pallets—wherever they found themselves. Wind pounded the ship and made the sails snap. The timbers creaked and groaned. The ship heaved deep to port."

"Make for Messina, mates," bellowed the captain. The westerly wind pressed hard on the starboard side, pushing the ship toward the coastline of Calabria.

"Luff the sail," shouted the helmsman as he pulled the tiller. He steered the ship toward the direction from which the wind came, and away from the rocky lee shore east of them.

"We quickly found ourselves in the center of the gale. The captain told the crew to make for the shelter of the strait of Messina. The island of Sicily will protect us from the wind. We struggled through rough seas, till at last the *Veronica* entered the strait between Italy and Sicily and the wind quit snapping at the sails."

"What happened next?" Sara sat down across from the *Veronica's* first mate. Juanito pattered around the table. She picked him up and patted his back. He leaned on her shoulder.

"We put into harbor and immediately the wind died down. We decided to wait out the storm in the safety of the sheltering waters there." Moretti grabbed a piece of bread and pulled off pieces and popped them into his mouth. He brushed off his uniform after each bite. He took a large piece of cheese and shoved it under the brushy mustache.

"Big." Juanito interrupted the narrative suddenly.

"What did you say, little one? Was that a word?" Sara held him at arm's length and coaxed a response out of Juanito. "Say it again, Juanito."

"B-big!" Juanito grinned and opened his eyes wide.

"Your first word. Well done, *niño*! My young one. You're not an infant anymore. We can have long conversations now, isn't that right?"

Juanito clapped his hands and wiggled his feet. "Be careful. I might drop you. Stop!" Juanito kicked against Sara with his feet.

"Big. Big." Sara laughed and put him down on his feet. Only then did she feel her cheeks color.

"Forgive my little one. He had something important to say." She smiled at Moretti and saw for the first time a warm light in the brown eyes above that notable mustache.

"You have a fine son, signora. And, may I say, you are an attentive mother." Now color crept up his neck. He wiped a finger across his mouth.

"Please continue, sir. You said you came to Messina harbor."

"As we came into the harbor, we became distracted by a galley nearby. One of the sailors threw a line to a hand on the pier, but missed. He quickly tried to reel it in. The *Veronica* kept drifting. Captain Ferlandini shouted for him to secure the lines quickly, but the ship continued drifting.

"'Slack the mainsail. Pull the boom hard against the wind, lads.' Two sailors dropped the mainsail. Then six pushed the boom hard into the wind. The ship came dangerously close to the galley, and struck on the rocks."

"Oh, no!"

"Boxes toppled. Passengers fell. And the boom shattered. Captain got a knock on the head and some large splinters in his leg." Sara gasped.

"We loaded him on a pallet and took him immediately, after we tied up, to a hospital in the town. His injuries were that bad." Moretti looked down at his hands.

"You must not blame yourself, sir." Sara looked at the tight tendons in his neck.

"But I do." He raised his caramel-colored eyes to meet hers. Sara looked away.

"I had to report to the crew and passengers that Captain Ferlandini received significant injuries, and the boat needed repair before we could sail another league. I had to take control, as the captain was in bad shape. He lost a lot of blood and was in and out of consciousness."

"I see."

"So, I decided the *Veronica* should undergo repairs before we could even limp back to Naples. We would have to give up the voyage to the Holy Land, and Captain Ferlandini, after he was in a stabilized condition, should be transported to his home, where he could best recover. Many of the passengers were unhappy about my choices."

"Indeed. I imagine many dreamed of reaching the Holy Land," said Sara.

"So, that is the long tale of our misfortune," said Moretti. "Many requested their money back. The captain is at home and would be happy to receive you in the near future. I would be happy to escort you there, at your convenience, signora." First Mate Moretti stood up, straight as a mast, which made him seem taller than he was. Sara stood, also, and saw that she must look down to meet his eyes.

"May I contact you--perhaps tomorrow? I would gladly come to see Captain Ferlandini. He has been a friend and great help to me." Sara ushered the officer toward the door.

"Send a message to the *Veronica*, and I will come." Moretti bowed and Sara made a short curtsy. He placed the magnificent hat on his neatly trimmed hair and stepped out into the street. Sara pushed the door till she heard a click. She sat back down at the table.

How fortunate it is I stayed here. I made the right decision.

Chapter 6

❋

"How does Captain Ferlandini seem to you, sir?" Sara broke the pleasant silence between them. She and Moretti were walking the streets of Naples. Sara had Juanito slung over one shoulder.

"Tired, weak, and worried. He has some important message he wanted you to hear directly from his lips."

"I hope it's not bad news."

"He wouldn't tell me. Ah, here we are." Sara stood before a three-story building of light sandstone bricks. The street contained many mature trees and each doorway opened onto a marble porch of three worn steps. Inside, they ascended a narrow flight of stairs in a dark hallway. "This way, please." He pulled back a curtain hung on a rope stretched around a bed. "Wait here, signora, and I'll wake the captain." The first officer disappeared.

"Captain Ferlandini, your visitor is here. Captain, are you awake?"

"What, oh, Moretti, thank you." She heard the captain clear his throat. "Is my hair combed? Am I presentable?"

"Sir, you have been wounded. She will understand if you're not perfectly attired."

"But do I look passable?"

"Yes, sir."

"All right, send Sara in, please, and Moretti—"

"Sir?"

"Leave us for a while."

"Very well, sir." He turned. "Sara—signora—please come in." First Officer Moretti led her to a chair by the captain's bed. Then he bowed and backed out.

"How are you feeling, Captain Ferlandini?" Sara leaned forward and patted his arm. "You've been through a trying time." Ferlandini grabbed her hand and gave it a squeeze. Sara withdrew her hand after what seemed a proper amount of time.

"Dear Sara, thank you for asking. I am doing poorly at the moment. Barely held together by a spider's thread, it seems. The doctor sewed my scalp back together, and he picked out some wood splinters from my thigh." Ferlandini indicated the bandaged area.

"I'm so sorry."

"I hope it doesn't smell too bad. I fear it's not healing cleanly. Festering--"

"No, not this soon." Sara kept from breathing in. "I'm glad I could come to see you. You have been a true friend and, really, truly a lifesaver on a number of occasions."

"Glad to do it, Sara. Glad to do it. Now, if you would listen to the ramblings of an old man—"

"You're not old," Sara protested.

"I'm fifty-one and a fool for not speaking to you earlier."

"Yes?" Sara's brows flew up like ravens in flight.

"Just listen, please. I want to tell you something. I've—admired you since I met you a year or two ago. You're beautiful—so lovely in appearance and kind-hearted. Brave and resourceful."

"You praise me too much, sir."

"You deserve it."

"I guess you have rescued me twice, haven't you? I must be a bother to you." Sara joined in the laughter.

"So, what do you think?" Captain Ferlandini sat up as straight as he could, wincing when trying to move his leg.

"About what?"

"Well, I'd love to be your husband, but I know you have one. So, will you think of me as your special friend? I'd do anything for you."

"Oh, captain. I already consider you a dear friend." Sara felt her burning cheeks, as she shifted Juanito to her other arm. "I think I should go now. I've made you tired."

"Yes, and I've said something foolish in my weakened state." Sara patted his arm again and tiptoed out.

"Did you hear?" Sara whispered. Moretti gave a slow nod. Sara walked away and back down the hall. Moretti caught up to her.

"It's none of my business and I won't tell anyone."

"What are Captain Ferlandini's chances of survival?"

"He was treated quickly and his wounds cleaned out. Sewed his scalp back together and dug out the splinters in his leg."

"But?"

"It was difficult to get out all of the splinters. They may fester. If he develops a fever, we'll know it's gone bad."

"Amputation of the leg?"

"Perhaps."

"He's a dear. I hate to think of him suffering. Let's stop talking about it and enjoy the walk back." They strolled along the streets and back to Sara's residence. Juanito clung heavily to Sara's shoulder. First Officer Moretti saluted. "It's been my privilege to escort you today." He bowed. "I hope you felt safe."

"Quite safe. My thanks." Sara curtsied. She turned and walked up the stairs, glad to finally put Juanito down. Sara closed her eyes and wept silently. *Captain Ferlandini is a dear friend. I hope he recovers completely. And I just realized I haven't given up that Juan may return. He will, won't he? Please let it be true.*

* * * *

"Naples feels like home. I could live here," she said to Juanito. "Let's get to Raul's and tell him all the news about the captain. There's so much to tell." Sara took big strides along the streets, taking in the sights and smells that were now familiar. "Juanito, let's go see Uncle Raul and Aunt Beata. And Angela, your friend." She found her way through the streets. The sun was setting and shadows had grown long. "Finally, here we are at Raul's house." She paused and readjusted Juanito. She heard Raul's voice through the thick door. Then she heard another deep voice. *Do they have guests? Well, it can't be helped. I just arrived.* She lifted the latch and entered.

"Hi, you two. I'm here!" She moved toward the voices.

"Who's that? Sara?" Raul came running toward her. "Back again? What's happened?" He kissed her on both cheeks and looked at her. "I have a big surprise for you. Come." Sara let herself be led to the eating area. What she saw next made her gasp and cry.

"Hello, Sara. I'm back, too."

"Juan!" Sara put Juanito down and closed the space in an instant. She flung her arms around him and held him close.

Juan enveloped her with his arms and planted a kiss on her lips. They held the embrace.

"I don't want to let go, Juan."

"I don't, either. I love you, Sara, but I'm weak. I've had a fever. I need to sit." Sara let him go and Juan sat on the bench. Sara picked up her little boy.

"Juan, this is your son. Juanito, this is your daddy." Juan's eyes grew large as he inspected every part of his little boy, touching fingers, nose and ears.

"He's just like you, Juan. He even has your green speckled eyes." Sara sank to the bench next to Juan and fitted herself into his arms. "Oh, Juan." She laid her head on his shoulder and let the tears fall. Juanito squeezed out from the middle and planted his feet on the floor.

"Da-da." Juan and Sara laughed through their tears, and continued their embrace.

"Oh, Sara. *Te amo.* I love you so much." Juan whispered in Sara's ear.

"And I love you, Juan." She kissed him with her whole heart and her desire rekindled as an ember fueled again to flame.

"Sara, you scare me," he whispered. "Your passion is too much." He kissed her gently.

"I feel like we're intruders in our own house. Don't you, Beata?" Raul talked behind his hand, a little too loudly.

"Yes. Let's excuse our selves and go to the living room. They need to be alone. It's obvious." Beata lifted Angela into her arms and exited the tender scene. Raul followed quickly, slapping Juan on the back.

"Good to have you back." Juan kept his arms around Sara, but jutted his chin out in acknowledgment. How long they held their embrace neither could tell. After a long while, Sara became aware that Juanito had wandered away from the table. Juan began stroking her back. Then came the crash. Sara jerked her head up.

"Where's Juanito?"

"Hm? I don't know." Now Juan was alert, too. They got up to see where the noise came from. It was Juanito. He had pulled down a jar of flour, cracking the ceramic pot and sending white powder everywhere. Puffs still floated in the air, but most rested on Juanito. "A little ghost." Juan chuckled. He picked up Juanito who started to cry. Sara took him.

"It's all right, little one. It's your daddy. He loves you, too." Sara tried to brush the flour off, but it stuck to her hair and her dress. "You're a sight and so am I."

Beata and Raul ran in, saw the scene and burst into laughter.

"Sister, you need to watch your son, not kiss your husband." Sara blushed but laughed. Juan came near and put his arm around her shoulder.

"What's this restaurant I've been hearing about, Sara? Have you really run a restaurant all by yourself this past year?" Juan looked at her with eyes wide open.

"I've had help, of course, waiters and cook's helpers," said Sara, "but, yes, I used some of the money you gave me to start a business. I needed a job, and there's not much translation work here. At least, I haven't discovered any."

"Actually, I arrived here just after I got off the boat from Spain. I saw your restaurant and looked for you. But it was closed, I guess. But I did talk to Leonardo."

Sara stared at him. "I guess I was out. I did take a walk with Juanito."

"Show me. Can you take me there now?"

"Yes, and you can see the apartment I have above it. It's almost re-furnished now. I did have a fire. Did Raul tell you? Oh, there's so much I want you to know." She squeezed his hand. Let's go." She turned to Raul. "See you later."

"Don't worry. I'll come by later. Goodbye, Mr. and Mrs. Sánchez. Go home and get re-acquainted." He winked at Juan. "And be gentle with Juan. He's still not well."

Juan and Sara, with Juanito in her arms, walked the few blocks to her apartment. Juan stopped several times to get his breath.

"Don't despise me if I have to rest a bit when I get there."

"Rest as long as you want. We have all the time in the world. I'll close the restaurant for a few days. It isn't every day my husband returns from the dead."

Chapter 7

✳

"Well, Señora Sánchez, you've tired me." Juan held Sara's hand as they arrived at her apartment and restaurant. "I feel like an old man. I should be taking you in my arms." With effort showing in his face, Juan put his arms around Sara who was holding Juanito. Juanito squeaked and Sara let out a giggle. Juan planted kisses like a hungry man devouring a long-awaited meal.

"Juan, enough! Please, I can't breathe," Sara's cheeks colored crimson. Juanito's face clouded at the closeness of this man he didn't know.

"I want to love you as you deserve." Juan's whiskers scraped against her cheek. "But I'm out of breath after this short walk." Juan sighed.

"Let's go inside. I want to show you my—our—place. I think Leonardo has seen to some repairs." Juan contented himself to follow Sara. Inside, Leonardo stood by the brick oven. The yeasty smell of bread baking filled the restaurant. Sara walked back to the cooking area and greeted him. "Leonardo, have you met my husband, Juan? He's come back from the New World. It's a miracle, isn't it?"

"Sì, signora. And you're back from your journey--so soon."

"Never left. It's a long story. I'll explain later."

It's a pleasure, Juan. No need for swords?" Leonardo inclined his head. "Now you want to return to your family, I think. So, I will tell you what I've accomplished, then wish you *buona fortuna*." He gestured toward the kitchen.

"Workers replaced the counter and shelves for storing plates and food supplies. And, if you turn around, you can see a few new tables, chairs and benches. More are coming from Carlo." He looked to Sara.

"I think those can wait till we begin making money again," said Sara.

"Show him your apartment," said Leonardo. "A lot has happened in the last two weeks. Come and see, Juan."

"Since I decided not to flee to the Holy Land," said Sara. "Leonardo has helped me so much."

Leonardo opened a newly made door and pointed to rebuilt steps. "You'll see the carpenters have been busy. And wait till you see upstairs." He let Sara and Juan go ahead of him into the apartment.

"Oh, wonderful! Juanito's new bed, of course, and—" She looked at Juan. "Ours." She smiled. "Do you like the carving on the headboard? It matches the two chairs I had done." She pointed to a corner. "The table has special carving, too."

"You chose wisely, Sara. It's sturdy and well-made, as well as handsome." Juan took her hand and kissed it. Sara blinked a few times. Juanito laid his head on Sara's shoulder.

"Juanito's getting tired. Hold him a minute while I prepare his bed." Sara gave Juan a limp little boy. Juan took him with arms held out from his body. Gradually he eased Juanito against his chest and patted his back. Sara spread out a blanket she found and let Juan ease Juanito down onto his new bed. They all tiptoed out and down the stairs. "You handled him like an expert, Juan. Well done."

"I've worked with small children in my medical practice," said Juan. "But not for a long time. And now, I have my own son to care for. I can scarcely believe it." He smiled at his wife. "You're beautiful."

Beryl Carpenter

"Juanito's a wedding night baby." Sara blushed. Leonardo cleared his throat.

"I think it's time I left. You need your privacy." He turned to go. "Will you be needing me tomorrow?"

"Leonardo, we'd like a few days to ourselves," said Juan. "I have a family to get reacquainted with, you understand. Sara and I want the place closed for a few days."

"I understand. Send me word when you want me to come back and bake bread."

"Thank you, Leonardo, for all you've done," said Sara. "I truly appreciate it." Leonardo nodded and let himself out.

Sara and Juan looked at each other. They approached one another like strangers. "It's been so long, Juan. I feel shy." Sara put her arms around Juan and leaned against his chest. "You're thin, Juan. You must have suffered a lot."

"I've had my troubles, dear Sarita. It's a long story ending with a recent high fever that keeps coming back. I confess I'm weaker than I want to be. "He enfolded her in his arms and placed a tender kiss on her mouth. "Let's go upstairs. We have missed out on two years of married life. It's time we were husband and wife again." He took her hand.

"Juan. I love you so."

* * * *

"I forgot how wonderful it is to be married." Sara whispered to Juan in the middle of the night. She got up on one elbow and looked at her sleeping husband. His face was smooth, at peace. He breathed deeply. "Poor man, you fell asleep so quickly a few hours ago." Sara brushed a finger along Juan's chin and over his lips. He smiled in his dream and turned toward her. She lay down again. "I won't wake you. You need your sleep." Sara hugged herself and felt again the intense joy of seeing Juan and feeling him close beside her. *Thank you, God. I'm so grateful.* She closed her eyes and slept.

In the morning, a knock at the door woke them all. Sara put on a robe and ran downstairs. "Who is it? The restaurant is closed."

"It's me, Raul. Open up."

"Raul, what are you doing here so early?" She opened the door a crack.

"Early? It's ten o'clock. Why are you still in bed?" He winked.

"Silly, Juan is exhausted and still ill, I think." Sara rubbed her warm cheeks. Raul clumped in.

"Can I see what Leonardo's been doing here? Did he get everything fixed already? That's fast." Raul craned his neck here and there while walking through the dining area and kitchen. "Very nice."

"He did a wonderful job. I need to settle expenses with him, but other than that, it's all done." Sara tied her belt while following after Raul.

"Raul, welcome." Juan made his way down the stairs a little later, carrying Juanito. His little boy turned his face away from Juan but wasn't crying.

"How's the little family?"

"Never better."

"Like you've never been apart?"

"I wouldn't say that, but we're working on it." Sara ducked her head. Raul laughed. Juan put Juanito down and he started walking toward his mother.

"Good man, Juan. I brought you some food. Beata said you wouldn't have time to shop. I see she was right." He handed Sara a cloth bag. Sara peeked in.

"Eggs and cheese and bread. Beata's a dear! Would you like some eggs, Raul?"

"No, I already ate. You two are keeping wedding week hours." He patted Juan on the back and gave Sara a hug. "I'll see you later. You need a sign on the door: 'No visitors'."

"I can do it," said Juan. "I live here, too."

"Of course you do," said Sara. "I've just become accustomed to making all the decisions since you've been gone."

"Well, I'm back. And I can help." He turned to Raul. "I'll make a sign. We're closed for a few days—the restaurant, that is. But, of course, you and Beata are welcome." Raul waved and shut the door behind him.

"Do you like the restaurant, Juan? It seemed like a good idea. I love to cook and I needed a job."

"Did you work while you were with child?"

"I had to. I needed the income. But, I hired some help— waiters and a kitchen helper."

"And Leonardo."

"Yes, he came later and repaired the brick oven and taught me how to make bread. It's a popular offering."

"How clever you've been. I'm proud of you!" said Juan taking her hand.

Sara smiled and kissed him. They heard a crash.

"Juanito. Where is he?" Sara looked around with saucer eyes. She ran in the direction of the sound. "Juanito? Where's my big boy?"

"Big. Big." Juanito sounded pleased with himself. Sara ran into the kitchen and exploded in laughter. Juan was right behind her.

"There, you are. And a mess!" Juanito sat in a puddle of oil next to a cracked jar. "Oh, no! Oil's everywhere." Sara waved her hands in the air.

"But Juanito is all right, I think." Juan held his sides while laughing hard.

"Big," said Juanito, oil in his hair and all over his face, on his clothes and between his bare toes.

"Yes, big mess, Juanito. This means a bath. I can see I need to get more sets of clothing for you. You are an active little boy now. And I need to watch you carefully."

"My mother used to complain I always had mud on my hosen," said Juan.

"Just like Daddy," said Sara. Juan scooped up his little boy and lifted him up high.

"Off you go to get a bath, Juanito." He handed him to Sara. "I'll clean up the oil while you bathe him, Sara." Juan stopped to catch his breath after Sara disappeared with Juanito. *Should be stronger! This fever has caught me by surprise.*

That night, they went to bed early, Juan protesting he was tired. "I think maybe you are just impatient to—" She stopped midsentence and blushed. "I need you, too." She reached out her arms and drew Juan closer. Juan's love overpowered him and Sara's emotion kindled like a newly laid fire.

"Oh, Sara!" It was Juan's outcry that woke the child, but Juanito's whimpers subsided and he returned to peaceful sleep. Sara and Juan covered their laughter with a kiss. Juan fell asleep immediately. Sara watched his face relax. Later, she awoke as Juan reached for her. "Sara, I missed you so! I was so lonely in La Navidad—just married and then shipwrecked. How would I ever get back to you? It was impossible." He covered his face with one hand.

"When I heard you hadn't returned with Columbus, I was crushed," said Sara. "And I was pregnant! Without you to share the time with me, it wasn't so happy."

"I wish I had known. I would have taken care of you. And now, I'm so fatigued all the time. This fever must be different—something I caught in the New World. It holds on and won't let go."

"It's all right. We can be patient. You will get better soon." Sara stroked Juan's back and caressed his cheek.

"I need to tell you my story. It's long, but maybe you'll understand what I endured to get back to you."

"I want to hear it—every detail," said Sara. She sat up and listened.

Chapter 8

In the New World – November 1493

"Here's how it happened." Juan started his tale of survival.

"I walked with difficulty to the Admiral's quarters. My feet made a slow slap-step-slap sound outside the building. I asked to see Columbus. I heard the orderly say there was someone to see him—urgently."

"Columbus wanted to know who it was. The orderly said I looked strange—like I'd been in the jungle too long. Maybe that was true. I had no idea. I hadn't seen my image in a mirror for a long time."

"I think Columbus was intrigued to see who it was, so the orderly showed me in.

"Admiral Columbus?" I said. My voice rasped. The words came out with difficulty. I hadn't spoken Spanish to anyone for weeks."

"The Admiral, or should I say, the Viceroy of the Indies, looked me over. I was a stooped figure in front of him. He noticed the stink of stringy hair and beard and the shredded clothes first, but didn't recognize me. 'You need a bath, sir,' he said."

"I pleaded with him immediately. I told him I needed to go back to Spain as soon as possible. 'That my life in the New Worlds was over. He demanded to know my name and why he should take me back."

"'I'm Juan Sánchez, your surgeon,' I said. 'You left me at La Navidad months ago.' I raked my greasy hair back. Then he saw my face."

"'Sánchez, man! I never expected to see you again,' "he said. 'We thought everyone had perished in the attack on La Navidad.' He started to get up to slap me on the back, but thought better of it when he noticed my grimy clothes. He sat back down and said he wanted to hear my story. He indicated a chair near his desk. I eased myself into the chair and sighed. I guess he saw my skeletal frame and offered a bit of wine. The cabin boy saw to it and soon I took a gulp of the red liquid. I thanked him and then related all that had happened to me. Since the shipwreck of the *Santa María* on Christmas Eve, the thirty-nine members of that ill-fated ship's crew had to stay in the New World, while Columbus limped back to Spain in two ships."

"I explained that the crew felt abandoned, and decided to do whatever pleased them until the food ran out. This meant taking many women. The Admiral didn't understand and wanted to know why we didn't plant the seeds he left and raise vegetables. I said there was no point in doing that. The sailors all thought they would die soon, so why not take pleasure where they could. And the seeds didn't grow well, as it turned out."

"Who attacked the fort?" said Sara, sitting up straighter.

"It was Indians, but I didn't know if it was the peace-loving Tainos or the warlike Caribs. Discipline had declined rapidly and several times a week we had skirmishes with the locals. They resented the crew bothering their daughters and wives. Columbus told me again he had warned the crew to act as Christian gentlemen. 'That didn't happen, sir,' I said."

"Columbus wanted to know if I was the sole survivor."

"I told him, 'I don't know. I've been hiding in a cave near here. A Taíno woman has treated my wounds as best she could and brought me food and water. I lay in the cave for days. Her herb tea and medicinal plants cured me.' Then I asked him if he sent news of the La Navidad destruction back to Spain. He said yes and urged me to continue my story about the La Navidad tragedy."

"'This is what I remember, but my mind is clouded by forgetfulness.' I told him as many details as I could so he would feel it vividly."

* * * *

"It was in October it happened. The heat and choking smoke of burning wood subsided at last. I stirred from my lethargy. The dampness of night in the jungle had soaked breeches. Or was it blood?"

"I was barely conscious. I thought I should move—get up. Where was I? I didn't know, because it was dark. And something tickled my face. It was a huge spider!"

"I tried to brush away the furry monster, but my arm felt as heavy as the *arquebus* I'd been issued at the fort." Juan blushed. "It was called the latest in weaponry, but I considered it worthless in a hurry. I felt for my sword. My fingers inched along my thigh until I felt cold steel. The spider paused and gazed at me with multiple eyes."

"I was talking to myself. I was that unnerved. 'Don't move now, *hombre*. Not a muscle.' Two jointed legs, puppet-like, drew up and took a step. Just one. 'Don't breathe! Wait, man!' The spider took another step with kitten soft legs, and edged over my nose, eyebrow and forehead. I flicked it away then and smashed it with my bloodied fist. I wiped spider guts on my pants leg."

"The Admiral intervened. 'Keep to the point, Sánchez.' Columbus changed positions in his chair and I continued."

"I called into the darkness, 'Luis, where are you?' Then I heard a voice from the leaves, 'Senor Juan?' It was Yari."

" 'Who is Yari?' said Columbus.

"She was a Taino woman I knew. I treated her young son for measles. Columbus urged me to go on. But he drummed his fingers on the desk."

"Yari came out of the bushes and I told her I was injured."

"' I have an arrow to the thigh,' I said. "And one to my shoulder. Can you help?' She yanked out the arrow in my thigh. I had already pulled out the one in my shoulder, but there was dried blood there. She urged me to stand and get my bag. We needed to get to shelter."

"I think I complained that my leg hurt like the devil. With a lot of effort, I braced myself on one elbow then bent my good leg under me and somehow, I rose. The pain seared every sinew."

"Oh, Juan, I'm so sorry," said Sara, tears in her eyes. Juan brushed them away.

"I'll continue," he said. "I need to get this burden off my shoulders."

"Yari flung my arm over her shoulders and held on. '*Guárico.* Come,' she said. I protested that I wouldn't go to the Taino village. 'And where's Luis?' I stopped walking and dug my feet in, although it cost me a great deal of pain. I demanded to know where Luis was. Then she told me Luis was dead."

"I protested. 'No! He can't be. She said she dragged his body to a place in the bushes and would show me after I rested. I think I slumped against her, suddenly weakened in my grief. I must have been delirious, because I don't remember I lot after that. I had to trust her as I dragged my injured leg over rocks and branches, up an incline and into the deep forest. I do remember that. It seemed to take forever. We came to the top of a knoll and then as we got closer, I saw the cave."

"I think she gathered branches to cushion me on the hard ground, because that's what I saw when I woke up later. She promised to return in the evening at sunset, so nobody would see where she went. I think she asked about food and I did find a bit of bread and old cheese in my bag later. After she left, all I could think then was, 'I must get back to Sara'."

Juan closed his eyes and stopped speaking.

"Oh, Juan. That's a stirring story!" said Sara, gazing at her husband.

"Columbus said the very same thing, Sara." Juan shifted his position.

* * * *

"'That's an impressive story, Sánchez,' said Columbus. 'You still don't look so good, though. Can you survive the voyage home?' I remember asking him again if he sent news of the massacre back to loved ones at home. He said he did. 'I sent a boatload of *hidalgos* back already,' was his reply. That made me more determined than ever to go back—now. I said, 'Everyone will think I'm dead when the news gets out. I need to prove them wrong.'"

"He wanted to know if I was fit enough to make the voyage. I said I was doctored with strange new herbs— *epasote*, *neem* and *non*i juice. I had regained my strength."

"I almost shouted it out: 'All I need is a bath and a shave. I'm strong enough to brave the Ocean Sea.' I pushed my weak body up and stood as straight as I could, to show the Admiral."

"Columbus tried to calm me. 'That's fine, Sánchez, I believe you. Sit down.' Then he said he would be sending some ships back, since there were no gardens and no shelter for the thousand or more *hidalgos* who came along on the second voyage. But, he wanted to leave his present location tomorrow to find another more suitable site to start a new settlement, somewhere along the northern coast. 'La Navidad was hastily built and now it's destroyed. We'll begin this venture again, in a more livable place,' he said."

"I pressed him to know when the ships would return to Spain. He said soon and urged me to get some clothes and a bath. He ordered his cabin boy to escort me to a private cubicle and attend to me. Food and a long sleep were the next orders."

"Before I followed the cabin boy, I asked the Admiral, 'Do you know where my wife Sara is? She sailed on the *Veronica*. And her brother, Raul Torres had plans to settle in Naples.'"

"He said he heard from Captain Ferlandini that you settled in Naples and didn't go to meet me in Bethlehem— 'a romantic notion,' he added."

"I told him I meant to get to Naples as soon as I could arrange it. He urged me to write a letter and he would forward it as soon as they reach Spain's waters. "No time, sir," I said. 'I mean to get there quick.'"

"Columbus asked again: 'By the way, do you know if Luis Torres died? He was a promising translator.'"

"I had to tell him, and this, Sara, may cause you distress." Juan grabbed her hand. Sara looked at him with wide eyes.

"This is what happened. Luis was hit by one arrow in the first attack. After that, I fell unconscious from my wounds. When I woke, Yari, the Taíno woman, told me Luis was dead. I saw his body later and identified it from the clothing on it."

Sara put a hand to her mouth.

"I'm sorry, dear Sara. It's a sad tale, and the next question of Columbus is embarrassing to me, but I want you to know."

"He asked, did I get to know this Indian woman? 'Yari, is that her name? Sounds rather cozy, being nursed by a half-naked angel of mercy.'" Juan blushed, but looked directly at Sara as he related the next statement.

"I never acted on my desires, thank God." I hung my head for a moment, and then raised it again. "God was merciful. Now, I want to get back to my bride, Sara. We've lost so much time together."

"Oh, Juan," said Sara.

"Columbus said, 'Good man, Sánchez,' and laid his hand on my shoulder. He told me to rest on board for a day or two, and 'get cleaned up!' I was filthy. I watched him making a notation in the ship's log. 'Found: one survivor from La Navidad, Doctor Juan Sánchez.' He put down the twenty-eighth of November as the date."

Juan stirred and got up. "I need to stretch. My legs are stiff." Sara nodded. Juan returned to tell the story after a few minutes.

* * * *

"I followed the cabin boy who got someone to row me out to the admiral's ship. He went along and on board saw to it I got a quiet room and a tub full of cold salt water.

"He warned me, 'We can't spare fresh water for baths, sir. It's only for cooking and drinking.' I asked if I could I get some hot fresh water for rinsing."

"That was permitted. The cabin boy said he'd come with some clothes for me. Then he'd bring me some food, too. 'Looks like you haven't been eating much.' the boy said. I smiled and nodded. I peeled off my hosen, still dirty though I had tried to clean them in a stream while recovering. The wound in my thigh had closed, but it still pained me. It seemed to have some putrefaction, too—a slight oozing. It has finally healed now, though. I removed my doublet and under shirt with care, because my shoulder still hurt when I tried to move it fully."

"I deposited all my clothes in a heap, found a lump of soap and tested the tub of water. Not too cold. I worked my way in, lowering myself little by little into the tub. It was round and made of wooden slats, definitely an old wine barrel, now in service for washing. Guess I can't expect a tub fit for a king. I chuckled. My attitude was changing. It was amusing to wash one place and then the other in that small tub—comical. I had to stand up and plunge my head into the now tepid water to wash my hair. I hoped I could borrow a comb from someone later."

"When I lowered myself into the tub again, my legs hung over the edge. But my torso felt the last warmth of the salt water. I let out a sigh and closed my eyes. Just for a minute, because the cabin boy returned bringing clothes. He warned me they might not be long enough. 'You're tall,' he said. Then he promised to get my other clothes washed, although they were tattered rags, and oh, the smell!"

Sara let out a low giggle. "I can picture it," she said. Juan laughed, too.

"The cabin boy said his goodbye and returned to Admiral Columbus. A washer boy brought a bucket and scrubbed the smelly wad and hung it up on one of the ship's lines. 'These can serve as rags, at least,' he said."

"Your story is vivid, and so funny," said Sara. She chuckled again.

"I scrubbed my torso," Juan continued. "The washer boy brought another bucket, this time of stinging hot water. Two rinses. I guess I was very dirty. He told me there was a plate of food for me in the mess. I stood up and a pleasant ocean breeze blew over my skin. It was such a relief to get clean. I took the bucket and dumped it over my head. Soap ran over my shoulders and into the tub. I grabbed a rough towel and rubbed myself dry, hair and body."

"By the time I finished, my skin prickled with little bumps. Brr. I was cold already. I remember that time so clearly. I still had a fever, or my wounds were still affecting me, I thought. I hurried into my underthings, hosen and doublet. They were short, for sure. But the soft shoes were comfortable. I took time also to shave with the razor and small scrap of mirror provided before heading to the mess."

"I wanted to shove the food in my mouth. Roast beef and turnips, a thin gravy but nicely seasoned, and carrots and onions! But I ate slowly. I knew I'd get sick if I overate. When I was recovering, Yari fed me some kind of starchy plant, like a turnip. Daily."

"I drank the watered down wine I was offered and asked for more. I drank two more cups of the mellow, red liquid and finally felt mellow myself. I got up and found the cubicle I'd been offered, *a toldilla*. I'm grateful and I'm going to sleep—now, I remembered thinking. I fell into the narrow bed and slept better than I had for months."

Chapter 9

✼

"I woke when the ship lurched and began to glide through the water. 'Sails up, mates and make for the north coast.' Someone yelled the command to the crew. The timbers groaned and so did I as I turned over, to look through a crack. The sky had changed color—it was afternoon—and a few clouds plumped the sky with orange pillows. Doesn't that sound poetic? I want you to picture it, Sara. I sat up and tried to stand. But I felt weak—tired. I fell back onto the hard pallet and went back to sleep. I felt the ship rock in gentle waves and curl along the large island Columbus had found. At least, I think that's what happened. I heard later where we had traveled. Columbus still claimed Quinsay was just around the corner."

Sara smiled at him and took his hand. Juan took a sip of wine she offered.

"Later, I slowly became aware that the ship had anchored. All was quiet. Then Columbus' voice boomed out. 'Our new settlement shall be called Isabela, after our beloved Queen.' I stretched and sat up. I wanted to investigate, because I was feeling better. I slid my legs over the edge of the pallet and put weight on them. I felt somewhat stronger, so I found the nearest ladder and climbed up to the deck. What I beheld dropped my jaw. Lush greenery so dense the plants fought for space to grow. Sweat beaded on my forehead in no time. Sailors launched boats to land on the sand that framed the small harbor. I planted myself in one of the launches and enjoyed feeling the salt water spray my face with each pull the sailors took on the oars."

"On the beach everyone noticed clouds of tiny flying insects. 'What are those?' I asked a sailor. He said he wasn't sure, but some other mates said they're like stinging flies, *moscas*, only smaller. Someone called them *mosquitos*, *'little moscas,'* and that seemed apt. Columbus landed in a launch just then and the sailor helped him disembark. The Admiral, clad in his most impressive clothing, including a shiny sword, led the exploration party inward. 'You stay here, Sánchez. You're not well yet,' he ordered me."

"I found a bleached log and lowered my frame onto it. I closed my eyes. A light breeze stirred up the cloud of bugs. Some hovered over me and soon I started slapping at the pesky things and scratching the welts they left. I listened as the breeze carried men's voices to my ears. Someone said the area looked promising. 'There are natural defenses here' and 'there'll be no threat from Indians here—and we can divert the water source' were other comments. Columbus proclaimed this would be the new settlement site, La Isabela. 'Place a flag here. We'll begin work tomorrow,' said the Admiral and Viceroy."

"For the next weeks, sailors unloaded timber from the ships' holds and the tools to cut, measure and erect a fort and houses. If all the ships' passengers stayed at La Isabela, it would become a village of one thousand or more in no time. However, I heard rumblings of protest from among the *hidalgos*. They complained bitterly that Columbus had misled them. 'Where was the gold littering every beach?' Where were the large estates they could claim as their own? Most important, where were their personal servants? Life in the New World was not at all what they expected. A group of them badgered the Admiral almost every day."

"They demanded to be sent back to Spain. They no longer wished to settle in the New World. 'Spain has its refinements, and that is what we wish to return to.' Columbus was astute. He folded his hands behind his back, paced the floor and listened without comment."

"After the first week at the new site, I began to feel dizzy and weak. My forehead was hot and my cheeks rosy. My joints ached. Doctor Chanca, the surgeon for the flagship, looked at me and pronounced I had the tropical fever that a number of other men had contracted. He told me to go to bed, get some rest and he would send medicine. I observed that about one third of the crew had come down with this malady. They all had multiple mosquito bites, which made them doubly irritable. Days passed as I and others lay in our bunks, too weak to get up and eat. Orderlies brought bowls of broth, but nobody felt like eating."

"Columbus himself succumbed to a mysterious illness, which confined him to his cabin. I was anxious to hear when the *hidalgos* would sail back to Spain. I will be on that ship if I have to crawl to get there, I vowed to myself. That same day, I asked the date. "December 11th, sir. But, I'm afraid not much will get done until Admiral Columbus feels better.' I asked what was wrong with the Admiral. I asked Doctor Chanca one day if it was the same sickness most of us have."

"He told me the Admiral's symptoms: a paralysis on the right side of his body, 'from the sole of his foot to the top of his head,' Chanca said. He says it gives him considerable pain, like a hundred bites of the mosquitos all at once. These signs were much different than the plight of so many there, I commented. Doctor Chanca folded his hands behind his back and planted his feet wide. 'It does sound different.' I went on to say I was not an authority on tropical sicknesses, but the constant practice of the men consorting with Indian women produced sores on the body and backs of the hands, symptoms worse than anything seen in the port cities of Spain. That was my observation. He conceded that was true. I walked back to my hard bed and stayed there I don't know how long."

"Finally one day, I managed to get up and find my way to the mess hall. I actually felt hungry! I couldn't remember how many weeks I had been sick. I sat next to a deck hand and asked him to tell me the latest news."

"He said two boats were launched the week before in search of the goldfields that must surely be nearby. One went to Cibao on the large island, and one to Niti, where Caribs, the cannibals, live. Both have returned with reports that gold can be found in the sand of the rivers and on land. They have samples—large nuggets to show our Spanish sovereigns, he added. A most interesting tale, I thought."

"Then I asked again when would the ships be returning to Spain?"

"The sailor answered me fully. He said since gold has been found, Admiral Columbus is ready to release those who wish to go back to Spain. And he wishes to rotate some of the men back to Spain, to bring back those that are healthy and fit to establish La Isabela. Twelve ships, I think he said, are soon bound for Cádiz. 'But many men have decided to stay, too. I have.' He ended his long comment."

"Of course, I wanted to know the date of departure. 'It's the second of February, sir,' he said, 'when the tides are favorable. The harbor here is small for all the vessels that are anchored now. It will certainly give us more space to tie up.' I thanked him for the information and took my wooden plate to the slop tub. I almost skipped to the ladder. Back in my room, I planned my departure. 'I, Juan Sánchez, will be on one of those ships without fail. And soon after that, I'll see my darling Sara.' The next ten days dragged by, but I felt increasingly stronger during that time. Even my wounds didn't bother me as much. I guess I had something better to occupy my mind."

Sara squeezed Juan's hand. Juan continued.

"Columbus, however, still kept to his room and to his bed, everyone said. On the night of the first of February, I climbed up the ladder one last time. I walked quietly over the deck. I drew close to the Admiral's cabin and put my ear to the door. I wondered if the Admiral was still awake. I heard a loud snort followed by a short silence. So, I knew. He's asleep, just as I thought. I turned the knob and slipped through the narrow passage. The old Admiral's gray hair splayed in all directions. His nightshirt open at the chest revealed more gray hair. I thumbed through the ship's log and found the date, November 28. I ripped the page out and folded it into my sleeve. I preferred to remain anonymous to history. Snorts and snores covered the sound of my activity. I tiptoed out and went back to my *toldilla*. Sara, I'm coming home, I said."

Chapter 10

"Do you want a drink? You must be parched after such a long story," said Sara. Juan shook his head and kept on with his tale.

"We did leave and I was on one of the ships, as I vowed to do. Many days later, I stepped on deck just as a sailor called from the main mast, 'Land, ho, Cádiz ahead.' I furrowed my eyebrows and squinted into the fog. The flagship glided forward, aided by the prevailing currents. Those paths in the sea had pushed us east and north all the way from the New World. When the fog parted, I saw a dark mass on the eastern horizon. As we drew closer, the shape of the harbor appeared."

"I asked the date. A sailor replied, '7 March 1494, sir. We've made good time.' I noticed Cádiz lay on an oblong island. A causeway on the south end big enough for carts and horses connected the island to the mainland. The northern part of the island contained a cluster of buildings. A cathedral occupied a prominent place, its gold dome catching the sunlight as it broke through the fog."

"'The captain said, 'Tie up, *hombres*.' Everyone put his muscle to it. They furled the sails, secured lines and prepared to dock. After a dozen deck hands strained to bring the ship under control, the ship came to rest at one of the piers along the inner harbor. Antonio de Torres, the captain chosen by Columbus welcomed us home. 'You are discharged from your obligation to this voyage, except for the crew who must secure the vessel first. Once that's completed, those of you on the crew can get your pay from the purser.' Captain Torres turned to the band of gentlemen bedecked in sweeping capes, wide hats with curling feathers and boots above their knees. '*Hidalgos*, collect your belongings. If you have anything to discuss with me, I'll be on the ship tomorrow, but for the rest of this day and tonight, I'll be on shore leave.' He stretched his hand out in a salute 'and ordered the gangplank should be dropped."

"The *hidalgos* jostled one another in an effort to each be first off the vessel. 'What, no carriers?' one of them said. Murmuring turned to shoving. Someone knocked off another's *sombrero*. Shouts and volleyed insults followed. I watched with a twitching lip and then a snort of laughter. I made my way off the vessel, along with a few other men, once the *hidalgos* cleared the way. A crowd of onlookers greeted us."

"They had many questions: 'Tell us, *hombres*, what was it like? How long did it take for you to return? Is it really the place Marco Polo wrote about, as Columbus said?' So, I turned to the crowd and answered them. I said Admiral Columbus put Antonio de Torres in charge of the returning ships and sent a letter with him to Queen Isabella and King Ferdinand. The captain navigated well and the weather was favorable. He made good time.' I started feeling weak and so I leaned against the pilings on the dock before continuing. 'Torres led the band of discontented men back home. You just saw them, the *hidalgos*.'"

"'Is this everyone?' They wanted to know. 'Well,' I said, 'Columbus did send one ship ahead to bear the news of the destruction of La Navidad. You did hear about that, didn't you? To which, they nodded. I told them the ships still waiting to dock have scores more men. Then, I gave them a lesson. I said that Torres retraced the path of the westerly voyage, taking an east-southeast direction along the northern shores of a string of islands Columbus discovered: first Hispaniola, then Puerto Rico, Virgin Islands, Santa Cruz, Montserrat, Guadalupe and Dominica."

"I paused, and then reeled like a drunkard. 'I don't know what's wrong with me—pardon. I feel dizzy,' I said. The listeners nodded their heads and kept their eyes riveted on my face. I tried to keep going with the details. I said that with clear skies and mild waves our twelve ships headed northeasterly toward the southwest coast of Spain. We've made land in twenty-five days, arriving here today, the seventh of March 1494. We have on board treasures from the New World—gold for Their Majesties, spices and natives. Some are cannibals. At that point, I lurched forward and would have fallen on my face, but one or two of the group reached out to hold me up."

"I told them I was not drunk, I just felt so weak—and I needed to lie down.

"They decided to take me back to Doctor Chanca who was still on board. Two men supported me and led me back up the gangplank to a pallet, a station where Chanca treated the men. I told them I'd felt unwell during the whole voyage. They left to find the doctor. I lay down on the narrow bed provided and closed my eyes. The infirmary, though small, exuded quietness, and smelled of herbs. I sniffed the pungent monk's hood, earthy rue and aromatic lavender, all used to cure ills."

"My mind was in turmoil. I needed to get back to you, Sara! I rolled onto my side and got back on my feet, my thoughts wild. I'll just look for some things to help my condition. After all, I'm a doctor. I ran my hand over the bottles and jars lined up on two wall-mounted shelves. I'll take this and this--something to ease the fever and something to help me sleep. I ducked my head to miss the clumps of drying herbs hanging from the ceiling. I pocketed the bottles and walked out the door. From the corner of my eye, I saw the erect and proud Chanca advancing across the deck."

"Chanca hailed me. 'Sánchez, is that your name?' I pretended I didn't recognize the name. I just kept walking and sauntered down the gangplank, not too fast. Doctor Chanca called again, '*Caballero,* you there. May I assist you?'"

"I turned my head to speak to the doctor. "Sorry, I didn't know you were speaking to me. I'm quite all right. I just went to retrieve something I left in my *toldilla*. He allowed he might be mistaken and then said good day to me. *Buenos dias*."

"I tipped a salute and strode down the pier. I'll need to repent later for that lie. Now to find a ship bound for Naples. I kept the pace until I got past several ships and out of sight. Then I stopped and leaned against a railing to think. I thought to myself: 'The best way to find a ship bound for Naples is to ask any sailor. I'll wait for one to walk by'." As the fog melted under the piercing rays of the sun, more and more people crowded the harbor promenade. The briny air mixed with the smell of sweat from the sailors passing by and the occasional clinging scents of cologne and hair pomades of the *hidalgo*s. I enjoyed standing there. Then I called to a sailor stumping by in dirty work clothes. The man stopped and shifted a sea bag from one shoulder to the ground."

"I asked: 'Sailor, do you know of any ships leaving for Naples soon?'"

"He scratched his head and thought a minute. He spoke in his rustic way. 'Must be one or two. Them Italian ships run a route up the coast to Lisbon and then back through the strait to Italy.' So I asked where the Italian ships were located. Again the colorful talk: 'You're almost there, sir.

Just a couple more slips on the left.' He pointed toward the cathedral. 'Right by the church.' The sailor promptly shifted his sea bag to the other shoulder and marched off."

"I followed the curve of the harbor and soon came to a fine vessel named the *Celestina*. The crew on the *Celestina* was busy scraping barnacles and applying pine tar. The dark pitch smelled of forests I remembered from my childhood. I hailed one of the sailors and asked when they were leaving. 'We're bound for Naples tomorrow.' I couldn't believe my luck. I asked the direction they were heading: Were they heading north to Lisbon first? He said, 'No, *signor*. We already traded there this trip. It's on to Naples via Tangier and then Barcelona.' I asked if they had room for another passenger. He said 'aye' and directed me to the purser to make arrangements. The purser said I could stay on board tonight. 'We leave early with the tide,' he said."

"I promised to come back later, but I wanted to get my midday meal on land. I left and ordered a hearty meal at a welcoming restaurant, as was customary for the midday meal. But when the first course came, my stomach lurched. The stuffed eggs made me gag. I ate some of the roasted chicken, but pushed away the large pieces of sweet peppers. I threw down a few small coins and pushed away from the table. The wine I drank contributed to the dizziness I had felt all morning. I struggled to get back to the *Celestina*. I took measured steps all the way back. I paused at the gangplank to take a breath and lifted each leg slowly. I asked for the purser and was directed to him. I shuffled across deck and got out my money pouch. 'Passage to Naples and a private room, if possible. I can pay.'"

"The purser collected his coins and pointed me to my cubicle. He noticed my unsteady gait. 'I'll call a boy to show you the way,' he said. 'Do you feel unwell, sir?'

"I made an excuse--that I was weary with traveling. 'All I need is a good rest,' I said and stumbled once as I followed the youngster to the ladder."

"'I bet you'll enjoy your siesta today, sir'," said the cabin boy. I asked his age. He said he was eleven—almost a man. 'I've been with the *Celestina* since I was seven." He drew himself up and straightened his soiled shirt and directed me down the ladder. I navigated the ladder by concentrating on each step as a separate task. He showed me to my space and I asked his name. 'Tomasso, sir.' The boy grabbed my bag and hefted it onto the bed. Then he said. 'Bye, *addio*.'"

"Before he left, I asked Tomasso to bring me a bowl of soup that night, as I'd like to stay in my room. I shifted my bag to the floor and shoved it under the bed. The chamber pot tilted. I righted it quickly. It was empty. I retrieved the two bottles I'd taken from Dr. Chanca's infirmary. A few drops of each should ease the fever and help me sleep a long time, I thought. I replaced the stoppers and wondered where to put them on a rocking vessel. I finally stowed them vertically in a crack in the floor. I pulled off my boots after a struggle and removed my outer garments. I hoped the medicine would begin to work on me soon. The fever was worrying me."

* * * *

"Tomasso coughed and shuffled his feet a few times and then brought in soup. I turned and lifted my head. I was on fire! My cheeks were burning! Tomasso noticed. He said I looked ill. I sat up. 'It's nothing, a slight fever,' I lied. 'Bring me the soup.' The steaming bowl smelled of chicken and herbs. 'Thank you, Tomasso. I'll feed myself.'

"Tomasso replied, 'If you please. I need to stay and take the bowl when you finish.' So, I told him I was slow today. I sucked the broth off the spoon as quickly as I could. It warmed my mouth and throat. I thrust the bowl back. 'Take it, and thanks'."

"I lay down and turned toward the hull wall, my cheek heating the cool bedding. Tomasso bowed out, I think. Tomasso brought another bowl in the morning. I slept I don't know how long, my dreams full of strange voices and incoherent imaginations. I was vaguely aware of Tomasso's comings and goings, I at last awoke with a faint feeling of hope. I had two questions: 'Where are we now? and what's that stink? Animals?' And I heard strange words outside."

"'It's Tangier, sir,' said Tomasso. 'You've slept two days and four hours or more.'"

"Sara looked at him with wide pupils. "If I'd only know what you suffered."

"It was worth it all to get back to you, dear one," said Juan, and kept on.

"Later on in the voyage, I awoke to a darkened room. Chills came in waves, washing over my body, taking control. My limbs tensed and shook. Then I became too hot! Sweat poured from my face. I felt the ship rock as waves lapped against the hull. I knew we must be underway, how long? I struggled onto one elbow and felt my forehead with the back of my hand. So hot! I needed more medicine—laudanum and a rosemary infusion. I reached down and fell out of bed as another wave of chills wracked my body."

"Where were the bottles? I felt around, fingers finally closing on the bottles. I sat up and took a few drops of each potion. I pulled myself up, took a breath and put my knees under me. Then one more push and I fell onto the bed. Now I was thirsty. I slept till light leaked through the ladder opening in the deck above. My lips stuck together and my forehead still felt hot. My stomach churned, but I gladly accepted the broth Tomasso brought. He mentioned the doctor was coming to see me. I said I didn't need a doctor, but I did need lots of purified water."

"'I'll do that,' he said, 'but the doctor is on his way, sir.'" Tomasso disappeared as the man strode in. 'What's the matter, sir? Not feeling well?' He approached me. I said I had just a simple fever—and a roaring headache. I clutched my head with both hands, and then asked for the chamber pot. I leaned over and vomited a bit of soup into the pot. I lay back on the bed and took a labored breath."

"The examination continued against my will. 'Any chills or further digestive problems?' The doctor felt my forehead and put two fingers to the side of my neck, at the pulse point. 'Normally, I'd bleed you. Your humors are sadly out of balance. I told him I was a doctor, also, and didn't want to be bled yet. 'I need sleep and water, and more broth. Just the simplest of remedies for now.'"

"He conceded. 'As you wish. I'll check on you tomorrow and note your progress. I have poppy juice to ease your pain.' He handed me a small vial. 'Be judicious—only a few drops.' I thanked him and asked him to send Tomasso back with purified water. Tomasso brought a tall wooden mug and held it to my lips. I let the drops trickle down my throat slowly, swishing the water around to moisten my mouth. 'I'll just stay with you for a while, sir. What's your name?' he asked."

"Juan, you can call me Juan." He took a few drops of the poppy juice. '*Signor* Juan. I will help you to get well. Do not be afraid.' Tomasso said. I closed my eyes and told him, I was in his hands." Tomasso tiptoed out sometime before I dropped off to sleep. When Tomasso returned a few hours later, he brought a pot and mug with him."

"'*Signor* Juan, I have some traditional remedies for you. Sit up and drink this tea. It's spearmint and very good to settle the digestion, to stop the vomit. Let me help you.' Tomasso put his arm behind my neck and propped me up. He urged me to take a sip. I said it tasted pleasant and took the mug. I drank it all. 'Another cup?' Tomasso handed the refilled mug to me. I drank it."

"What time is it? What day is it? Where are we?" I looked at Tomasso who shrugged his shoulders. I said I thought we were underway because I felt the ship surging on the waves and heard the sound of the ship passing through the sea. Tomasso said we were, indeed, sailing from Tangier to Barcelona now. 'It's a long voyage, maybe three days if the winds favor us. It is a good time to rest.'"

"'How is the fever?' The doctor entered and abruptly felt my forehead. 'Still very hot.' I said I woke up with sweat-drenched bedding and was out of ideas how to treat the disease. 'I've run out of ideas.' He said it took time for the fevers to leave the body."

"These chills and shakes tire me, too. When will it stop?" I grabbed the doctor's shoulders and shook them. 'Do not worry, *signor*. The doctor extracted himself from my grip. "He promised to have the cook prepare a plaster of sage for your chest. After it was on my body, I would sleep better. The sage plaster stops some of the sweat, he said, and told Tomasso to see to it. And he was gone."

"I lay back, feeling shrunken in body. 'I'm in your hands, Tomasso. *Grazie molto.* Many thanks. And please bring water.' He promised again to help me. 'I will get the plaster now,' he said. 'Then you can sleep.' But, I woke sometime during the night. The ship surged and rocked gently in the waters of the Middle Sea. My thoughts raced like dolphins before the waves. 'Won't this boat ever get there? How far could Barcelona be? And this plaster—it's intolerable. It itches. It stings. And my heart is beating fast!'"

"I staggered to my feet, wanting to get the plaster off of me. I shuffled to the basin of water on a small side table. With an effort, I pulled off the shirt covering me. I soaked a piece of toweling and dabbed at the thick plaster. Over and over, I wrung out the towel and applied the water again. Finally, dripping wet, I blotted my chest with more toweling. I felt such a relief, but now I was shivered. I fetched my shirt off the floor and staggered at the sudden wave of dizziness. What was this illness, I wondered. Back in bed, my cheeks warmed and a wave of chills sent spasms through my body. I felt a presence in the room. Was I dying?"

"Sara? Are you here?" I spoke into the darkness. I listened to the whisper of the waves against the ship's hull. 'Sara, pray for me. I need to reach you—soon.' The freshening breeze sent its airy message—Woo—Juan—Juan— Was I feverish or was I just losing my mind?"

"Oh, Juan. I wish I had been there to comfort you," said Sara.

Juan kissed her hand and paused for a minute. "Almost done with the telling."

Chapter 11

"The next thing I heard was the command to tie up in Barcelona. I opened my eyes and analyzed the situation. I felt better but wondered if I could stand. I pushed myself up to sitting position and slung one leg and then the other over the side of the narrow bed."

"'*Signor* Juan,' said Tomasso, 'how are you today? You've been in bed feverish for thirteen days.' Tomasso bustled in like an old grandmother, though he was only eleven. He brought a set of clothes and polished boots. He laid the pile next to me and the boots hit the floor nearby. He told me the doctor wanted me to get dressed today and to get some fresh air."

"I tested my legs—they felt wobbly. Then I asked the date. My mind had been floating in a feverish fog."

"The date was 22 March 1494. I would have time to walk around town and get a good meal. Tomasso grimaced at the water basin and wadded toweling. 'Did the sage plaster make you sweat less, *signor*?' he asked. I told him it felt like fire! Besides the fever and shaking, my heart was beating wildly. I suspected the plaster did it. I just wanted to be rid of it! I told him all this and reached for the snowy shirt. I maneuvered it over my head, but winced."

"He knew my problem. 'Sore arms, *signor*?' he said. I told him he was a good nurse. Yes, I ached everywhere. I pulled my soiled hosen off, kicking it aside. I grabbed the fresh garment and reached down to insert my right foot. Tomasso said he'd get clean water for me, if I could manage my clothes. I said I'm not an invalid yet. I straightened my hosen, put on a doublet and pushed my feet into the polished boots. By then, Tomasso brought back warm water and a clean bit of toweling with soap. He told me to be careful. 'You are still sick, *Signor* Juan. I know these things.' Tomasso held up his chin. I chuckled at his protective ways—he was like a mother hen. I soaped my face and neck, and promised to behave myself."

"I said, 'I want to go up on deck for a short time and walk around till I get tired. Thank you, my friend.' I saluted my short helper and climbed the ladder slowly, taking one rung at a time. Slow as an old grandpa. The sea breeze hit my face, I remember, as I came up on deck, cooling my red cheeks. I sauntered around the deck, taking short whiffs of fresh air. I shivered and realized I should have worn a cape. That was when I met the captain."

"He introduced himself by saying, 'Good day, *signor*. I haven't seen you on deck during this voyage.' He was a tall, stocky man with curly black hair and a three-cornered hat. I introduced myself, saying I was Juan Sánchez. I bowed as best I could, through the cloud of his dizziness that came on me then. 'Ferlandini,' he answered. 'Niccolo Ferlandini. Perhaps you know my father, Domenico Ferlandini. We run ships between Italy and Spain mostly, and sometimes take pilgrims to the Holy Land.' The younger Ferlandini looped his fingers around the hilt of his sword and assumed a wide stance."

"'Does he captain the *Veronica*?' I wanted to know. I met him some months ago in Palos." We started chatting. I remarked it at the time of the Expulsion. He said lots of Jewish people needed passage to parts far and wide. 'Where did you go?' he said.'"

"I told him I'm not Jewish, but my wife is. I said you left Spain, Sara, bound for Naples to join your brother, I thought. 'Now I'm trying to re-unite with her,' I said."

"He ventured to say that I was most likely impatient to be there, and wanted to know your brother's name. 'Raul Torres,' I said and explained your brother and his wife left Spain almost two years ago, before the official deadline."

"Was that wise, to share Raul's name so openly?" said Sara, shifting her position.

"I wanted to find out what he knew about you,' said Juan. "And I judged him to be a decent and discreet man. So, I asked if they got on his ship. Of course, he didn't remember, but offered that their agent might have the ship's log on file. Then he asked where have I been these past months? I said, 'On a long voyage, with no way to get a message out.'"

"He scratched his head and said he seemed to remember his father talking about a young woman who took passage on his ship, and got married just before leaving. Attractive woman, coppery hair, he said. 'That's my wife, Sara!" I said I was there to get married and then we parted till now. He was curious, asking where'd I disappeared to all that time? 'Leaving a pretty wife, too?' I told Niccolo it's a long story— 'couldn't be helped—a shipwreck and all.'

"And now, you're ill. Going home to die, or to be nursed back to health?"

"I said, 'What do you think? I can't wait to have my wife minister to me.' His question made me angry. But he replied, 'Good man,' and slapped me on the back."

"I questioned him closely about whether he had any information. 'Did your father say anything about where Sara is living now—and how she's doing?' I wanted to know. He said his father talks about you often. The woman seems to have lots of troubles. Had to leave Spain. Had someone stalking her. A religious man, he thought. 'Morales!' I exploded. Niccolo said, 'Sorry, *hombre*. I don't mean to scare you. I'm sure she's fine.'"

"I said I am more determined than ever to get back to you. At that point I stopped talking and tried to stop the wave of chills coursing through my body. My muscles tensed visibly."

"Oh, Juan! How sad." Sara had tears in her eyes. Juan kissed her hand.

"Captain Ferlandini, the younger, was concerned and urged me to get back to rest. Urged me to recover on the last leg of the voyage and go see 'that beautiful wife of yours.' He said, '*Buona fortuna*. Good fortune to you.' I took shuffling steps back to the ladder. I placed each foot with care. I'm sure my knuckles whitened as I gripped the rungs and descended. I found the way to my cubicle and bed and slumped on the pallet. I removed my doublet and pulled each boot off, to drop where they fell. Angling into the bed, I sighed and closed my eyes. Chided myself for tiring so quickly. Such a small bit of exercise and I'm exhausted. I talked to my self. 'Get well, hombre. Enough of this! Find your wife and take care of her!'"

* * * *

Juan stood up and paced the floor while talking.

"Later, I heard the noises while it was still dark in the ship. The congenial shouts, the creaking of wooden boats and clanking as anchors got hoisted—all these provided mental entertainment for me. I imagined fishermen must be underway to find the best seafood—giant lobsters with viselike claws, elusive shrimp that propel themselves through cobalt waters, clams to be dug and mussels to scrape from crusted rocks. All these would end up in a rice and seafood dish called *paella*, a specialty of Spain's Mediterranean coastal towns. Rice from Valencia with a pinch of golden saffron from the purple crocus on the plains of La Mancha made this concoction truly Spanish. I really got poetic in my imaginings. Then, I knew that I must be feeling better. So I decided to go into town. Tomasso brought me some food soon after, which I slurped quickly, cutlery in constant motion. 'Ah, that was good.' I wiped my mouth, backhanded, and stood up."

"Tomasso asked, 'You're all right, *Signor* Juan? Are you going off the ship?' I nodded. 'Bravo, *signor.* I also think you are well,' he said."

"I told him the fever left me late in the night. 'No shaking, no muscle pain and my headache is fading.' I held out my arms like an actor taking a bow. Tomasso clapped. *'Perfetto, Signor* Juan. Perfect.' He told me the *Celestina* would leave that night on the tide's turn so I should be back on board by sunset."

"I promised to be back before then. Since I still didn't have my strength back. But 'I plan to enjoy this sunny day, Tomasso!' I headed for the ladder and popped my head out at the top in no time. I ambled across deck and down the walkway to the wharf. A wide promenade led up from the wharf."

"I'd like to describe the scene in detail—it was so unique! On each side, hawkers praised their oranges and lemons, their mounds of teardrop-shaped almonds, half-moon lentils and wrinkled chickpeas. A vegetable stand sported piles of spring asparagus, blood red beets, celery, eggplant, leeks and lettuce. Herbs in pots and tied in neat bundles with string sat up straight on another table: basil and garlic, baskets of black pepper, pungent cloves, coriander, bulbous roots of ginger, round nutmegs and cinnamon bark, procured from India were available for a price. Burlap bags bulged with rice, nutty barley and wheat. Olives of all sizes and shapes occupied another booth, and with it jars of gleaming olive oils: the fruity dark green extra virgin, first press of the harvest, and the lighter golden oils so practical for everyday use. The smell of frying stopped me."

"I heard the hawkers say, 'Come get the spring onions, *señor*, sautéed with garlic. And we have the freshest shrimp cooked with garlic, as well.' I got a coin out of my pouch and took the food offered. After savoring that, I headed for the bazaar tables: bits of jewelry, scarves and fans. 'I must find something for Sara,' I thought to myself. 'After all, I haven't seen her for almost two years.'"

"I walked through all the bazaar booths, exotic trinkets from faraway places befuddling my head. Finally, I saw something sparkle in the sun. "What is that, señora?" A woman dressed in a silky dress with many folds and arranged over one shoulder looked up and smiled. She had a ring attached to one nostril and a red mark on her forehead."

"'You have a discerning eye, señor,' she said. 'These are pearls from India. Fashioned to hang from a silver chain. Your lady would be thrilled to receive such a gift.'" So, I asked her how she came all the way from India to Barcelona. She said she married a merchant seaman, in Goa, a Portuguese colon on the coast of India, and sailed many places with him. On one trip, he was washed overboard in a storm. She found she liked traveling in ships and trading in port cities. So, instead of returning to India she built up a business importing pearls and making fine jewelry."

"Not sure I believed her, but the pearl seemed to be of good quality. The woman tossed her head and put both hands on her hips. Silver bangles caught the sun and jingled as they fell back into place on her arms. She asserted forcefully that they were the best."

"I said, 'If the price is agreeable, I'll take this one.' I pointed to a large, teardrop shaped pearl. It shimmered in a way I've never seen. Like foam on a wave, maybe."

"She perceived I was enchanted by it, so we bargained till we reached a satisfactory agreement. She offered me tea and I accepted it."

"It is beautiful, Juan. I love it." Sara fingered the luminous jewel at her neck.

Juan smiled and resumed the story.

"Later, on board the *Celestina*, I took the necklace out of its brocaded pouch again and hoped you would love it. It still shimmered. I put it back in the pouch and tucked it in my bag. Captain Ferlandini strode up to me and remarked that we'd be leaving soon. He noticed I looked much improved in health. I told him the fever left me and the other ailments are becoming less bothersome. 'I'm very grateful.' Then I asked him to tell me a little about Naples."

"He mentioned the political situation is precarious. I said I didn't follow Italian politics, so he said the King of Naples, Ferdinand I, died in January, and his son, Alfonso II assumed the throne. But his son is just as despised as his father. The treasury is depleted. The noblemen are disgusted. He said all this."

"I asked him, 'What do you fear will happen?' and leaned closed for the answer. He said Charles VIII of France fancies he can take over the Italian duchies in the north, that he's preparing an army now. He said, 'I hear that even Ferdinand of Aragon, a cousin, I believe, may assert a claim to the throne of Naples. Who can keep track off all these princes!'"

"'And the Neapolitans—what will they do?' I asked. He said they would fight back. But it's all so disorganized—there is no unity, he conceded."

"I wondered, 'Why are you telling me this? Should intelligent people leave before this happens?' He said very clearly: 'I'd recommend it. Find your wife and leave.' I promised I'd consider it and thanked him. 'But the only priority now was to find Sara.'"

"He wished me *'Buona fortuna'* and *'Andare con Dio,* go with God, *signor.'* We clasped arms and parted. Immediately, Ferlandini pivoted and yelled a command to the crew. "Sails up, mates. It's on to Naples." The now-familiar routine began again and soon the *Celestina* slipped out of the harbor. I remember thinking: 'We have been fortunate with weather— no sudden squalls—so we should make Naples in just a few days.'"

"However, the next day that all changed. The sheets flattened with no wind to fill their expansive volume. The sun was a blazing orb, and the heavens sent no cooling breezes. I gazed at the watery blue tablecloth spread before me. Not a wrinkle disturbed its perfection. On the horizon, I saw a surge. It moved speedily through the inky depths getting closer to the ship. Suddenly, a silver form burst into the air right in front of me. It splashed seawater onto the deck. A dolphin! Hah! I exploded in laughter and delight. 'Well, you're one being that's not disturbed by the calm we're in.' The dolphin passed by again and nodded its head at me."

"One, two, three days of calm. 'When will the winds pick up again? We need to get to Naples. I need to get there!' I paced the deck and wrung my hands. My imagination constructed wild possibilities. *'Sara was burned in the fire. Sara lies injured at Raul's. Sara lost all the money I gave her. Sara is dead!'* Wait! *I'm making myself sick again. 'Calm yourself,'* I commanded. I climbed down the ladder and back to my cubicle. I whispered a prayer. I dozed but when I awoke there was still no wind."

Sara poured Juan a cup of wine. He sipped and cleared his throat.

Chapter 12

Juan continued:

"The *Celestina* sailed into Naples on 15 April. I watched from the deck. Naples harbor is wide and crescent-shaped with an abundance of wharves and piers. An imposing fortress guards the harbor."

"A breakwater extends from a prominent point on the northwest side into the ocean. In the inner harbor another breakwater complements a long pier. The *Celestina* found a slip and tied up there. As I sauntered off the boat and then stood on the wharf, I surveyed the view out to sea. A large mountain loomed across the way, 'a wisp of lacy *mantilla* gracing its cap,' as I recall."

"The captain announced, 'Naples is a lively seaport, a center of trade and fishing industry, offering fine leathers, wines and pasta.'"

"I must be off to find my Sara. I said goodbye to the long-winded Niccolo Ferlandini and his audience. *If I keep listening to him, I'll never reach my darling Sara.* My eagerness gave me extra energy. I took long strides up Harbor Street. *This looks promising.*"

"Cobblestones covered the street in perfect squares. This street had a lot of traffic, many people walking, and a few horses clopped along, too. Unloading took place on other streets. The pleasant chatter and yelled greetings mingled with the cries of merchants in sidewalk booths and cubbyhole shops along the way. Several food stands offered roasted pine nuts or *taralli,* a rolled and twisted bit of bread, a handful for a bargain. I bought some and let the vendor drop them in my pouch."

"I looked up ahead and saw a charred building. The leftovers of a sign said *'Spagnola.'* Could that be Sara's restaurant? The place had burned recently. A pile of timber sat by the front door and bits of charcoal still littered the scene. I hurried to the door and knocked. 'Anybody here?'"

"Nobody answered. My hopes fell flatter than a cod fillet. How would I find her? Then the door opened and a man with floury hands greet me."

"'Yes?'"

"I'm Juan Sánchez, looking for my wife, Sara. I saw the sign outside, and she's Spanish, so I thought maybe— Do you understand Spanish?" I hesitated. "I just got back from a long voyage. I've been sick. Do you know her?"

"Juan. Glad to meet you. I'm Leonardo, the manager."

"Oh, sorry I bothered you. Must be mistaken— I turned to go."

"Wait. I do know Sara. This is her restaurant. It was burnt recently. She asked me to manage it, to help get it repaired and running again."

"Is she here? What about Raul Torres, her brother? Does he live in Naples?"

"No and yes, to your two questions. Sara's not here, she went out for a walk. Maybe you'd like to see Raul. He should be the one to explain everything."

"What do you mean?"

"Just ask Raul. I'm not the one to tell you."

"'Tell me where she is.' I drew my sword and held the point to his throat. 'I have been gone almost two years. During that time I traveled with Columbus to the New World, endured a shipwreck, was left to guard the swiftly-built fort there, survived an attack on the fort and two wounds to my body, contracted a jungle fever and finally returned to find my wife. Besides that, I am personally acquainted with the Viceroy of the Indies. Tell me where my wife is.' By the end of the speech I was shouting."

"I told you she'll be back soon,' said Leonardo. 'You can wait outside. I don't want to be skewered. Or you can go to Raul's house. Which I recommend, under the circumstances.' He gave a few quick instructions. I withdrew my sword and sheathed it. Leonardo stepped back, gestured with flour flying off his hands and floating down to the street. Then he shut the door in my face. And I heard the bolt set in place. I pounded on the door, but no answer. After all, I'd threatened Leonardo."

"I made a quick exit and sped up a few streets and turned once or twice. I came to a pleasant street with trees overhead and ceramic-potted geraniums. Tile patterns in blues and yellows covered the lower wall and tiny rocks inlaid in dirt pathways graced the neighborhood. The sound of children's voices could be heard up and down the street. 'That must be Raul's house.' I rapped on the door."

"Yes?" A man opened the door. "Who is it?"

"You have a visitor from afar," I said. Raul turned his full attention to me and recognition dawned on his face. 'Juan, is that you? Could it be? Are you really here—and alive? Come in!' Raul embraced me. His nose gave a soft whistle as he took a breath."

"Raul, what a relief. You are here. But where is Sara?"

"Come in, sit down. Beata, could you get our guest a drink?"

"Beata looked up at the two men entering the family area. 'A miracle! It's our brother-in-law!' She jumped up and raced to give me an embrace. 'We heard rumors you were left in the New World. Then we heard just recently that everyone died there. Sit down and tell us about it.' She went to get a bottle of wine."

"'But, where's Sara?' I kept asking. 'Why won't anyone tell me?' I stood right where I had entered and looked around."

"Sara, I'll try to tell the following conversation word for word as it happened," Juan said to Sara, "Since it happened so recently." Sara grinned and nodded.

"'She's in Naples, Juan.' Beata handed him a wooden cup of fragrant red liquid. "'That's not a good enough answer. I've come thousands of miles to find her.' My voice rose. 'Tell me now!'"

"'Raul told me, 'Did you stop at her restaurant?'"

"Leonardo told me she was out for a walk.' I took a sip. I slumped down on a bench."

"'Then she probably is. She and Juanito.'"

"'Who's Juanito? I'll kill him. You mean she left me and took up with another man?'" I stood up fast, fists clenched. You can imagine I was furious."

"Raul and Beata giggled. 'No, silly,' said Beata. 'Juanito is your son. I guess you don't know.'"

"'What? A son?' I choked on the wine. I put the cup down and held my head with both hands. 'I don't understand. I have a son?'"

"'Born last April. He's one year old now.' Beata grinned."

"'There's much to tell you, Juan,' said Raul. 'Come, eat with us. Are you well? You look pale.'"

"'I was in the attack on La Navidad, hid in a cave, begged a ride on one of Columbus' returning ships and hopped a vessel to Naples, so yes, I'm tired. I think I had a jungle fever, too.' I put my head down on the table, my arms a cradle. 'What kept me going was my desire to see my beautiful bride, but you say she's not here. Why? Why? Why?' My eyes clouded over and I started to have chills."

"'You have a story to tell, and so do we. Much has happened to Sara. She's a brave one, my sister, but she just made an important decision. Please stay with us. Dinner will soon be ready and night is coming. Let's talk about everything over our meal.'"

"'That sounds like something Sara would say.' But, I will leave now—this minute.' I began to feel the fever returning I got up and walked circles around the room."

"'Your face is as red as *tinto,* Spanish wine. And you're shaking,' said Beata."

"'I know I should rest, but I just want to find my wife.' I raked a shaky hand through my hair. 'If I sound desperate, I guess I am.' I must have fainted, then."

"A few hours later, I tried to get up from the bed they had taken me to, but I felt the weakness again. I called to Raul and Beata."

"'Do you think you can go back to Sara's restaurant now? You don't look so well.' Raul patted me on the arm. You need a doctor."

"But, I got up with an effort and made my way toward the front door."

"Take a cloak," said Beata, as I strode down the hall. In my mind, I retraced with Raul the route back to Sara's. My mind was so confused. How could everyone be so calm! I walked with a purpose, though it was hard to negotiate some broken tiles on the sidewalk. By the time I reached the wharves, my cheeks and forehead felt cooler. I walked straight to the restaurant and knocked. Nobody answered."

"Where is Sara?"

"I trudged back toward Raul and Beata's, but collapsed on a low bulkhead halfway back. Raul walked up after just a minute and hired a cart."

"I was worried you wouldn't get there. Too sick! Come back to my house. I'll send a message to Sara. I don't know why she's so hard to find today."

"By the time we reached Raul's place, the fever raged again, sending waves of shaking spasms. Raul helped me down the hall. I pulled off my boots, removed my doublet and hosen while Beata went to fetch a pitcher and wooden tumbler. I sank into bed. Beata had made it with soft white sheets, a mounded pillow and a light blanket—so comforting! 'Beata, I need more blankets,' I said as she returned. 'I feel so cold.' She felt my forehead. 'You're hot with fever. I'll make some herbal tea that will help that condition.' I nodded and closed my eyes. I felt a pressure in my head. Something was pressing against my skull. *And it's getting harder to breathe. How will I sleep?*"

"Beata brought a steaming mug of lavender and basil tea. Good for relieving headaches. 'And a bit of chamomile to put you to sleep,' she said. I drank it all. I lay back and pulled the covers up. Beata spread another blanket over me. She promised to check on me. She urged me to sleep and get better. I gave a slight nod and relaxed. In spite of burning cheeks and pressure in my head, I slept. But it was short lived."

"I awoke as the pressure to my skull increased. *And now my chest feels heavy, too.* By evening I was panting like an overheated dog. Beata dabbed cool water on my face and neck. She helped me take some pure water. She brought me clear soup, but I refused all but a few sips. 'We need a doctor, Raul,' she said. 'Please go find one for Juan.'"

"Raul brought an portly, white-wigged surgeon who tapped on my chest and listened to me breathe. The gentleman doctor spoke only Italian, so Raul did his best to explain my maladies. Juan held his head and moaned. "Ahh," said the doctor. "*Mal di testa e liquido nei polmoni. Non bene.*"

"'Yes, not good, doctor. I understand that.' Raul leaned over the doctor's shoulder to get a better view of me. 'Headache and fluid in the lungs, too,' I think you said. What can be done? '*Che rimedio*? Is there a remedy?' The doctor shrugged his shoulders."

"'*Olio di menta piperita.*' He brought out a small bottle and demonstrated what to do. I was to breathe what was in the bottle, not drink it, as he motioned several times.

"Raul said, 'I understand. *Capisco.*' Beata and Raul thanked the doctor and gave him some coins. The white wig bobbed out of the room. Beata told me to sit up and breathe in the oil. 'Whew. It must be peppermint. It's strong!' I inhaled a deep breath and sputtered. I tried again, with not so deep a breath, and a third time. My panting subsided a bit and I slept."

"And now you know everything."

Chapter 13

Juan came to the end of his story and sat down on the bed, next to Sara. She watched him with tears glistening in her eyes.

"I went that day to visit Captain Ferlandini. I guess I should have told Leonardo or Raul. Why didn't they leave me a message? I came back in the evening." Sara looked at Juan. "But, I finally found you. And I'm so sorry. You've been through so much, Juan. No wonder you're tired."

"I want to be strong. Be your protector." Juan's voice halted.

"You will be. You are. Always." Sara kissed him lightly and laid her head on his chest. Juan relaxed, still feverish, and held her till sleep caught them.

Morning came, and with it a crowing baby boy. Juanito let out a yell.

"Big!"

Sara ran to him and said, "We'll have to teach you some new words." She picked up the squirming Juanito and tossed him up to her shoulder. She got him fresh diapers and washed his face in some tepid water left in the ceramic basin from the night before. "Today we get more clothes for you, big boy. And also, for your daddy."

"Da-Da."

"What's this? Did I hear my name?" Juan strolled in rubbing sleep out of his eyes. He picked up a clean little boy and bounced him around. "Want to fly like a bird?" He held

Juanito at arm's length and made squawking noises like a crow. Juanito squealed.

"Da-da."

"That's me. Shall we go get food, Mama?" Sara nodded and followed them downstairs. She cut up cheese and broke the stale bread into pieces. Juan held Juanito in his lap at the table and let him reach for bits of food. "I think he likes to gnaw on the bread. Maybe he's getting more teeth." Sara smiled and nodded. *Life is good again.*

The three days sped by like any ideal situation. Mornings were filled with Juanito's antics and his parents' smiles. Juan took every opportunity to become acquainted with his little son's mannerisms and preferences. He was quick to observe that walking delighted Juanito. He toured from room to room picking out things of interest—a flower in a vase, spider on the wall, a puffy cloud outside. At mealtime, Juanito cried loudly for food and hated to wait for Mama to prepare it.

Evenings were filled with Juan and Sara expressing their love for each other in tender words and caresses. A canopy of stars and velvet darkness provided the privacy and intimacy they both craved. A single kiss could take Sara's breath away and the powerful love Juan felt for his wife made him dizzy with joy and desire.

"Juan, you don't have to make up for all our missed nights together so quickly," she said, teasing.

"When I think of what I've lost all these months—" Juan reached for Sara again. Laughing, she pushed him away.

"I love you dearly, but I think Juanito is waking up. And today, we really should re-open the restaurant. People will wonder." Sara jumped out of bed and planted a peck on Juan's lips. Juan groaned and rolled over. Sara dressed quickly and brushed her long auburn tresses. She arranged them on top of her head and ran to get Juanito, who was making little squawks. "I'm coming, Juanito."

Sara began the daily routine with Juanito, taking him downstairs for food. Juan joined them some time later. "I've sent word to Leonardo to come today," she said. "We need to make plans to open the restaurant. We need to start making money again." She smiled at Juan. "You have a dreamy look in your eyes, Señor Sánchez."

"Just in love with my beautiful wife." He kissed her neck and took Juanito. "I'll handle the little one today so you can make your preparations."

"Juan, you're an angel. That would help me a lot." She jumped up and grabbed her shoulder bag. "I need to head to the market before Leonardo gets here. I need some things."

"Goodbye. Enjoy the shopping." Juan winked and tickled Juanito. The day went quickly, filled with buying herbs, ordering sacks of flour and salt, placing orders for eggs, chicken and fish and having a new sign made. Leonardo showed up about mid-day. He and Sara conferred. "We'll open the day after tomorrow, Leonardo," said Sara. "That's when the sign is ready."

"Good, because it takes a day to fire up the brick oven. An even temperature and all that," said Leonardo. "I'll start making the rustic country bread everyone loves. It was popular before the fire. I'll add different herbs, of course, for those who like that."

"Wonderful. I'll start with a basic menu—soup and frittata—and bread. Let's see how it goes for a week."

"Will your husband help you?"

"With cooking? I don't know. But he's willing to take care of Juanito for some of the time. Oh, I should contact Clara, my former baby caretaker." Sara wrote a note and put it in her pocket.

"Waiters?"

"Allegra and Beppe will return first, and then Stefano and Silvia as we get more business." Leonardo nodded.

"May you be as successful as you were before."

A shadow crossed the threshold.

"*Signor* Alessandro, you always seem to know what I'm doing." Sara brushed a loose curl back from her forehead and straightened her work clothes. Leonardo disappeared into the other room.

"*Buon giorno, signora.* I'm glad to see you have opened your restaurant again. I was just passing by and saw your preparations." The magistrate bowed low. He cleared his throat. Juan strolled in. He had donned his best doublet and combed his hair.

"Who's this, Sara? A visitor?"

"Juan, this is *Signor* Alessandro, the local magistrate and collector of taxes." Juan bowed and held the man's gaze a long time. "My husband, Juan Sánchez, sir."

"What does he want?" Juan turned to his wife.

"*Signor* Alessandro hasn't told me yet." She turned to her visitor and raised her eyebrows.

"*Signora*, since your restaurant is working again, you will need to pay taxes. I see you have done a fine job of restoration."

"How much is due, and when?"

"It embarrasses me to say you need to pay by Friday."

"That's only three days. I can't do it." Sara placed both hands on her hips.

"We can make an arrangement again, as we did before."

"For an added fee, I imagine," said Juan.

"It's customary, *signor.*" *Signor* Alessandro looked down at his shoes.

"No! Nothing more than the amount due! You'll not take advantage of a single woman anymore." Juan folded his arms and puffed out his chest.

"But, *signor*—"

"Send us a proper invoice from the mayor's office and we'll pay it. But nothing more! Goodbye, *signor*." Juan motioned toward the door and *Signor* Alessandro took his leave quickly.

"Juan, what have you done?" Sara wrung her hands. "I hope we don't have problems with him later."

"I doubt it."

"He's caused problems before, though. You should be more cautious." Another shadow crossed the threshold.

"Is there a *Signora* Sánchez here or someone named Juan Sánchez?"

"Who are you?"

"The postman. I have several letters to deliver." He held them out. "All from Spain, and you're the owner of *La Donna Spagnola*, right? The Spanish Woman?"

"That's right," said Sara. "Oh, look, Juan, one is from Ana, my old family housekeeper. There's another from Moguer, a woman named Catalina Torres. Oh, and look a letter from Córdoba." Sara handed it to Juan.

"From my family." He fingered it and shot a glance at Sara. "What's all this? Three letters in one day? Do you always get so many letters?"

"Never. I'm as amazed as you." They strolled inside and sat at a table to examine the letters. Sara ripped open the letter from Ana. She scanned the message. "Oh, Ana is sick. She may be dying. She wishes me well and would like to see me one more time." A single tear slid down Sara's cheek. Juan reached for her hand.

"I'm so sorry! Let's see what my family has to say. Did I tell you I sent them a letter when I arrived in Cádiz? I wanted to go there, but the fever kept me low. So, I just came to you." He broke the wax seal and unrolled it.

"This is a letter inviting us to come live with them. 'We are ecstatic to see you, your wife and child'." Sara clapped her hands. Juan smiled.

"What does the third letter say? Have you ever heard of this Catalina Torres?"

"Let me read the letter and I'll tell you." She scanned the contents.

'Dear Sara de Sánchez Torres,

I write to you as the widow of your brother, Luis. He married me only a few weeks before he left on the fateful voyage with Columbus. As you see, I am now alone. Luis gave me a baby, but it was delivered stillborn and before its time. I weep as I write to you. I am alone. As your sister in law, I beg of you to come live with me. We will be two *viudas*, widows together, at least. Our time on earth will be less lonely if we can be together. I think that King Ferdinand and Queen Isabella will grant a small pension to anyone whose relative perished at La Navidad. I have already applied for it. Maybe you could come and ask for one, too. Together, we could find a way to live. With affection, Catalina de Torres.'

"What an amazing letter, Sara. How did she learn about you?"

"Luis must have told her about me and Raul. I don't know how it got to us here in Naples, though."

"Maybe Columbus forwarded it."

"What did you want to tell me before?"

"Luis told me about Catalina just when the Indians attacked the fort at La Navidad."

"So, she really is Luis' widow? Luis was always running off somewhere. Now I know one place he visited." She gave a half smile. "We must visit her sometime."

"What about these other letters? And why three in one day? It's a sign."

"Perhaps. It does make me want to go back to Spain."

"*Igualmente*. And me, equally."

"I dream of Spain almost every night." Sara sighed.

"Don't you like Naples?"

"The lush gardens, the hot sun, the flowing, tinkling water. Wouldn't you dream of it, too?"

"I did dream of it. When I wasn't dreaming of you."

"Oh, Juan. It's a wonderful dream. But that's all it can be. How could we ever go back?"

"Well, Morales is no longer a problem for you, right? Does anyone else know your history? Especially in a city other than Granada?"

"It would take a very strong reason to get me to return. I am afraid of being followed again. It haunts me." Juan put his arm around her.

"You have endured so much, Sara. But maybe it's over. Think about it."

"I will try." She stood up. "Now, I need to finish my plans for opening *La Donna Spagnola*. 'The Spanish Woman' has come back to life."

Chapter 14

The restaurant opened two days later, a large sign announcing the date and giving the seasonal menu, based on what was available locally at peak freshness. Leonardo arrived early that morning, forming loaves of crusty bread and sliding them into the hot brick oven. When Sara came downstairs, wonderful smells filled the kitchen. "Your delicious bread will bring in a lot of customers today, Leonardo."

Leonardo wiped his forehead with the back of his hand. "It's my pleasure, Sara. I love making bread." He clapped his hands together. A puff of flour filled the air around him.

"It's about time to open the doors. I wonder where—"

Two people scurried through the front door. "Here we are, *signora*." Allegra and Beppe entered smiling. Beppe hopped from one foot to the other. "We are glad you opened the restaurant again."

"Let's get started. It's almost time," said Sara. Allegra and Beppe ran to set the tables with cutlery and plates. Soon, the first customers entered. "It's the mother hen and her chicks," Beppe whispered.

"Fortunata, welcome," said Sara, as she moved forward to embrace her friend.

"Hello, *amica*. I'm very happy to see you rebuilt and started your restaurant again. It was always full of people before. It will be again." She paused to take a breath. "Now, Luisa, mind your manners. Don't hit your little brother. Luigi, no pulling of Luisa's hair." The children paused to listen, and then stuck out their tongues at each other. "I have news to tell you, Sara, but first we need a bite to eat, don't we, children?"

"Sì, mama. Sì." All five of them circled around and fought for chairs. "I want to sit there. That's mine!"

"When it's quiet, I'll order." Fortunata lifted her chin and looked around the table. Each child settled in a chair and looked at her. "Good. Now, Beppe, I'd like to order two frittatas and a basket of that good bread you make here. It's available today, right?"

"Si, *signora*. Herb bread or plain?"

"Plain, I think. The children prefer that. And a pitcher of lemon water."

"Grazie, *signora*. I'll place your order quickly." Beppe ran to the kitchen to tell Sara. "Your first order, *Signora* Sara."

"Thanks. I must do some prep work. If I need to feed Fortunata's brood and the other customers coming in today." Sara wiped her forehead. "I forgot about getting organized. Send Allegra to me." Beppe filled up a pitcher of lemon water and set cups at Fortunata's table. Allegra walked by while greeting a customer. Beppe laid a hand on Allegra's arm.

"Allegra, *Signora* Sara needs you in the kitchen for a while. I'll manage the orders."

"There are three new tables of people and more walking in now. Right this way please. I'll seat you." She led a group of four to a window table and returned. "All right, I'll go to Sara now."

Allegra nodded her head and ducked into the kitchen. She washed her hands and put on an apron. "What shall I do first, *signora*?"

"Chop lots of onions and then mince a bowl of garlic." Sara cut thin slices of eggplant. She built a mound of the purple vegetable and then started on a mountain of snowy turnips. Allegra shook her curls in acknowledgment and grabbed a knife. The steely edge swished through a bag of onions, making neat slices and then another pile of chopped bits. Next, Allegra took pains to peel each section of the garlic head and then chop them extra fine.

"Nice work," said Sara. She reached for the garlic. "I need that now!" Beppe swooped in. The bowl of garlic turned over and landed on Beppe's boot.

"Clean it up and start again! And be careful, everyone!"

"I'm sorry, *signora*," said Beppe. "I'll get the bread for Fortunata and get out of here."

"Clearly, I didn't plan well for the first day," said Sara.

"People are so glad you opened your restaurant they all came at once. I think it will become more settled after a few days, *signora*."

"Perhaps you are right, Allegra. We'll keep working here to keep up with the orders and tonight I'll make plans to smooth things out." Sara smiled at Allegra. "I need your help for another half hour, then you can help in the dining room."

"Very good." Allegra and Sara put their heads down and replaced the spilled garlic and also cut more vegetables and made *limonata*. Soon the rush of orders slowed. "There, we did it, *signora*," said Allegra.

"Thanks to you. Now go join Beppe in the restaurant." Sara wiped her hands on her apron and got a drink of lemon water. The sharp flavor puckered her lips, but the honey flavoring the water also soothed her dry throat. "Ahh."

Beppe returned. "Please, *signora*, you are needed in the restaurant." Sara followed him and met Fortunata and children just as they were exiting the door. "What's your news, Fortunata?"

"I guess it's not a secret." Fortunata blushed. "There will soon be another Amato in the world. I am with child." She looked at her hands.

Sara embraced her. "My best wishes. Another home-on-leave baby."

"Yes."

"I'm pleased to hear—"

"Come quickly, *Signora* Sara." Beppe touched her shoulder.

"What's the matter?" Sara brushed back her hair.

"Something terrible has happened. Come and see." He gave her a nudge. Sara followed on his heels to the front of the restaurant.

"*Signor* Alessandro is just leaving." Beppe motioned to the front door. Sara stepped outside. There a large sign had been nailed over the restaurant's bill of fare.

"What's this all about, *signor*?" Sara's voice rose in pitch and volume. "Beppe, get Juan." The teenager ran through the door toward the apartment steps.

"*Buon giorno, Signora* Sánchez." *Signor* Alessandro, clothed in a flowing doublet of brocaded satin, bowed low. Two men of lesser grandeur stood on either side of him. One held a hammer and one a small ladder. "I hope you are well."

"What have you done?"

"Your restaurant is now officially closed because you have not paid your taxes." With a sweeping motion he gestured toward the fresh sign. It was a parchment covered with finely scripted writing and two large seals, one in each corner, accompanied by a wax impression. "See the mayor's official mark."

"Wait—"

"We asked for an official invoice, not this!" Juan exploded through the doorway onto the street. The tax collector backed away and his helpers moved closer to him.

"'By order of the mayor,' it says: 'From today, The Spanish Woman will be closed until it is properly registered with the local authorities'." *Signor* Alessandro's voice echoed off the walls of the nearby buildings.

"You have embarrassed us, sir. This will affect our business." Juan's hands clenched and his knuckles whitened.

"What can we do to get the restaurant opened again?" Sara wrung her hands and looked at the tax collector.

"I will come by tomorrow to make arrangements, but you must do as I say. You must cooperate."

"We must pay your bribe." Juan shook a fist.

"As you say." *Signor* Alessandro's head dipped in a nod. He adjusted his doublet around his ample middle and turned to leave. "However, until you make proper payment, your restaurant is closed." With a rustle of garments, he left.

Chapter 15

"I don't know if I have enough to pay the taxes!" Sara covered her face and shook her head.

"And the bribe." Juan put his arm around Sara. She leaned into him.

"Yes. With all the rebuilding and making of furniture, I just don't know. But let's count it out tonight." Sara dismissed Beppe and Allegra and shut the door for the evening.

"Don't worry, dear Sarita."

Juanito let out a shriek, which sent both of them up the stairs. Juanito stood at the top of the stairwell on shaky feet, arms held out to aid his balance. Sara closed the gap quickly. "Juanito, what a big boy you are! Are you ready to try the stairs?" She took his hand and showed him how to back down the stairs, hands on each tread. "It's like crawling backward, big boy!"

"Big!" said Juanito, and wriggled backward and down a step.

"Know any other words, Juanito?" Juan rolled his eyes at his little boy.

"Da-da!" Juanito waved an arm at Juan and grinned.

"Good boy!" Juan scooped up Juanito and raised him high in the air. Juanito giggled. Juan and Sara headed up to their apartment home. Juan stoked the fire in the bedroom brazier.

"I'll go down and heat up something for our dinner," said Sara. She descended and found some cooked pasta. She quickly prepared a cream sauce and added bits of meat and vegetables. She tossed in with the warmed pasta and cut a few slices of Leonardo's bread. Sara carried up the stairs and put it on the carved table and slid the carved chairs up to it. "Come, Juanito, let's have some food."

After the food was consumed and Juanito's face and hands got cleaned, Sara ran to the wardrobe and felt in the back for the money pouch. She found it and pulled it out. "It's not as heavy as before." She raised her eyebrows.

"Bring it here and let's count the coins." Juan cleared off the table and put Juanito down.

"Be careful of the brazier," said Sara. Juan scooped up Juanito again and held him on his lap. "I'll hold the boy, you count the coins."

Sara made piles of each denomination of coin, then counted each and added the numbers. "Did *Signor* Alessandro give us a number?"

"How much do you have?"

"Three hundred."

"He said two hundred and twenty."

"Well, we have some savings left, then, but there may be other bills from the carpenters."

"What's most important is to get the place open again—and quickly."

"Sure. We also need to build up our savings."

"We'll pay the taxes tomorrow, Saturday, then we can re-open Monday. We'll make a lot of money from your eager customers and then see if we can pay the rest of the renovation bills. It'll be all right, you'll see."

'It's such a worry, trying to run a restaurant and pay all the food suppliers as well as keep track of taxes. *Signor* Alessandro always finds me in a tight situation."

"You've managed well to this point. I'm sure you will set everything right again."

"That fire was a big setback."

"I'm here now and I'll help in every way I can."

"I'm glad I have you to help me talk through problems, Juan." She leaned across the table and kissed him.

"*Te amo,* Sarita. I love you. Let's put Juanito to bed, so we can have some private time." Juan lifted Juanito to sit on his shoulders, then pushed away from the table and walked him to his bedroom. Juanito gurgled and squealed his delight. Sara prepared Juanito for bed and rocked him. She opened her bodice and let him nurse.

"Only at bedtime now. He'll soon be too old for this."

"You're a wonderful mother, Sara." Juan stroked Juanito's head and placed a single kiss on Sara's cheek.

"Juanito's body relaxed and went limp. Sara gathered him up and placed him in his new bed. She straightened her blouse and went back to Juan's arms. "How I missed you when you were gone! It will take time to repair that empty time."

"Then let's start now, dear one." Juan drew her to their bedroom and reached out to her. They shared again the anguish of separation and the joy of reuniting.

In the morning, they dressed, counted out the necessary coins and put them in a pouch. "I wish we could teach Signor Alessandro a lesson. So he'll never bribe us again."

"I imagine we're not the only ones from whom he extracts extra money." Sara smoothed her hair into an upswept style.

"I have an idea that might work. Do you have a piece of parchment?" Sara looked and found a small square, on which Juan wrote something. "I wonder if the mayor knows that Signor Alessandro takes a little extra. Let's present this money directly to him and see what happens."

"Clever idea." Sara put a miniature doublet on Juanito and planted him on one hip. "This little boy is getting big and heavy."

"Big!" "Boy!"

"Very good. Let's go." The family ambled down the streets toward city hall. When they got there, they found the mayor's office and walked directly to his door. Since it was ajar, Juan called out,

"*Signor* Mayor, may we come in?"

"What's this? Who are you?" A middle-aged man, bald but otherwise handsomely arrayed, stepped to the door. "How can I help you?"

"We have a tax payment to pay, *signor*." Sara set the pouch on the man's desk and Juan place the parchment next to it. "Our tax collector is *Signor* Alessandro. He closed our restaurant yesterday because we hadn't paid our taxes."

"This is really not my concern. One of the clerks can take it if *Signor* Alessandro is not here."

"We thought you'd like to know that he always asks a bribe and gives very short notice. Is that standard practice?"

"What? No! Let me read the parchment." The mayor took up the parchment and read it carefully. "Hm. I see. I'll speak with him. And thank you for the information. Please get a receipt for your payment from the clerk in the other room. *Buon giorno*." He bowed and ushered them out of his office.

"Did the mayor look surprised? Do you think he'll do something about *Signor* Alessandro?"

"We can hope he does." Juan and Sara clasped hands and walked along with Juanito slung over Juan's shoulder. "The rest of the day is free for us, since the restaurant is closed. What shall we do?"

"Let me show you Naples. It's an interesting town and has a lot of history."

"Well, I'm not too enthralled with history, but show me a couple of things before Juanito tires." They walked down to the harbor. "There's Castel Nuovo, with its five towers and brick façade. Built many years ago, I think."

"I saw that when I landed. How about going to a scenic point?"

"There's a mountain in the distance, Vesuvius. Would you like to see? I know a good place to view it."

"Sure. Maybe Juanito would, too. It's funny. We now have to consider Juanito's likes and dislikes when we do something."

"Yes, he's a little person already." Sara chucked him under the chin. Juanito lifted up his head from Juan's shoulder as if it were a boulder. His eyes looked glassy.

"What's wrong, little man?" Juan followed Sara until they came to a rocky knoll with a view across the crescent-shaped bay.

"I think he's getting sick, Juan. Let's not stay too long." She put a hand on Juanito's forehead. "He's hot."

"Since we're here, I'd like to spend just a minute to admire the view. How often does that mountain spew lava?" Juan planted his feet and rubbed Juanito's back.

"I don't know, but the local people tell stories. They seem to think it's something to be feared." Sara eased a blanket around Juanito's shoulders. He burrowed his head in deeper.

"Hm. I saw a mountain spew ash when we were sailing with Columbus through the Canary Islands. Exciting but disturbing."

"Sure. Something that's far beyond anyone's power to control or predict."

"It's awe-inspiring." They stood a moment longer to take in the purple smudge of the hill and wisps of clouds that made up the mountain. "How's Juanito?"

"His cheeks are hot and he's panting like a dog." Sara took him from Juan's arms and covered him with the blanket. "We need to get back." Juanito began to squirm and by the time he was placed in his bed, he was crying with all his might.

"Let me give him something to calm him." Juan found a small bottle in his bag and poured a few drops onto Juanito's tongue. "His throat is red, he's feverish and his nose is running. Does he get ill often, Sara?"

"No. Never! This is the first time he's had more than a running nose. Could he be teething?"

"No. It's more than that. It may be influenza, or perhaps ague, like I've had. Ague causes those waves of chills and shaking."

"Oh, Juan—no!" Sara's voice broke and she cried out. "My baby, my baby." She rubbed Juanito's belly. His sobs subsided.

"Don't worry too much, my darling. We'll give him the best of care. He'll come through this." Juan put an arm around Sara's shoulder. She turned and put her head into his chest. "Go, sit down for a while. I'll watch the little one."

They took turns through the day and late into the night and the following day, as well. When it was time to awaken for a new day of work on Monday, only Sara's will pulled her out of bed. "I'm so tired." She stumbled around in the dark and found her clothes draped over the chair. *That's not like me. I usually put my clothes away.*

"I'll take care of Juanito today, so you can work. It's important you open the restaurant again."

"How is our little one?" She placed a hand on Juanito's cheek and brushed hair back from his forehead. "Oh, still warm."

"Yes, but better, I think. And I haven't seen him shivering like before."

"I've got to go," said Sara. It's time to get started downstairs and maybe find some food to eat first." Sara adjusted her everyday dress and smoothed a little olive oil lotion on her face and hands. "I'll send someone to relieve you." She pecked him on his cheek like a chicken seeking sustenance, and felt the stubble that had grown there in the last two days. "Get some rest, my love." Juan gave her an unreadable look.

The day was full of demands: orders for food and for loaves of bread, suppliers bringing meat, eggs or vegetables and waiting for payment, and a myriad of decisions about how and where to store the food. Sara looked up when the church bells chimed three. "I haven't eaten lunch, and I haven't thought a minute about Juan and Juanito." She brushed flour off her apron and tidied her workspace before looking for food. Some leftover frittata filled her stomach, then she remembered: "Oh, no. I promised to send someone to help Juan. I wonder how he's doing. I wonder how Juanito is doing, too."

Sara dismissed the workers and ran up the stairs. "Juan, I'm sorry I forgot. How are you?" She met him on the stairway. Juan put his hand over her mouth. "Shh, quiet! Juanito is finally asleep. Don't wake him. Where have you been?" His eyebrows knit together and the corners of his mouth drooped down. Sara wriggled out of his grasp.

"Don't do that. I'm not a child." She whispered, "I've been so busy I just forgot. I'm sorry."

"I'm absolutely exhausted and want to get out of here for a while. I'll see you later." Juan turned on his heel and took the stairs two at a time.

"Wait, Juan. How is Juanito? What should I do to care for him?" Juanito let out a cry and sat up. "Da-da!"

"You look awful, little one. Flushed and tired." Juanito squirmed around and rubbed his stomach. A few gags and up came his lunch. "Oh, no! All over the bed coverings. I'll have to clean you and the bed." Sara scooped up Juanito and took him over to the basin of water. She stripped off his clothes and dropped them on the floor. "Horrible smell! I bet you are wondering what's wrong. Poor Juanito!"

Sara took a piece of toweling and dampened it, then cleared the vomit off of her little boy—face, mouth, ears, body. She put some rosemary in the water to take away the odor. She dabbed at the debris that had gotten on her dress while working with Juanito. "Now, let's get a clean nightshirt for you, dear one." Juanito whimpered and squirmed. Sara gave him some tepid water and sat him down on the floor while she pulled off the bed sheets. "Lots of laundry. I hope that doesn't happen again." She covered the ruined bed with a thick towel and laid her little boy down. She looked for some medicine to help settle Juanito's insides. "I don't know what any of these bottles are for." She looked at Juan's shelf of vials and terracotta bottles. "Where is he? Why did he leave so fast? And this laundry is piling up."

Juan returned later, looking pale and pinched in expression. "Juan, where have you been? What's the problem?" Her voice sounded shrill in her own ears.

"The problem is I had to vomit, so I ran outside rather than make a mess here. And then, I decided to seek an apothecary and get some remedy for this. I think I caught it from Juanito." Juan held up a small vial with a stopper.

"Oh, I'm relieved," said Sara, "and sorry I just yelled at you. You're sick, too, aren't you?" Juan nodded and rubbed his middle.

"I'm beginning to think I'll never get well again," said Juan. "First, the jungle fever, sweating, waves of shivering and shakes, more fever and weakness, and now after finally feeling well, I get the vomits." Sara advanced to his side and rubbed his back and then hugged him.

"Dear Juan. How discouraging. I suppose I'll get the same illness soon, then, being around you two. I better get Clara to come and nurse us all, and wash the laundry we'll all need cleaned."

"Juanito looks so limp. Did you give him anything?"

"No, I don't know your medicines and what they do. Can you help him and explain about the different vials so I can help when you're not here?"

"Of course." Juan took a vial and dropped one or two drops unto Juanito's tongue. "This should soothe him and let him sleep again. "He may vomit again before the day's over, though. I already cleaned up one mess before you came."

"I'm tired and I know you're tired. Let me go and send a message for help right now." Sara walked slowly to the stairway and down. She opened the front door and called, "Young man, do you know where Clara Díaz lives?" He nodded.

"I need her help. Today, if possible. She knows us—Sara Sánchez at 'The Spanish Woman' restaurant. Here's a coin." The youth turned and ran as if in a race.

Chapter 16

❋

"I never thought we'd all get well! There was always someone vomiting or raging with fever." Sara sat at the carved table and looked at herself in the hand mirror. She stuck out her tongue. "I'm still not over it. I look terrible! Coated tongue, dark circles under my eyes."

Juan sat on the edge of the bed pulling on hosen and a linen shirt. "I'm so glad you called Clara. She's taken care of all of us. And this shirt smells clean. The stink of the last several days is over." He pushed himself up to standing. "I'll get Juanito. I hear him making little-boy noises."

"He must be well, then, finally." Sara took up a brush and worked at the tangles in her hair. "I haven't brushed my hair for two days!"

"Did Leonardo shut the restaurant? Did your workers manage it all?"

"I've no idea. I felt so awful the last few days, I just wanted to curl up in the bed and stay there forever." Sara went to the wardrobe for a clean dress. "I hope Clara didn't catch our illness."

"I didn't, *signora*." Clara came bustling in with folded sheets and towels and several items of clothing for each of them. "Do you feel like eating, any of you? I have soup downstairs. Come down and have some." She laid sheets over the chair back and put the folded clothing into a chest. Then she took to the stairs.

"Thank you, Clara. We needed you and you did it all." Sara stood up and took Juanito from Juan. "You're all dressed and you look eager to get up." Juanito eyed his mama and waved his arms.

"Ma-ma."

"A new word! Good for you. Learning even while sick." She squeezed Juanito and he giggled. "Let's go downstairs for soup. That sounds good for this invalid. How about you, Juan?"

"Yes, soup it is. Easy on the insides." They all made their way down the stairs and into the kitchen. "Mm. Smells good."

"My stomach is lurching," said Sara.

"You're not going to be sick again?"

"No, no." But she rubbed her middle.

They ate their soup slowly. "It feels good to eat again and hope to keep it down," said Juan.

"This soup is as good as Ana's used to be. She was our housekeeper after my mother died. She kept our family from falling apart."

"That was a difficult time, I imagine."

"Yes. And since I got that letter from her, I can't stop thinking of our life in Spain." Juan took her hand and squeezed.

"What are your favorite memories?"

"There are so many: the sun warming the golden sandstone buildings, the tinkling of water as it flows through water channels in the patio garden, the coo of doves that can sound like laughter and the fragrance of wisteria—"

"Wow, you've really thought about it."

"It's enchanting. A good garden, like in the Alhambra, should contain large pools and narrow channels that carry rushing water to every part. That cools a person on a hot day. And the sound of moving water is so calming on the ear. Fragrant plants like wisteria, orange blossoms and lavender spice the air. So, eyes, ears, nose and skin all nourish body and soul."

"Your descriptions sound like gardens in the Alcázar of Córdoba. Sorry to say, I've never seen the Alhambra gardens."

"What makes your heart beat faster?"

"Besides you? The rich history, guitar music picked one string at a time, air-cured ham, the wonderful Arabian horses—and the trip with Columbus to the New World. I feel proud that our king and queen championed this voyage of discovery and found a whole new realm."

"Why is the trip so important to you?"

"I personally learned so much about the native peoples there. It was full of danger, but also knowledge. Does it sound unmanly for me to say I'd like to tell people all that we discovered—the animals, birds and plants, and our contacts with the native people? It's now a part of our history that people should know."

"Maybe you should write down your thoughts. Look back at your journals—the ones Columbus sent to me on his return from the first voyage. I hoped to have you home back then, but your journals helped me in my disappointment that you were left at La Navidad. Write about what you observed and did. Columbus kept a log, right?"

"Yes, but he had a duty to the queen and king to report. And he worried so much about finding Cathay and gold."

"Write a book like Marco Polo did long ago. People are curious about the voyage. Why don't you do that?" Sara looked up. "I'll get Clara to come every day so you can spend time writing."

"I do love caring for my little boy," said Juan. "But, I admit I'm a bit restless. What's ahead for me in Naples? And do you intend to stay here forever?"

"I don't know."

"Do you consider it your new home?" Juan held her gaze a long time, as if the answer might appear as an image in a reflecting pool, clear and bright.

"No, but I don't dare hope for anything else. We were expelled forever."

"Well, we can write about Spain and dream about it. I like your suggestion. I will start writing." Juan got up and grabbed his cloak. "I'm off to buy parchments and a new quill. And I'll dig out my journal and read it again." He gave her a soft kiss. "Say, did you get it from Columbus? I asked him to take it to you when he returned from the first voyage. Since I stayed behind in La Navidad, not knowing if I'd ever get back, I wanted you to have that part of me."

"Yes, of course. I do have it and I treasure it. Columbus delivered it personally. I read and re-read about all your experiences in the New World. It was a comfort in an uncertain time. I'll find it before you return and leave it on the table. I'm off to work today. I'll arrange things with Clara, too, and pay her for her recent nursing care." Sara waved as he rushed out the door.

I'd like to read that collection of Andalucían poems my father once owned. I'll look for it tonight, too. Sara sighed and lifted Juanito from her lap to her hip. "You are so heavy now, Juanito. You're a big boy!"

"Big, big!" Juanito kicked his legs and squirmed to get down. Sara let him go. "Clara's coming today. I'm glad I asked her. We can talk and make plans that will let Juan have free time to write. I'll wait for her and then run to the restaurant before the lunch crowd arrives." Sara sat down to watch Juanito explore the room, occasionally removing an object that would break or hurt him. "So curious!"

Clara entered after a few minutes. Sara arranged to have her come three times a week for half a day. "I'm sorry I can't come every day. I have another family that needs me, too. You understand?"

"Of course, and thank you, Clara. Can you start tomorrow?" She nodded and waved her farewell. Juan returned with a package and a smile on his face. "Oh!" said Sara. "I need to get your journal." She ran to the wardrobe and reached to the back. On a high shelf her hand wrapped around a set of parchments held together with a cord. She withdrew it. "This I remember." She presented it to Juan. "This came when I needed it and was a joy to read. Finally, I knew what you were experiencing."

"Say, sometime I'd like to read the journal you kept. Do you have it?"

"Yes. And I'll let you see it anytime. Let me know." She kissed Juan and he returned her affection. "I really must go, or would you like me to put Juanito to bed for a nap first?" said Sara.

"Don't bother. I can do it. Will Clara be helping us with child care?"

"Oh, I forgot. She will start tomorrow. Three days a week for half a day. Bye." Sara slipped out and down the stairs to the restaurant. She put on an apron and went to the front door. She retrieved the box of vegetables and began chopping the fresh herbs that had just arrived. *Juan must have received this. I'm late today.* As the church bells tolled from across the street, Beppe and Allegra breezed in.

"Here we are, at ten exactly. It's a beautiful day outside." Beppe went to the basin and washed his hands with a slab of homemade soap. Allegra mimicked his actions and then got an apron.

"*Signora*, what shall I do to help you?" She reached for a knife and found a cutting board. She looked up.

"First slice onions and then do a bowl of chopped onions, followed by a small bowl of minced garlic."

"That will keep me busy a while. What about after that?"

"Then I'll have a mound of vegetables to prep."

"Here I go." Allegra poised with her knife and then grabbed some onions, easing off the translucent skins. Soon she started a rhythm—grab an onion, slice it thin and fast. Sara watched her a moment. "You're a good prep chef now. Quick!"

Allegra looked up, but nicked her finger. "Oh, no. Let me clean and bandage that! I'll be back. Just a minute." Once that was taken care of, Sara also set up a chopping rhythm. *Soothing! My friends will think I'm loca—crazy. Chopping like I'm beating a drum.*

Beppe prepared the dining area and called out, "First customers coming." He welcomed and seated an older couple and brought their orders to the kitchen. "Do we have chicken this morning?" Sara looked and nodded.

"Juan received it, I think. What's the order?"

"Baked chicken with lemon and rosemary and caponata salad."

"For two?" Beppe nodded as he went to fill their drink orders.

Sara checked the ice level in the chicken container. It was cold. She found a plump chicken and washed it in tepid water. "Slice a couple of lemons, thin, Allegra, and pass the bowl of sliced onions."

"Si, *signora*. Here they are." Sara rubbed rosemary into the inner cavity and then splashed olive oil on the outside. Next she stuffed the inside with rice, lemon slices and onions. She placed them on a shallow metal dish and shoved them in the hot bread oven. "I hope Leonardo doesn't mind." Next she chopped a variety of vegetables, including shiny purple eggplants and mixed them in a bowl with a few herbs and olive oil.

"*Perfetto*," said Beppe when he came to get the finished dishes. "These people will love it. They must know about you, because they said they loved your cooking."

"Tell me when they finish, and I'll come say *buon giorno*."

"I think they're Spanish. They have a different accent."

"Go take the chicken to them before it cools." Sara waved him off. She peeked out the door but couldn't see their table. A bit later, someone knocked and then opened the door.

"May I come in, Sara?" Sara started and then let out a shriek.

"Margarita—and Rodrigo." Sara ran to embrace her friend, garlic bits bristling from her hands. "I've missed you so much!" The two women squeezed each other tight for a long time laughing and grinning, until Rodrigo asked for a hug, too. Sara broke away and squeezed him around the shoulders.

"I'm glad to see you both. Why are you here? Just a visit?"

"No, we've left the Holy Land permanently and we're looking for a new home. It's a long story. And Rodrigo is in poor health, too." Sara looked to him, eyebrows knit.

"My heart. It beats very fast sometimes and scares me. When it does, I have no energy. I want to find a good doctor who can help me."

"Aren't there doctors in Jerusalem?"

"There's really not much there at this point in history. Life is random with many dangers."

"Such as?"

"Theft, lack of roads and tainted water."

"It's totally unorganized, and the officials are dishonest."

"I know somebody like that here," said Sara. "You'll have to come for supper. Perhaps we could find a place for you to stay, too."

"We accept your invitation, but we have lodging for a few nights."

"Why are you in Naples?"

"We came to see you."

"Juan has returned from the New World," said Sara. "It's a miracle."

"How wonderful! We must hear all about it. But we should get out of your kitchen now. We'll talk to you both at dinner." They waved goodbye and left.

"Beppe, please tell Juan we're having company for dinner before you leave. I'll be shopping at the market for a little while." Beppe nodded and trotted up the stairs to inform Juan.

Sara worked feverishly to clean up the kitchen and close the restaurant till tomorrow. *I must get some things for supper. What a busy day!* She searched for the freshest vegetables, fruits and meats among meager remains. *I wonder what Margarita went through—she and Rodrigo. Sounded grim.* She hurried back and took over care of Juanito, and then prepared a simple supper with all the fresh findings she could bring together. Margarita and Rodrigo returned just as the sun was going down on the lengthening spring day.

"*Buenas noches.* You remembered our Spanish traditions! Supper in the cool of night." Sara welcomed them in and Juan directed them to be seated.

"What a delight to see you again, *mi amiga*," said Margarita. "I've missed you, but I see you have a new roommate." Margarita smiled widely at Sara.

"I'm still getting used to having Juan back. It's lovely, though." Sara's face glowed like the setting sun. "You came back at a good time. We just got over a siege of sickness, all three of us."

"Are you well enough for company?"

"Of course," said Juan. "And we want to hear about your time in the Holy Land. You must be tired from your recent travels. Come and eat, and tell us what you experienced there. Did you receive a blessing being in the land of our Savior?"

"Come, sit at the table," said Sara. "Here are some seasonal vegetables and some local cheeses and our own bread made by Leonardo, our baker." Everyone sat down and passed the platters around. Conversations began over the breaking of rosemary herb bread and vegetable *caponata*. White cheese interlaced with fresh basil filled another plate and a plate of poached, chilled fish another. Amid comments about the food and inquiries about recent events in Naples, Margarita and Rodrigo shared their story.

Margarita began: "You remember we married here in Naples and then took a ship to the Holy Land. That old pirate Kemal Reis must stop every ship that passes through the eastern Mediterranean. He stopped ours."

"Took all our money, although we managed to hide some, grabbed a few sailors to man his vessel and, unfortunately, took some young women for his own pleasure." Rodrigo's fists turned white. "It angers me he can commit such heartless acts and get away with it."

"Well, we continued on to Acre and discovered it to be in ruins. It's been that way, locals say, since the Crusaders left. The port was destroyed so no Crusaders could return." Margarita paused for breath.

"A long story, I'm afraid. We went ashore in boats hired for the purpose, since there's no place for larger vessels to dock. It's a wild, rough place with much lawlessness. Everyone trying to cheat you out of your money."

"We had a place to stay with an old friend of Rodrigo's, but day-to-day life was a struggle. Going to market and never certain what you could find for food. The fish was good, though. Daily catches."

"How to earn money to live? Impossible! I finally set up a shop employing a few weavers. They made clothing. For a while it was profitable, but later a city official wanted a share of the income. That's when we closed."

"About that time, Rodrigo began experiencing this fluttering in his chest and a dizziness that didn't go away. Alarming!"

"Did you consult a doctor?" said Juan.

"There was only a very old Knight Hospitalet, but he had the palsy and had lost his sense, too. Mumbled when asked a question, and could barely stand."

"We left Acre then, and have been on board ships till today." Margarita looked at her husband. "How are you faring today, Rodrigo?"

"No flutters now. It comes mostly when I walk up a hill or climb steps."

"I will examine you, tomorrow, if you wish." Juan placed a hand on Rodrigo's back.

"Bless you." Rodrigo turned to his handsome wife. "I am feeling tired, Margarita, dear. Could we go back to our room now?"

"We have more to tell you two," said Margarita, rising to help her husband stand. "And a favor to ask of you."

"Come back tomorrow and let's talk after Rodrigo's examination."

"*Vaya con Dios.*"

"*Igualmente.* Likewise."

Chapter 17

The older couple returned the next day, a Saturday. Sara had arranged for Leonardo to supervise the running of the restaurant for the day. Rodrigo entered a few steps behind Margarita, and silent. Juan ushered him up the stairs and into the small bedroom, which he'd prepared for the examination.

"How do you feel today, sir?" Juan listened to Rodrigo's chest.

"Not so bad at the moment. But I can't walk as fast as Margarita."

"Any stiff joints causing that?" Juan took Rodrigo's arm and put two fingers to the upturned wrist.

"No, sir. I'm fit in all other ways."

"Do you eat plenty of fresh vegetables and fruits?"

"Well, my wife was a vegetable seller for many years, so I do get a goodly amount." Rodrigo chuckled. "It was a bit harder to find fresh-grown things in the Holy Land, however. The climate is so dry."

Juan thumped on Rodrigo's chest and then turned to his back. Tapping, tapping, he asked, "Any pains?"

"Now? No, but sometimes I feel light in the head and dizzy. Sometimes my eyes don't focus, too. And the flutters in my chest are disturbing."

"But not overpowering?"

"No, I can almost manage. I'd like to know how to slow my heart down a bit when it gets this way, though. That would make Margarita happy, too." He sighed and stretched.

Juan stopped his prodding and sat across from Rodrigo. "The news is you do have a weakened heart, maybe from a childhood fever. But, there are many things you can do to relieve your distressing symptoms, though."

"I may have had such a disease. I don't remember. Why should it affect me in old age?" Rodrigo shrugged. "What can I do now?"

"I have some ideas and some medicines I can give you. Let me write them down and then Margarita will know, too." Juan spent the next minutes showing the older man one medicine and another, from lemon balm to yarrow, poppy juice for calming an extreme incident, and lavender and rosemary to use in a bath or as a chest rub with olive oil. Rodrigo stood up and clapped Juan on the shoulder.

"Thank you, doctor. You have given me hope."

"Call me Juan. And I'll help you get all these remedies as you need more." He guided Rodrigo out of the bedroom door and down the stairs to where the two ladies awaited.

"How is he?" Margarita's face stretched taut, jaw to forehead. She reached out a hand to Rodrigo.

"It could be worse." Rodrigo sat next to her.

"He will be able to manage very well. I gave him instructions." Juan put several small bottles into a cloth bag and handed it to Rodrigo.

"Too much fuss, woman," said Rodrigo. "I'll tell you later."

"You said you wanted to ask a favor," said Sara. "What is it?"

"You see, Rodrigo's spells come upon him without warning. It's difficult when traveling to stop and deal with it. We need traveling companions to help when a spell comes upon him."

"So, you want us to be those traveling companions?" said Sara.

"Would you mind going with us at least till we get to Spain? You could leave us then and return, or—"

"I don't know. This is so sudden," said Sara, rubbing her forehead.

"We've been thinking of Spain recently. We miss it," said Juan. "What do you think, Sara? Should we go with them?"

"Go and then return, or go and stay in Spain?"

"It's a dilemma."

"We need time to think about it," said Sara. "Yes, we'd love to help you, but do we leave Naples forever? We—I— have a lot invested in this city. Running a restaurant, owning a residence. But, I thought about fleeing Naples just a month ago. Fears about the Inquisition seeking me out keep coming to mind."

"Is it Morales again?"

Sara nodded.

We'll give you time. I'm showing Rodrigo the sights for the next few days. Castel Nuovo, Mt. Vesuvius, the central market square where I once sold vegetables—" Margarita rose. "We should leave you now. We'll keep in touch." She took Rodrigo's offered arm and together they strolled out the door and glided down the cobbled street. A puff of air swirled in. Sara grinned.

"Let's get Juanito—I think I hear him—and take a walk. I know a park where he could play while we talk." She jumped up. "I'll bring some food, too."

"Good. We have momentous decisions to make, but we don't need to act so seriously. I'll get Juanito; you put together some food. A portable meal!" Juan took the stairs two at a time. By the time he returned, Sara had wrapped up some cooked chicken and cheese, fresh cherries and bread.

"I had to close my eyes and not watch the workers as I skirted through the kitchen. But, I think they are managing well. Leonardo is a dear."

"Ready to go?" Juan nuzzled Juanito and grabbed Sara's hand. It was another wonderful day outside. It was fully spring now, and the tender lime green shoots of the wisteria had swirled themselves around wrought iron grates and spilled a purple mantle over every balcony and gate. An aura of delicate sweetness perfumed the air. Ceramic pots of red geraniums spiked the walkways and congregated near the bubbling fountains. Stray dogs chased each other, tugging at the same sticks and nosing into dubious piles of small animal bones.

"Let me take you to my favorite quiet spot in the city," said Sara. "I didn't have much time to go there while working and caring for a baby, but here we are now and we have time today." Sara pulled Juan and Juanito ahead by the hand. "There are trees, and benches to sit on and a tiled area for Juanito to walk around." She led them a few blocks to the left and a few to the right. "It's small and hidden, and that makes it special. Here it is." She flung out her arm and pointed. Juan looked from side to side.

"I don't see it."

"There. Down the stairs and over behind that big sycamore tree."

They followed her pattering steps and turned around a bend. What they saw made Juan gasp. Juanito's eyes became big as cobblestones. The sound of water lifted on the air. A giant fountain filled with statuary and leaping sprays of liquid light caught their eyes. Water moved from the central jet over a second bowl of stone frogs, beavers and water birds. The droplets found their way between the animals frozen in time and place and cascaded down to a third level where it pooled in a large vat. Orange and coral fish battled for place as Juan put down Juanito and both ran to splash their hands in the gigantic vessel.

Under a tree sat a lone bench. "I'll sit there, while you two play with the water," said Sara. She watched Juan enjoy his little son's antics, slapping the water to see the fish disperse in all directions. The game repeated every few minutes for the next half hour. "Look at his persistence."

"Are you hungry, Juanito?" called Sara. Juanito nodded, so Juan brought a dripping boy over to the bench. "I hope you have a towel, Sara." They sat down and took the food she offered them. Juan tore it into chunks for the little boy. "Now, when we're done eating, we can go back and wash our hands in the fountain," said Juan.

"Do you have any thoughts about helping Margarita and Rodrigo get to Spain?" said Sara. She inched closer to Juan and the squirming Juanito. She took her little boy and bounced him on her lap. His dark wavy hair lifted and fell.

"I'm in favor of it," said Juan. "I would like to leave here permanently. I think you know my heart is in Spain. And I'd like to go see my parents and meet this Catalina your brother married. What about you?"

"Of course, but I have responsibilities here in Naples, and Spain is dangerous. The Inquisition makes it so." Sara gazed at him.

"Morales is gone."

"Yes, but will I be trailed by other members and found to be lacking some good grace? And, it will be hard to travel with a young boy and an ailing couple."

"They're our friends and they've come to us for help." Juan responded.

"Do we have enough money to get there? Will it be stolen or confiscated at the border? And you know how difficult it is for a *converso* to demonstrate their orthodoxy. It's exhausting." Sara sighed.

"Do you want to be continually bothered by *Signor* Alessandro, the dishonest tax collector?" Juan patted Sara's hand.

"Good point. But is Leonardo competent to run the restaurant?" Sara's face had beaded with sweat as the discussion continued.

"How has he done to this point?" Juan took Juanito and laid him against his shoulder.

"I trust him," said Sara. "And he is careful and a trained cook."

"And, he knows Naples. He's lived here for years, he told me." Juan patted Juanito's back and lowered his voice. "We'd lose a lot of money just leaving the restaurant."

"We could make an arrangement with Leonardo. He could send payments by way of Columbus' agents in Spain."

"There is one other consideration." Sara's face tensed into tight creases. "I'm afraid to go back." Juan reached over and gently smoothed her worried face.

"We can do it. It's our true home. Nobody is chasing you anymore, dear Sarita. And we can trust God's direction and guidance."

"And, we'll accompany our best friends." Sara smiled. "You have persuaded me, I think. I'd follow you almost anywhere, but you know this is a difficult choice. Let me just think about it overnight." She planted a soft kiss on his cheek and patted Juanito who had relaxed into sleep on Juan's shoulder.

"Let us make plans. Tomorrow. I'm anxious to return. I long to see Spain and introduce you to my parents. They need to see their grandson!" Juan got up. "Let's go home and put the little one to bed." Sara nodded and gathered up the remains of the food before following her little family home.

What have I committed myself to do now?

Sara thought about the future and knew before morning what her answer would be. After tending to Juanito the next day, she looked through her belongings and found that book of Andalusian poems she had remembered. She took a few minutes and immediately felt the tug of the words on her heartstrings.

Here's the one I was looking for: It's all about the Guadalquivir River. It snakes all the way from the foothills, going past Córdoba and Sevilla to the sea. Wow! These are startling images of love and violence, but I like the part that says, 'and then doves laughed.' She put the book down, and thought for a moment.

It's always the same. Whenever I read poetry, I feel I could fall into the middle, like falling down a well, and submerge myself forever.

I've watched a cormorant before. She sits on the surface in her black feathers, takes a breath and dives for the bottom to find choice minnows or mosses. That's the way it is! To feast on tender morsels—sweet images, lovely words, great thoughts. I could spend all day immersed in such a sea of poetry.

I love the phrase we have in our language: Al fondo--to go to the depths or the utter end of the farthest point. That's poetry for me. It goes al fondo, into the very depths of my soul.

Sara sighed, put the book away to read later and went to make dinner.

Chapter 18

"We accept your invitation and will accompany you to Spain," said Sara as she embraced Margarita. Juan slapped Rodrigo on the back.

"Wonderful! I'm excited you decided so quickly."

"When do you want to go to Spain, and what's your expected point of entry, Rodrigo?" Juan grasped hands with the older man and listened for his reply.

"As soon as possible, but I know you may need time to re-arrange things."

"True."

"An unexpected entry point seems best—a smaller city?"

"Perhaps. But for now, let us write to our friends and family to let them know we're coming back. And get their sense of the safest way to return." Sara passed a bowl of bread and some olives. "Soon we'll have real *manzanilla* olives again. I can hardly wait." They sat around the table, eating a late supper of fish, cooked vegetables and crunchy bread. Juanito had long ago been settled into bed.

"Shall we set a date to go back, maybe one or two months?" said Juan.

"I'll do my best to train my workers, and Leonardo." Sara smiled and hugged herself. "I feel light-headed with excitement."

"I'll do all I can to help you, Sara," said Margarita. "I'd gladly take care of Juanito. After all, he's almost a grandson to me. I'm almost his grandmother!"

"His godmother, too." She patted Margarita's hand.

"We should visit this Catalina de Torres in Moguer," said Juan. "She apparently is Luis' legal wife."

"Really?" Rodrigo turned his head toward Juan.

"Sara received a letter recently from her. It seems she wants Sara to come and live with her, two widows together, to subsist on a widow's pension. Guess you'll have to show her you're not a widow." Juan winked at Sara.

"I would like to talk to her and hear her story of how she met and married my brother Luis. He traveled with Columbus, you know, but didn't survive the terrible tragedy at La Navidad, in the New World."

"Was his body ever found, Sara?" Margarita looked long at Sara.

"Juan told me his body was identified by the clothes he was wearing, and by an arrow still lodged in his decaying body." Sara shivered and looked to Juan.

"Yes, I was there, too, you know. A Taino woman, who I had helped earlier with her sick child, rescued me. Otherwise, I'd be dead, also. She led me to the place where she had moved the body. I saw and can confirm his death."

"Juan said the natives just left the bodies where they had fallen, the ones not burned in the fortress."

"Columbus found those bodies when he arrived in late November, but I guess some men had left the fort earlier, because of all the strife. Nobody could agree on anything, and the person left in charge couldn't control them. It's shameful. A blot on our glorious history."

"Juan's started writing the account of his adventures with Columbus. His perspective as a doctor is much different than Admiral Columbus' and I think the world, or at least the Spanish people, would be curious and glad to hear what actually happened."

"How is it different from Columbus' log book?" Rodrigo leaned forward.

"I was interested in the people we met, the Taino Indians and a few Caribs from another island. I look on the discovery as a chance to learn from this unknown and isolated group of people. There is a wealth of plants and animals we've never seen before. Could there be a plant remedy that would benefit us in the Old World? I collected and dried a few things and found them useful. The Taino woman showed me."

"The same one who nursed you to health?" Rodrigo narrowed his eyes.

"I was always true to you, Sara. I never wavered." Juan's neck colored.

"I never doubted it." Sara took his hand.

Juan cleared his throat. "They have a unique language, too. It's not Aramaic like Columbus expected and it's probably not from Cipango or Cathay. I started recording it." Juan continued. "We collected a number of plants that the natives seemed to value. They grow tall leaves, dry them and then roll them and then light them and inhale their smoke. Not an unpleasant smell. Also, there's a globelike fruit, oblong and bumpy with the sweetest yellow flesh. I know our people will like that. We brought back native peoples, too, but Queen Isabella was distressed we made slaves out of any of them."

"Your tales are curious and fascinating," said Margarita. "I hope you will get them published upon our return."

"You're a second Marco Polo," said Rodrigo. He got up and slapped Juan on the back. "We should go, my dear. It's getting late." Margarita nodded and joined him at the door. "By the way, Juan, your remedies are already helping me. I sleep much better and I've had less trouble with my heart. *Muchas gracias.*" He saluted Juan as Margarita waved goodbye.

"We'll keep talking. We'll inquire about routes and schedules. *Adios.*" Juan and Sara fell into bed, happy but exhausted. Embracing, they whispered late into the night of plans and dreams and hopes. Their passion following their separation had not faded but mellowed into a sweet contentment as they fell asleep.

A few days later, before Sara went down the stairs to work, Juan said, "I think I'll finish up a first installment of my book and send it ahead for publication tomorrow."

"How do you do that? Where should you send it?"

"Let me think about that—maybe to Queen Isabella?"

"You would certainly get noticed then—sole survivor and eyewitness of the tragedy of La Navidad. She has much influence."

"Indeed. Do we want that publicity?"

"Would it reawaken the Inquisition's search for me?"

"I don't know. Maybe it would give you and me a certain status—a Christian hero and his *converso* wife. Maybe you'd be praised."

"Send it off, maybe to your parents' home, and they can present it to the court. I wonder where Queen Isabella and King Ferdinand are residing now? They move their court every few months. I think it's a wise way to keep tuned to the needs of each region of the country." Juan nodded.

"My parents will tell us." Juan kissed Sara. "Time to go to work?" He embraced her and gave her a nudge toward the stairway.

"I'll see you later." She trotted downstairs and Juan got out his writings. "I wonder," he said. "Will our people want to know the truth or will they believe the sometimes fantastic claims Columbus makes about finding gold?" He settled down to work on the parchments. Margarita had already come and whisked away Juanito to the inn where she and Rodrigo stayed. "Ah, a whole day to think and write! I'm a fortunate man." He blushed. "But what kind of man lets his wife work? It's shameful. It must come to an end."

Sara found Juan still at work when she closed the restaurant and ran upstairs. "Look at you—the author! Did you have a productive day?" She came and put her arms around his neck.

"Look at this, Sara, and tell me what you think." Juan pointed to the parchment in front of him and Sara leaned a bit closer to read it.

The land is full of all manner of leafy plants. Vines with knife-like leaves twine up a tall palm, while shiny leaves that look as if they were chopped by a giant knife grow in clumps throughout the jungle floor. Birds chirp and caw and show off their garish colors of orange, flame red or shiny obsidian. They nod at us with fans on their heads or long yellow beaks. Crawling insects exhibit claws, hard backs or dozens of legs.

The New World is truly a feast for the eyes and ears. The Taino people who inhabit the region are gentle, mild and peaceful. Not like the Caribs, who live, we think, on a neighboring island and are rumored to be cannibals. Columbus maintains that these islands are off shore from Cipango or Cathay. The people call themselves Taino, but Columbus calls them Indians, because he believes we were exploring east of India.

After a few minutes, Sara made a noise of approval in her throat and placed a kiss on her husband's stubbly cheek.

"That's so interesting, Juan. Well written and clear. It shows thoughtful insights into the lives of the Taino people. A unique presentation."

"So much praise." Juan raised his eyebrows. "But I'm glad you liked it. I want others to see and understand the lucid marvels of that untouched place. I'm afraid it's already been affected, though. Many of the locals contracted the same diseases we Europeans brought over on the ships. They seem to have no defenses. Many more will die." Juan raked his fingers through his wavy brown hair.

"Another issue I should write about is slavery. Columbus keeps taking groups of natives to be slaves. He tells the Queen that this is a profitable idea. But, the Queen keeps reminding him she wants the natives to be treated with courtesy and kindness. If I expose the extent of Columbus' slave-taking, I could be in serious trouble." Sara gave him a blank look.

"Has Margarita come yet?" Sara walked into the bedroom and took up her brush. She unpinned her hair, letting it cascade down like a coppery waterfall. She took up her brush to smooth it out, but Juan put down his quill and appeared behind her, putting his fingers in her long tresses.

"What did you say, my love?"

"Is Juanito here?" Then she turned around to receive his adoration. "I'm a fortunate woman to have a husband like you."

"Mm," said Juan, burrowing his face into her abundance of hair. The door downstairs opened and slammed. Sara heard coos and babbling talk.

"Margarita, we're up here." Sara gave Juan a tender kiss and then went to the stairway to watch Juanito get closer. "I missed you, little boy." She reached out to Juanito, who said,

"Mama."

Margarita laughed and gave over her charge to Sara.

"He's been a good boy today, and had a long afternoon rest." She dropped his bag next to the doorway. "Laundry."

"Thanks again for your help. Juan will soon have an installment of his writings ready to send to Spain."

"It goes much faster without having to care for the little one." He poked his finger into Juanito's middle.

"You're welcome. I do hope we can proceed to Spain soon, though. Now that the decision is made, I have become impatient."

"Shall we get together next Monday night to see how all the plans are developing? We can have supper here—just soup and some bread, perhaps."

"We'll be here. *Buenas noches.* I'll be back tomorrow to get Juanito."

When Monday came, Sara set out a vegetable soup simmered in chicken broth. She tore a piece off a loaf of bread and handed the loaf to Margarita. "Please have some bread and soup and let's talk." She ladled soup for all and bit into the bread.

"We spoke to Leonardo about managing the restaurant." Juan paused.

"Yes?"

"It seems he wants to buy the place now. That changes things for us. We have to decide whether to leave forever now."

"What did you decide?" Rodrigo spoke softly.

"If Leonardo can work out a plan to pay us (and that's not clear yet), we will leave Naples with you—permanently." Sara let out a big breath of air and squeezed Juan's hand.

"You can see we now have to attend to a lot more details."

"We applaud you," said Rodrigo.

"Everything looks clear for all of us to leave on the *Celestina* or *Agostina* two months from now. Nico Ferlandini is a good man. He's keeping four spots reserved for us on the *Agostina* in July or the *Celestina* in August."

"So soon?" Sara's smile faded.

"It's well into 1494. We need to keep working on our plan," said Rodrigo. "What shall we tell him? July or August?"

"July it is," said Juan and Sara nodded.

The next days and weeks Sara trained Leonardo in her methods of managing the restaurant. "You probably know as much as I do. You have so much experience."

"I don't deny it, but I want to get a feel for the passion you put into cooking. It definitely appeals to a wide range of people. A restaurant for the people, and with the freshest and best local foods." Sara's cheeks got pink.

"A lovely compliment. I know you'll do well yourself." She showed him how she kept food cold, where she ordered vegetables from, and where to get the best chickens, pork and fish. They talked continually.

Juan went with Leonardo to the moneylender and worked out a system of payments satisfactory to both sides. "We take one-third now and when we get to Spain, we'll send our new address. Captain Ferlandini can bring a second installment to us in six months. You can depend on his honesty. A third payment will come a year from now."

"Agreed. I hope to be as successful as Sara has been. It's a very popular restaurant in Naples." They signed the papers to make it official and were promised copies in two days' time.

"We received a letter from your parents, Juan," said Sara. "They are thrilled to get our reply and want to see us plus Juanito, of course, as soon as we can get there. They sound like wonderful people." Sara handed the scrolled letter to Juan.

"I'm sorry Ana died before we could get there, Sara. She sounded like a special soul. Perhaps we could visit her gravesite sometime after we settle." Sara nodded and wiped at her eyes. "Have you heard from Catalina de Torres?"

"Not yet. Let's try to find her after we see your parents. In fact, I'd like to settle in Moguer, or near there."

"Why?"

"I have this image of a Moorish garden, with trickling water, vines and flowers, lacy arches, and fountains. And warm weather all year. You can only find that in Andalusia."

"You want to live in a garden?"

"No, of course not. But I want such a garden near my house."

"I could agree to that." Juan took both of Sara's hands and swung her around in an impromptu dance. She laughed and laughed.

"When I find the image I see in my mind, I'll know I'm finally home."

"I wish that for you with all my heart." Juan brought her close and enfolded Sara in his arms. "With all my heart." They both sighed then laughed.

"We'd better start packing."

Chapter 19

I weep at the thought of pearls
Spilling their lustrous glow
With only the stars to see—
And kisses offered fully.

In the garden at midnight
The laughing water is so beautiful
Almost it covers the piercing sadness
Of our last goodbye.

Sara put down her quill and sighed. *I can never express the beauty of thought and form that poets have mastered. But it's fun to try, like this attempt.* Sara fingered the gathering of small bits of parchment that each contained a poem to love, to beauty, jewels compared to water, to the assets of the beloved, to the beauty of God. *These poets caught the ache of desire, the exquisite feeling of falling in love, and the bitterness of separation.* She got up and walked around, trying not to wake Juan, or Juanito in the adjoining room. The candle sputtered. *I should get back in bed, but the loveliness of these verses stirs my heart. I wish I had more time to contemplate, besides just a few stolen moments. Oh, well.* Sara snuffed out the candle.

Juan stirred as Sara slipped back into bed. "Hello, my love. I'm here." She brushed her lips across his cheek and settled close to him. "Mm," was all he said as he turned toward Sara. *When do we leave Naples? Is it three or four weeks? Will we be ready? Must make a list of details to attend to—later.*

Sara awoke to an annoying sound. Someone was pounding somewhere. *What? Why?* As she roused out of sleep, she leapt out of bed. "Someone's at the door, Juan! Something's wrong. Hurry!" Sara took the stairs, hitting the steps as fast as she could. She threw the door open.

"At last!" Margarita blew in, panting. "Could Juan come, quickly? Something's wrong with Rodrigo." Her eyes scanned the room till she fixed on Juan struggling down the stairs, fastening his doublet.

"What seems to be the problem?" He jammed his feet into his boots and grabbed his bag and cloak.

"He can't catch his breath. Says his heart is thumping wildly. 'Jumping out of his chest,' he says. Please hurry." Margarita's voice caught. A sob escaped her lips. Sara gave her a hug before she followed Juan out the door. *Vaya con Dios.* Juanito let out a howl she could hear from the main floor. She turned and sped up to his bedroom.

"What's the matter, big boy?" She picked him up and cuddled him.

"Pa?" Juanito looked around, sniffling and gulping for air.

"Papa will come back soon. He went to help Rodrigo." Sara patted his back and held him close to the crook of her neck. Sara hummed a lullaby and Juanito laid his head on her shoulder. He relaxed as she patted him and walked around his room. Soon he fell asleep. She set him down and adjusted the covers.

I don't know when he'll come back and what his news will be. But I can pray. She sat on her bed and prayed for Rodrigo's health and wisdom for Juan. Slipping into bed, she felt the peaceful certainty of trusting all to God's hands.

The church bells across the street chimed eight o'clock before she knew it. She got up and fed and cared for Juanito before Juan returned.

"What's the news, Juan?" She gave him a kiss. Juan kicked off his boots.

"Rodrigo's resting, but he had a scary time of it for a while. I finally helped him by making an infusion of a plant I got in the New World—neem. I'm so glad I had it in my bag. I gave all the rest of it to Margarita and showed her how to use it. After that's gone, I don't know how to help Rodrigo." Juan sat down and grabbed a hunk of bread and smeared *mermelada* on it. "Mm, good jam," he said. "Do you have any cheese?" Sara brought him some.

"What will this do to our travel plans?"

"I don't know, but Rodrigo is otherwise strong and able."

"I wonder—will they give up their plans to return to Spain? It seems likely. We must ask them."

"Give them a few days, Sara." Juan yawned. "And now, I need to rest. Can I sleep for an hour? I don't think Margarita will come today to take care of Juanito."

"Yes, get some sleep. I'll watch Juanito till you get up and then go to work." She embraced him and gave him a nudge toward the stairs.

"Papa, papa." Juanito waved his arms and legs.

"Yes, big boy, I'm here and I love you." Juan played with Juanito for a moment and then gave him over to Sara. "Thank you," he mouthed.

"Sleep well, *mi amor*."

* * * *

Sara spent the hour talking and playing games with her little boy, watching him try to run on his sturdy legs. While she played with Juanito, in her mind she composed love poems in the Moorish style. *"Thieves of pleasure," "my most precious jewel," "water falls continuously like neck chains of silver and pearls," "the wine of her glance."* Sara sighed. *Such haunting images. My heart is full and bursting!* "I could never write half as beautiful poetry! Don't you agree, Juanito?"

Juanito looked up with questions in his eyes. "No." He grinned. "No."

"Another new word! Hooray!" Sara clapped her hands and Juanito joined her, laughing and saying, "No, no, no."

"Good, Juanito." She picked him up and swung him through the air.

"What's the celebration?" Juan entered the room, yawning and scratching the top of his head.

"Juanito said another word—no." Juan smiled and grabbed him for another ride around the room.

"Why don't you go now, Sara, and I'll take care of my big boy." Juan waved goodbye while Sara slipped out. Downstairs, Allegra and Beppe had already arrived and set the tables. Allegra was starting on the preparation work for the day.

"My day revolves around onions and garlic," she said. "Every day, chop, chop. And slice. Not much to talk about when I go home. My mother says I have a tiresome job."

"What do you tell her?"

"There's always something happening, I tell her. The tax collector threatens us, or an old friend comes in to see you, or even an enemy comes." Allegra's eyes lit up like candlelight.

"Who are you thinking of?" Sara shuddered. "I don't call that fun."

"That dark man with tall black boots."

"Montenegro?"

"Yes, that's him. He was dangerous . . .and handsome." She giggled.

"Don't wish for a dangerous man—he will prove his reputation to your detriment." Allegra wiped the grin off her face and looked down.

"You are right, of course."

"Have you seen Montenegro recently, Allegra?" Creases spread across Sara's forehead.

"Yes. No. I'm not sure. I saw a man dressed in black yesterday."

"Where?"

"He was standing across the street in the shadows."

"Was it a man with tall black boots and a cloak?"

"No, not Montenegro. More like a cleric. Long black robes. But he looked different."

"What do you mean?"

"It wasn't that old man, Morales, is that his name? It was a younger man."

"But a cleric, a priest?"

"Yes. That's it."

"Did you see him today?"

"No, not yet today."

"Please let me know when you see him again. Immediately."

"I will. And don't worry. We will help you. Beppe and I."

"I think we should get ready for our customers. It's opening time." Sara worked at a rapid pace, preparing orders as they came in. But she pondered the latest disturbing bit of information. *Has the Inquisition sent a new investigator? Am I under suspicion for being involved in Morales' death? If it's true, we need to disappear.*

Nobody saw a man in black that day. After work, Sara ran up the steps to Juan. "Guess what? Allegra saw a cleric watching our restaurant yesterday."

It's not Morales, so who could it be? Are you sure he's watching us?"

"I just know he is. Why does everybody persecute me like a hound after a bird?" Sara gulped and started panting.

"Calm yourself, Sara." Juan enfolded her in his arms and rubbed her back. "Breathe slowly, take a breath." Sara followed his directions and soon her panic subsided. She sat down and put her hands in her lap.

"What shall we do if it is true? I can't face the Inquisition again. It's frightening."

"We also need to find out if Rodrigo is able to travel. If he is, maybe we should leave sooner."

"I like that idea. It really is Leonardo's responsibility, anyway, now that we've decided and signed papers. I'm sure he wants to get started."

"Yes, he's waiting like the gentleman he is. But we need to let him take over. Let's slip out of town on the next available ship, maybe at night. I'll find out and book passage. But I'll check with Margarita and Rodrigo first."

* * * *

"Rodrigo feels weaker after this recent spell," said Margarita. Juan listened to Rodrigo's heart and checked him thoroughly. Rodrigo answered all his questions.

"No disease I can detect now, Rodrigo. Are you fit to travel?"

"I need to get to Córdoba as soon as possible. Take me home." Juan laid a hand on Rodrigo's back and nodded.

"I must say my goodbyes to Raul and Beata," said Sara, when she heard of Rodrigo's request.

"I'm sure we have time for that. Let's invite them and Rodrigo and Margarita over for a farewell dinner." Sara nodded.

"I'll make a wonderful Spanish dish to remind us all of our heritage. If only we could persuade Raul and Beata to come along, too."

"I'll go invite them all. Is tomorrow a good time?"

"Yes, Juan. And we'll talk long and late over delicious food."

The next day, Sara left Juanito with Margarita and walked to the central market area. Already, the market burst with people looking for the freshest vegetables at a bargain. Sellers yelled the praises of their own produce: the largest onions, the longest beans, the zestiest garlic and the sweetest cherries. Sara made her way to her favorite seller and purchased two onions, one head of garlic and a measure of rice, enough for four servings. At the herb seller, she bought a bunch of flat leaf parsley and some thyme. Across the street, she bargained with the butcher for a plump chicken, already cleaned and plucked. She bought olives at the next stand and a few strips of ham at the cured meats stand. Then, at the last stand, she bought a few eggs and some sweet cream. *Better get busy!* Sara hurried home to make the special dinner.

After the main course of roasted chicken with rice and ham had been consumed, Sara brought out her favorite: small plates of flan with caramelized sugar dripping over the tops of each one.

"Lovely, Sara!" Margarita took a bite and savored it in her mouth. Raul smacked his lips.

"Tasty. I almost want to return to Spain."

"Why don't you come?" said Rodrigo. "I'm sure we'd all love that."

"We left Spain to get away from the persecution of our people," said Raul. "We will never return until that edict is repealed."

"That will never happen, brother," said Sara quietly.

"Then, it's settled. How will you deal with members of the Inquisition sneaking around, looking for lapses in your Christian behavior?"

"I am truly in my heart a believer in Jesus," said Sara. "I don't have to pretend now, one foot in my Jewish heritage and one in my new faith."

"Are you renouncing your heritage?" Raul's nose whistled, showing his agitation. He pinched his nostrils to stop it.

"I'll never do that, Raul. But I want to follow Jesus, be his disciple."

"We think our behavior will show we are true believers," added Juan.

"I applaud you, Sara," said Beata. "But, for us, we decided long ago that we could not live under the rule of those who squash our beliefs and customs—our precious Jewish heritage." Sara got up and embraced Beata, then, and Raul. All the adults exchanged hugs and wished each other well.

"I will miss you two so much," said Sara. "Let's hope to meet again."

"Goodnight, all," said Margarita and Rodrigo. Raul and Beata left next. Juanito fussed. Juan picked him up and put him to bed while Sara cleaned up the dishes. Sara shed a lot of tears before she fell asleep that night.

* * * *

As soon as it could be arranged, four people and one small child dressed for travel. Rodrigo walked with halting steps and Margarita supported him, one bag slung over her shoulder. Juan carried their two bags and Rodrigo's, while Sara handled Juanito and one bag.

"How can we tiptoe through the night with all this bulky baggage?" Sara whispered. Juan just motioned for her to keep going. Each turn in the road, each shutter opening above them, caused them to startle. "Shh, Quiet, everyone!"

"Captain, our thanks and good evening," said Juan, when they reached the ship. Juan turned back. "By the way, have you seen a Spanish cleric on the dock?"

"It's hard to remember. Let's say I didn't notice any such person."

Sara heard Juan mutter under his breath, "They'll not threaten my wife, my family. Not while I have the power to prevent it." He turned to usher his charges—Margarita and Rodrigo—onto the ship. Sara gripped Juanito as she walked the deck. *God help us.*

Later, on the deck of the *Agostina*, Sara unpinned her hair and let the wind sweep it back from her face. *What a glorious feeling of freedom! If only for a moment.*

Sara paced the deck, brushing wild strands of hair back from her face. She scanned the sky. She noticed the sweep of some shearwaters, sea birds with knife-like wings. They sliced through the air and swooped close to the waves, following the swirl of the winds. *Magnificent.* Their gray-tipped wings and white bellies contrasted sharply with the deep blue sky.

The *Agostina*'s hull carved a path through the water and rode the waves in a rocking motion. Soon Sara relaxed and moved with the surges and dips. *It's like riding a horse.* She closed her eyes and felt the light touch of the breeze on her cheeks. The ship's timbers creaked and the sails snapped as they filled and re-filled after tacking left and right through the blue void. Juan came up on deck and joined her. "It's a magnificent sea, isn't it? Restless sometimes and then smooth as forged glass the next." He took her hand and kissed it.

"Yes, my dearest." Sara snuggled her head into the niche between Juan's chin and shoulder. "Your presence is a wonderful comfort."

"Trust all to me, and to the Almighty. My parents have influence, also."

"Juan, you will have influence after your travel journal is known."

Juan threw his arm around Sara's shoulders and placed a kiss on her lips.

"Juan," she protested, "this is too public. It's not proper." Sara blushed and looked around.

"We could adjourn to another location below." He winked.

"We'd wake Juanito." She smiled and gave a silly grin. "Do you know how far we've sailed?"

"Hardly a half day yet, Sarita. Perhaps fifty or sixty nautical miles. We have a couple more days of travel to get to Palma and then the final destination, Málaga.

"Come, Juan, let's go below and see if Juanito has awakened from his sleep." Sara took Juan's hand and together they strolled to the ladder and descended.

The next day, they came above deck with Juanito to watch the passage between the great islands. Corsica, and Sardinia.

"It's narrow. I can see them clearly," said Sara, viewing from the deck bushes and shrubbery on both islands. "But, it's hard to distinguish anything on either island." The sun rose in the sky. Juan shaded his eyes.

"Let's go below and find Margarita and Rodrigo. We need to talk with them." They found their friends in an adjoining cubicle.

All passenger spaces provided were little more than room for two beds, one above the other. Rodrigo smiled from his lower bed and Margarita above. "We'll be safe here."

Sara again spoke her fears and worries to her friends and received much the same advice: wait and trust. "We don't know what will happen until we arrive," said Rodrigo. "It's best to enjoy the journey and the fair weather."

"It is lovely," said Margarita. "We walked around deck earlier."

"I'm looking forward to returning to the place I was born—Córdoba." Margarita and Rodrigo waved goodbye as Sara and Juan with Juanito returned to their cubicle.

"It won't be long till we reach our destination," said Juan.

"Only a few more days. Nothing to worry about, right Juanito?" She tickled her little boy and he laughed.

"S-pain," said Juanito.

Five days later the *Agostina* docked in Málaga and began unloading cargo. All the passengers assembled on deck and gripped their bags, waiting for the gangplank to be lowered. *At last, we're home.*

Chapter 20

1 August 1494

"Let me see your documents." The official put out his hand to block their exit from the ship. Sara looked at Juan with eyes wide. Juanito began to cry.

"I don't have identity documents, Juan," she whispered. Juan reached into his shoulder bag and produced a small packet. He turned to the official.

"I think you'll find these in order. I'm Juan Sánchez, this is my wife Sara and our child, Juanito." The man's face showed no expression as he unrolled the scrolls. He looked carefully at each one.

"Hm. They seem to be authentic and complete. I see Admiral Columbus witnessed your marriage. There must be a story there."

"Yes, of course. We married aboard his ship just before leaving on his first voyage of discovery."

"I see. Not everyone returned from that fateful expedition. You are one of the fortunate ones." The official rolled up the scrolls and put them back in the packet. Juan took them and inserted the packet into his bag.

"You may proceed."

Juan ushered his family off the pier and away toward the town. "Juan, I've never been more scared in my life. I didn't know you had documents for us all, but I'm glad."

"I got Columbus' notary to certify our marriage. I had him check the logbook and write a document. I thought it might be important some day. Señor Rodrigo de Escobedo was his name, a man who knows his importance. He was one of the landing party when Columbus first stepped into the New World. Columbus had him certify right then that he, the Admiral, was claiming the territory for the Queen and King of Spain."

"You were right about it being important."

"We've entered the country without a problem. First step completed."

They clasped hands and grinned. Sara scanned the scene in front of them. Málaga had a wide harbor with a sandy beach along much of the shore. The ships docked to one side in a deeper channel. The sun shone with a fierce intensity. Gulls flew overhead, squawking, hoping that when the one holding a shell in its mouth dropped it on a rock, they would scoop up the contents first.

"Look." Juan pointed to a nearby hill. "I've heard of that fortress. It's called the Alcazaba and the castle next to it is Gibralfaro. One of the emirs of Córdoba built the Alcazaba long ago to protect the town against pirates."

Sara looked up and saw a grand sweep of weathered stonewalls with regular observation points, and at one end a castle, perched like a nesting bird on the cliff. "They would be able to see in all directions from that promontory," she said.

"A series of Moorish potentates lived there until recently. Who knows what will happen now." Juan shrugged his shoulders.

"Now to find transportation." Juan carried their bags while Sara hoisted Juanito to one hip and followed. It was a hot day but the sea breeze blew steadily along the strand. Once they cleared the docks, Juan and Sara moved quickly along the promenade, a tiled walkway lined by palm trees.

A great noise of many voices swirled around them. A dozen teams of horses hitched up to large carts lined the promenade and each driver made it his goal to get their business.

"Do you need a ride to Ronda? I have a fine team of horses."

"Fifty *maravedis* to anywhere in Málaga. Step right over here."

"Coach to Córdoba. Reasonable prices."

Juan chose a driver and negotiated a price. "And I need you to go back to the docks and pick up an older couple there."

"Very good, sir. Get in." The driver stowed their bags in the back and tied them down. Juan helped Sara get in. He turned around.

"Where's Juanito?" Juan looked both ways and then laughed. He scooped Juanito up from the cobblestones, holding a tiny crab shell in his fist.

"Here's your adventurer." Juan handed Juanito to Sara, before he climbed up to the seat.

"Drive back there at the second dock, the one with all the people standing around." Juan pointed. The driver flicked the reins and headed the two black horses in the right direction. The wooden wheels creaked and wobbled on the uneven tiles.

"Here we are, Juan. Over here." Margarita and Rodrigo called out and waved. They walked to the cart and gave their bags to the driver. He helped Margarita and then Rodrigo up the step to sit on a second bench seat behind Juan and Sara. Juan grinned. The driver threw the bags in back and tied them down before starting the team again.

"Where to, travelers? Are you going to the same place?"

"Córdoba. We're all going there. And Señor Galvan here in back will give you directions when we get closer. He has family there."

"Yes, sir. Córdoba it is. It's a few days' journey, so I have a *bota* of water in back whenever you get thirsty and we'll stop occasionally to rest the horses."

"Sara, I bought some cheese and bread from vendors at the dock. In case Juanito gets hungry," said Margarita.

"Or me, too," said Juan. "I think we'll all be happy to have a bit of that before we get to the big city. *Mil gracias.*"

"Put a hat on if you have one," said the driver. "It's a hot sun up there." Sara found a shawl and draped it over her head and also Juanito's, who was leaning on her shoulder. Juanito relaxed as the horses plodded along. The cart rocked rhythmically and even Sara found the creaking sounds soothing. She closed her eyes.

The cart came to a stop under a spreading tree. "Let's stop for some water, travelers, and a bit of food if you have it. The driver jumped down and got the *bota*. He passed it to Juan who held it up to his mouth and let the cool liquid hit his palate.

"Would you like some, Sara?" Sara startled and opened her mouth. Juan aimed the cool stream of water into her mouth. She laid Juanito down on a blanket they put between them. Margarita and Rodrigo had the *bota* now and made pleasurable noises of approval.

"Here's some bread." Margarita passed half a loaf to Sara. "And next, some cheese." She got out a knife and cut a few chunks to pass them. The hard sheep's cheese and the crisp bread brought little noises of happiness to their lips.

"Let's continue. We need to get to Córdoba in good time." The driver got out a bucket of water he'd stored for his horses and they slurped it readily. The team set out again and wound through the countryside and began climbing the hills. From the sandy tree-lined beaches of the coast to the rocky countryside, the sea breeze blew over valleys and through ravines dotted with scrubby bushes. The only green places were groves of olive trees and the banks of flowing streams. The streams, beleaguered by the drying wind and sun, showed their rocky bottoms and looked like they soon would become *arroyos*, dusty and useless till the rains came again.

Juan stretched and yawned. "Will this journey never end?"

"You're anxious to be home, and I don't wonder. It's been a long time, hasn't it?"

"Too long."

"Do they know you're coming?"

"I did send a letter from Naples. I hope it has already arrived. But, I wasn't able to say the exact date and time, of course. We may be coming a few days before they expect us. I hope they're home."

"They'll be there, looking down the road constantly till they see the dust of the horses' hooves and hear the chatter of our voices." She patted him on the shoulder.

"I look forward to meeting them. Tell me something about them."

"Sorry I haven't said much about them." Juan frowned. "When I first met you, I told you my father is a leather merchant. He wanted me to follow in the family business, but I wanted to become a doctor."

"I remember. And your mother?"

"She makes incredible pottery. That's become a small business for her after all the children grew up. Haven't I told you this before?"

"Wonderful! An artist. And we have been separated a long time, in answer to your last question." Juan laughed and continued.

"Yes, and she sells it through my father's shop. He fashions boots and bags and hats from leather, and she paints plates and cups and pitchers."

"How many brothers and sisters do you have?"

"I'm the third child, like you. But there are five of us altogether, an older brother and sister and a younger sister and brother. A very neat arrangement, no?"

"I won't ask you all their names now, but I'll need to know that soon."

"I wouldn't be surprised if we are greeted by the whole family when we arrive. Be prepared for a crowd."

"Are all the siblings married?"

"Yes. I received a long letter from my mother through Columbus' agent when I first returned. So, let's see, José Carlos, the oldest, married Teresa and has three children. María, the next oldest, married Martín, and has four children My younger sister Ana married Xavier and has two children, and my little brother Roberto married Josefina and they have their first child now." He sighed. "Don't ask me to say the children's names."

"So, José Carlos, María, Ana and Roberto. Your four brothers and sisters. And your parents' names?"

"You really are ambitious and so thoughtful. My father is Rafael and my mother is Carolina."

"I will try to commit the names to memory before we get to Córdoba."

"We'll get there about three days from when we started in Málaga, including stopping to rest the horses."

"So I have plenty of time to memorize names."

"I'm amazed."

The wagon rolled along. Juanito woke up when one of the wheels hit a rock and bounced him onto the wooden floor. He rolled over and looked up at his parents, unsure whether to cry or laugh.

"Hi, big boy. What are you doing on the floor?" Juan reached for Juanito and lifted him high. Juanito laughed. "Do we have a bit of food for this big boy, mama?"

"Yes, I have bread." She tore off a piece from the loaf. She went about changing wet diaper rags and settled Juanito on her lap. The sun burned down from above and Sara threw the shawl over the two of them again. They peeked at each other for a while till Juanito tired of that game. The dusty landscape plodded by, each step of the horses echoing off the field of boulders they crossed through.

"Such rugged territory," said Sara. "What will Córdoba be like? I've never been there."

"The Guadalquivir River snakes through the countryside for miles and passes by the city. The Romans built a great wide bridge held upon many arches. This time of year, it's very dry, though, so the water is only a trickle." Juan smiled. "And the city is past its zenith, but still majestic. You'll see it and love it."

"I'm sure I will." The driver rolled the wagon into a grove of olive trees.

"Time to rest the horses. Everyone should rest here, too. We'll be here an hour."

He got out the barrel of water for the horse, and they slurped noisily. The travel-weary passengers climbed down. Sara spread a blanket on the ground. Margarita and Rodrigo did the same, lowering themselves slowly to dry ground and deep shade.

"There's a town ahead called Antequera, a village on a hill with an abandoned Moorish fortress and an inn, where we'll lodge for the night." Sara lay down and closed her eyes it seemed no more than a minute before the driver signaled it was time to leave again.

The team of horses struggled up the winding path to Antequera. Sara looked up into the hills and noticed some unusual rock formations. It looked like plates, rounded and flat, stacked one on another, like dishes gathered for washing. Everyone jumped out of the wagon when they finally pulled up to the inn. Rooms had been arranged. Married men roomed with their spouses, avoiding the crowded room of *solteros,* bachelors and those men traveling without family. The innkeeper served up steaming bowls of stew and early figs in wine as a dessert. Sara looked out a small window, viewing a sweeping landscape in straw yellow, olive green and fig brown. The sky, tinged with peach and orange, resembled *salmorejo,* a cold, refreshing soup often served in this region. She sighed and lay down again. The hot air still filtered in. *It's too hot to sleep well, but I should try.*

The next morning everyone got up quickly and gobbled their portion of bread and a watered down cup of sherry. They loaded into the wagon and soon the driver directed his rested horses down the hill and onward toward Córdoba. A few hours along the path, they stopped and got water for the horses and themselves. Sara looked across the parched hills with limestone rocks pushed up here and there.

"How much farther to Córdoba, driver?"

"It's another long day's drive after today, *señora,*" the driver responded.

"I wonder what will be waiting for us there?"

"A celebration with our family, Sara," said Juan. "And perhaps some friends."

"We'll see soon enough," said Rodrigo. "I'll be delirious to get off this cart." They traveled the rest of the day and arrived dusty and weary at a small village called Aguilar de la

Frontera, a half-day's ride from Córdoba. The whitewashed stucco buildings glowed in the setting sun. Everyone was hot and tired from the very long day of travel. They filed into an inviting inn, ate a savory but thin garlic soup, abundant bread and a slab of cheese. Everyone slept soundly, even Juanito. The next day, they arrived.

The wagon reached the Roman bridge just as the sun passed its highest point in the sky. The hot wind licked at their cheeks and dried their lips. The water *bota* had only a few drops left for each person, and the food was just a few crumbs.

"There's a large group of people at the other end. Is that all your family, Juan?"

"My family's not that big. Who could they be?" He shrugged his shoulders and threw out his hands. "I do see my mother and father in front, though." The horse clopped across the cobblestone bridge surface and suddenly the group of people expanded and began to cheer and clap. "What's all this?" The wagon came to a stop in front of them.

"*Bienvenidos*. Welcome, Juan Sánchez, our own native son. And his family, too!" A man dressed in long blue robes and a puffy hat lifted his hand and continued to address the group. "We welcome Juan Sánchez, born and educated in Córdoba. Son of Rafael and Carolina Sánchez. We commend him for his writings and for his courage in traveling with Admiral Columbus. I proclaim today, Juan Sánchez Day. We will feast together and give thanks for his presence again in our midst and wish him every blessing in his illustrious life."

Juan's jaw clamped shut and then his neck colored. His eyes held questions as he looked at Sara and then around the crowd. Sara saw an older woman wave and wipe her eyes. "My mother," he pointed out. He jumped down and ran to embrace her. Then he turned to his father. "I'm so happy and honored to see you again."

"It's our honor and joy to have a son return from the dead. So we thought. And where is your wife and child?" He grasped his son's hand and then threw an arm around his shoulder. Juan motioned for Sara to come and she found her way through the crowd.

"This is Sara Elena, my beloved, and here is Juan Alonso, our child."

Juan's parents hovered around the two for a moment and then reached out to embrace Sara and then to take turns holding Juanito. They cooed and cuddled him and asked a hundred questions till the mayor spoke up and said,

"The feast awaits. Everyone come and follow me to the banquet over here in the covered patio. Tables are set out and servers will seat you." He directed Juan and the whole Sánchez family to sit at a raised table. He joined them, for he was to make a speech. After the food had all been consumed, the mayor stood up and raised a toast to Juan.

"I seem to be a hero, but I don't know why."

"Sir, your travel writings have been published and caught the attention of the king and queen. All educated people have been reading the startling account of the voyage. It's the first written words we've had on that famous expedition."

"Well. I'm honored to be recognized," said Juan.

"Not only that. The king and queen request your presence at court as soon as you may arrive. We didn't quite know what to tell them. But they are anxious to speak with you and reward you." The mayor beamed. "You reflect great credit on your family and our great city, Córdoba." He made a sweeping bow and then applauded Juan. Others joined the clapping until it sounded like thunder. Juan nodded to the crowd and sat down. Gradually the crowd dispersed to their homes. The breeze disguised the heat of the afternoon.

Juanito was fussy and weepy. "He's tired, Juan," said Sara. "We need to find a bed for him." Juan's parents picked up the bags where the driver had left them and walked with them into the city till they reached their home on Calle Encarnación. "Welcome, all of you."

Chapter 21

"A summons has come from Their Majesties," said Juan's father. "They are now in residence at the Alcázar here in Córdoba and request your presence as soon as may be."

"Oh, no! I have no proper garments to wear and I'm dusty from the road." Sara jumped up and paced the floor while talking.

"Did they give a time we should arrive?" said Juan.

"The notice says they are 'aware of the festival in your honor and, therefore, defer seeing you until tomorrow morning at ten.'"

"That's a relief. I guess I could wear the green dress Don Antonio gave me. What do you think, Juan?"

Juan scowled. "No!" he said, with voice taut. Sara frowned and looked away. She knew, then. It was a reminder to him of how close she came to shame and ruin.

She said quickly, "You're right, it really makes me look sallow. I should give it away."

"I may have something suitable," said Carolina, Juan's mother. "And perhaps you'd like a bath. Come with me."

"Juan, could you tend Juanito if he wakes up?" Juan looked up and nodded. Juan's father elbowed him.

"So you tend babies? Not the usual work of a father, is it?"

"It comes from my medical training. You know, tending the ill and suffering, and cleaning up the messy wounds of soldiers." Juan grinned. His dad laughed.

"I don't think you'll see the other fathers in our family following your example. It's women's work."

"Father, it came of necessity. In Naples, Sara had to work to survive, and that's the only work we had between us in the short time I spent there. I am not ashamed of helping my beloved wife." Father held his peace and stroked his beard.

"I hope you'll have time to show Sara some of the sights in Córdoba, after your royal visit."

"I thought a walk through the Jewish quarter and a trip to the *mezquita,* the great mosque."

"You'll no doubt walk through the gardens on the way to the Alcázar, the royal palace. Their majesties usually travel north to Segovia for the hot summer months. Consider it an honor that they have tarried here to meet with you."

"I'm uneasy about this meeting. What will they say? What will I say?"

"Don't speak unless spoken to. Be respectful and don't belch."

"I hardly think so, Father."

"Don't worry, son. Just answer what they ask, and then stop."

"Do you have a good doublet I could wear tomorrow?"

"I'm bigger around the middle than you, but I think we can find something." He slapped Juan on the back. "After the ladies are finished, that is."

The next day, Sara and Juan dressed in the finest clothes they could put together and made their way to the royal palace. They decided to walk, since it was only a short distance.

"You look lovely today, Sara. It's wonderful to see you in a gown that shows off your beauty." Juan clasped her hand and squeezed it.

"Your mother was so helpful. Don't you love this aquamarine damask and the black braid around the square neckline? It's a favorite color of mine."

"If you mention that, I'm sure my mother will give it to you."

"I didn't intend that."

"We need to compose ourselves. We're almost to the palace." They walked through the royal gardens, beside a long oblong pool with streams of water arching in perfect parabolas over and into it.

"The splashing of water always calms me," said Juan. The perfume of blossoming flowers permeated the air: scented geraniums, carnations and lilies. Lavish sprays of wisteria flung themselves across wrought iron grills and wound tightly around poles, ardent lovers embracing their true love. Their color was fading in the heat, their season almost over.

"Here we are," said Juan, as they walked around the last garden plot and reached a long promenade. "The throne room lies just ahead."

"I hope we're not late." Sara smoothed her gown and stepped forward, her heart beating a bit faster.

An audience with the queen and king!

* * * *

"You didn't tell me you knew the queen," said Juan as they strolled back to his parents' home.

"I don't know them."

"Queen Isabella knew you."

"I was surprised and flattered. I only performed a small act, carried a message, for her during the siege of Granada. And I copied a bit of writing for her once." Sara touched Juan's arm. "What did you think of the audience today?"

"It went well, I guess. I'm not sure she likes my writings." He sighed.

"She got angry that Admiral Columbus treated the natives so harshly."

"Yes, but I only reported it, I didn't do that myself."

"Sometimes people forget that." Sara stopped, opened her fan and waved it in front of her face. "She showed curiosity about herbal medicines and the Taino language. Didn't Columbus bring back some Indians to show her?"

"I wonder where they were? Maybe I could have talked to them."

"Most of them died, I heard. Couldn't survive the ocean crossing."

"That's so wrong!" said Juan, clenching his fists.

"How much money did they give you as a reward?"

"I haven't counted it yet, but it's a sizable pouch."

"Strange that they don't want your name and writings to spread beyond Córdoba. Did you understand why?" Sara looked at her husband.

"My controversial writings. Critical of Columbus, I guess." He shrugged his shoulders. "It reflects on the monarchs, I guess."

"Well, you won't get rich by selling lots of copies, then."

"I think we may be watched by someone connected to the Inquisition, so I'd rather keep our names out of everyone's conversation. Did you see that priest standing quietly to the back of the throne room? He may be an investigator."

Sara stopped and grabbed Juan's arm. "No! I can't bear it."

"I could be wrong, Sara. Oh, here we are. Back again." He opened the door and let her through first. "Let's enjoy Córdoba for a day or two and then move on."

"We need to say goodbye to Margarita and Rodrigo, too. I wonder where we'll go from here? Moguer?" Juan nodded his agreement and then turned to his family. They answered the many questions that filled the air and finally flopped on chairs.

"We're tired, everyone. Stop! Please." Juan held up his hand, palm out.

"Where's Juanito?" Sara looked around.

"Taking a rest."

"I need to get out of this gown and into something more comfortable."

"Would you like to see parts of Córdoba before we leave?" said Juan.

Sara nodded.

"I wish you would stay," said Mother Sánchez. "Juanito is so sweet."

"Perhaps we can stay awhile. Juanito needs to know his grandparents."

"I've heard about the grand mosque. Could we go there, Juan?" Sara unbuttoned the loops on her sleeves.

"Let me help you with the rest. And I'll change, too. Don't want to get your good doublet dirty, Father." Sara and Juan retreated to the bedroom they were using and rid themselves of their formal wear. When they returned to the *sala*, Sara was wearing her everyday dress and Juan his second best doublet. "We'll see you later, unless you'd like us to take Juanito."

"No. We'll keep him. It's fun to play with a little boy again." Mother Sánchez radiated a huge smile. Juan's father waved them off, too.

"The grand mosque is very old, Sara, and I think very beautiful. It's up the hill not far from here and, of course, has a grove of orange trees with a system of water rivulets the Moors always set up. It keeps the trees watered and also has a pleasant trickle throughout the day."

"I love the smell of orange blossoms," said Sara.

"This is not the right time for that, you know, but it's still green and fresh there. There's a well from which to get a drink, too."

"Can we go inside?"

"Since the Catholic Monarchs have conquered all of Spain, the mosque is no longer used as a place of Muslim worship. Instead, there is now a Christian chapel inside. So, yes, we can venture inside." They walked to the entrance.

"Can you feel the rush of cool air coming from inside?"

"Mm, it's so nice. The day is getting hot already." She shivered. "Thousands of feet have crossed this doorstep. See, the marble is worn down."

"I love this place," said Juan. "See—it's a huge open room with double arches everywhere. To me, they look like spreading palm trees. The columns are the trunks."

"Columns of so many kinds—I see green, red, black and gold streaks and even blue veins." Sara pointed at several nearby pillars.

"Taken from old Roman remains to be used again here."

"So practical."

"The Catholic Monarchs plan to build a Catholic cathedral inside of here."

"Where? It would ruin the architecture!"

"Shh. They're the conquerors—so it's customary."

"Let's get out of here." They strolled with soft steps toward the exit. "Do you hear someone following us?" Sara looked over her shoulder. "I thought I saw a man in black behind one of the pillars."

"You see a lot of men in black. Are you sure?"

"I thought I did." Sara looked at her feet. "Let's walk quickly but quietly. Maybe we'll hear something." They scurried across the threshold and hid around a corner of the building. They watched several people exit the great mosque but none in black. Sara sighed and they started walking again.

"You have an active imagination."

"I know what I saw."

"Well, let's go home now. It's almost time for our main meal."

"All right." They strolled arm in arm down the wide main street and found their way toward the parents' house. As they crossed the threshold, Sara looked back and saw a smudge of black disappear behind a potted bush. *I was right! So, we once again have to evade the Inquisition. I hope it proves easier this time.*

* * * *

After the mid-day meal and a siesta, Juan and Sara took Juanito with them. "Let's walk through the Jewish Quarter. It has a lot to see."

"I'd like to buy a leather bag from your father, and maybe a piece of pottery your mother made."

"Their shop happens to be in on Calle Encarnación. It's a good place to do business and the rents are reasonable. I'll show you when we come to it."

"The streets are so narrow—hardly enough for a cart to go through."

"It's hot today. These sandstone blocks are like a bread oven! Burning!"

Juan ushered her to a shadowy corner.

"Cool yourself here for a minute." Sara wiped Juanito's face and then hers. Meanwhile, she glanced at the shops tucked in the walls here and there. A clothing shop with hand-embroidered shawls and intricate fans. Next to it, a bookstore, or maybe just a place to buy paper and quills?

"I'd like to peek into both of these places," Sara said. "I could use a fan today. Yesterday, I borrowed one from your mother." Juan took Juanito while Sara meandered through the shop. She looked at all the fans—wooden slats painted with colorful flowers and designs on both sides, and some made of stiffened fabrics and bordered by lace. She hesitated, and then reached out for the green brocade with attached tassels. She dropped some coins in the storeowner's palm and slipped it in her shoulder bag. Sara stepped outside. She noticed Juan had moved on to the parchments store.

"Did you find something you need, Juan?" Sara strolled in and touched his sleeve. She took Juanito.

"More paper for my travel book. I've got lots of details I want to include. My mind is whirling." He went toward a stack of thick sheets with uneven edges. Fresh and supple and made out of hemp and linen rags, the shop owner announced. Juan chose three and dropped coins on the counter. Sara breathed deeply and remembered a long forgotten day working with her father in his translation office. The shopkeeper rolled them into a cylinder and tied a string around them. "Let's go farther up the street and turn the corner. That's where my father's shop is located."

They turned left at the corner after climbing ten or more terraced steps. Sara saw a shop with a large window. Arranged in a display: leather purses with long straps and some with no strap, but embossed with flowing designs and dyed in several spots of color. And the animal smell of the leather, earthy and permeating, conjured up for Sara the smell of her father's book pouches.

"These stores take me back to childhood memories. The smells, the feel of new parchments, it's evocative."

"I don't think a tanner's workshop would bring such happy memories, though, do you?" He held his nose. Sara's laugh shot out of her mouth.

"That stinky place, no!"

"It's down by the river at the edge of town, if you want a good whiff."

Sara moved on and came to the pottery. Platter-size plates were displayed on a wall shelf. The bright colors swirled about the center and a band of blue framed the edge. One plate held a profuse number of daisy-like flowers but in many colors: red, blue and yellow with green leaves strewn about.

Another plate depicted a view of Córdoba as seen from across the river, just before crossing the Roman bridge. The broad avenue of bricks led straight to the city's sentry tower, through the city gate. The walls of the grand mosque rose high above it all. Carolina Sánchez had painted groups of people making their way to the city, or stopping to converse. The costumes of the important and the country folk were all re-created in detail.

"Oh, Juan, can we get this? Your mother's work is so fine, so detailed. This will help me remember Córdoba even when we must leave." Juan strolled up and scrutinized the platter.

"That's typical of Mother's best work. Yes, I think we should have it."

He took it over to the counter where his father was at work on hand tooling a money pouch.

"Is there a shoulder bag or pouch you would like, Sara? Take another look." Sara knew just what she wanted and brought back a shoulder bag in the orangey brown color typical of much of the leather goods in Córdoba.

"A great choice, Sara," said Father Sánchez. "Juan, do you need new boots? I can give you them at a special price."

"Thanks, Father, but mine are in good condition."

"Carolina will be delighted you chose this platter. In fact, maybe we should just give it to you. A wedding present, though we missed it by two years."

Sara gasped and leaned over the counter to give Juan's father a kiss on the cheek. His neck colored, but he smiled widely.

"You got my father to smile, Sara. That doesn't happen much. I think you have made a good impression." Juan whispered into his wife's ear. Juanito laughed and clapped his hands.

"Big, big." Juan poked him till he laughed again.

"Say grandfather, Juanito. *Abuelo*." Juanito scowled and rolled his eyes like an owl.

"Aboo. Aboo." He clapped his hands. After Father Sánchez wiped a tear that had escaped his eye, he wrapped up the two articles.

"We'll see you at home, Father. It's been great to see your fine leather skills and Mother's ceramics." He waved to them.

"We might just stay a few more days, Dad. I'm so glad you can get to know my family—Sara and Juanito."

Juan and Sara stayed three more days, days that flew by like swallows, breathtaking in beauty but fleeting.

But a feeling of doom entered Sara's heart.

Chapter 22

The driver steadied the horses and tied the cart outside the door. "Time to go, Sara. Do you have anything else to load?" said Juan. He gathered up the bags and bundles set by the door and gave them to the driver.

"Coming," said Sara, scurrying down the hall. Juanito clung to her skirts and ran to keep up with her. "Run, Juanito, run!"

"Run," echoed Juanito, his legs working like a hunting dog's. He got caught in Sara's skirts and lost his footing. Down he crashed and let out a wail.

"You tore my skirt, Juanito." Sara dropped her packages and bags and went to set Juanito on his feet. "Are you all right? What a fast runner you are!" Juanito sniffled but started running again and got to the door before her. "You're the winner!"

"Yay!" Juanito shook his hands in the air.

"Let's not play now," said Juan, his smile turned down at the corners. "Give me those things and climb in the cart." Sara lifted Juanito up and joined him without delay. She spread out a blanket and plopped Juanito there next to her.

"We're ready," she said, voice tight and lips a thin line. Juan's mother and father came to the door and blew kisses to Juanito. His father clasped hands with Juan and his mother hugged him and planted a kiss on each cheek.

"*Vaya con Dios*, loved ones. Let us know when and where you settle." Juan reached the cart's seat in one giant step and put his arm around Sara.

"*Te amo*," he whispered into her ear. Her body relaxed. She leaned against him. "I will send a message as soon as we find a home, Father." He waved again. The cart creaked and started rolling. The two black horses clopped into the main road; hoof beats echoing off the sandstone walls. The sun rose higher in a cloudless sky warming the walls and pavement.

"How far do we go today? Do we have plenty of water?" Sara threw a shawl over her head and Juanito's.

"It's a hot day, so we'll stop in the shade some, for our sake and also for the horses. Be sure to drink water often. I hope to reach an inn twelve leagues from here, not quite half way to Sevilla, today." He scratched his head and re-positioned his hat. "We have to consider the little one, too." The driver wiped his forehead with the back on his hand. His black shirt and short tabard had a blot of sweat at the small of his back. Juan acknowledged his remarks with a small sound in his throat.

A puff of dust in the distance and then the sound of hooves on the trail alerted them all that several people were approaching. Sara gazed back at the road they had traveled. She pursed her lips.

"Who are they?"

Shading her eyes with one hand, she made out three men riding small horses—no, burros. "And all of the men dressed in black--Oh, no!"

"Now Sara, we don't know that they are following us." Juan patted her hand. "They might just be traveling on the same road. Let's wait here and see."

As the three priests got closer, they pulled up alongside the wagon and made the sign of the cross as a greeting. The driver stopped and so did they.

"Good day, friars. What takes you along this road?" Juan bowed his head slightly in respect.

"We travel west toward Sevilla, sir. A long journey but necessary, as our monastery is there." The one in the middle replied and Sara looked at him from under her shaded eyes. He sat tall in the plain saddle hitched on the donkey. The friar's eyes darted from Juan to Sara and rested a moment on Juanito's face. Sara gathered him up and against her shoulder, partially hiding her face.

"What business brought you to Córdoba, may we ask?"

"The bishop of the region commanded it. All the members of the Inquisition had to appear before the royal court."

"I see. A royal summons."

"Indeed," said another friar, short and with a belly that strained at the fabric of his robe. "An inspired speech by King Ferdinand to faithfully prosecute wanderers from the faith." He lifted his chin and put on a closed-lip smile.

"There aren't many, now that the Alhambra Decree has done its work."

"There are still those who pretend to faith but don't practice it. Also, we must root out blasphemy, as well. Those who slander the holy faith in word or deed." The third friar, a youth with eager eyes, jumped into the conversation.

"In fact, we heard of—"

"Silence, brother," said the middle one. "That is private information." He turned to Juan and Sara. "We bid you Godspeed and a safe journey." They all nodded and urged their mounts forward. Sara clasped Juan's hands, knuckles turning white.

"Let's begin again, driver," said Juan. "The day grows hotter and the road is long." The driver flicked the reins. Juan leaned close to her ear. "Sara, do not worry about the

Inquisition. They have no interest in or knowledge of you." Her smile didn't reach her eyes.

They stopped twice that day, once for a lunch on the grass under a grove of olive trees, and a second time as they neared their stopping point. Juan, Sara and Juanito all drank long from the *bota* bag and used a bit of water to clean the sweat off their faces. Juan's wide-brimmed hat showed sweat stains around the flat crown. Sara's hair lay matted in wet clumps around her face. Juanito squirmed and kicked his legs. "You need to get out and run around, don't you? Juan, could you get down and let Juanito run a bit?"

"No time for that, señora," said the driver. "We must push on and get to our inn before sunset." Sara sighed and bounced Juanito around, clapping his hands together and doing hand motions to make the little boy laugh not whine. The wagon rolled on and came to village on a rounded knoll. It overlooked a dry valley of rocks and dry creek beds. The breeze blew steadily, tossing dead plants into the air till they skittered over the rough hillside and formed brittle balls.

"Such a lonely place!" said Sara.

"The innkeeper is friendly and makes a good lamb stew." The driver got the bags out of the cart and led them into the stone structure. A covered porch in front held rough wooden tables and benches for guests. Sara stopped to look out at the barren vista.

"It's quiet here. Only the sound of the wind." She followed the others and soon they made their way to a room with a straw mattress on the bed frame, and a small cot for Juanito. "And the floors are swept."

"We can rest here. Let's go down to the dining room and get our supper." Juan picked up Juanito and they passed through the narrow hall. A door opened and Sara caught a glance of black robes. She stiffened and walked faster. The stew was thick and hot and full of onions and carrots.

"Mm. Delicious." said Juan, licking his lips.

"But the lamb chunks are little chewy." Sara wiped her mouth and gave little pieces of lamb and carrots to Juanito. "I think I'll take Juanito out to the field to run around," said Sara. "Then he'll sleep easier."

"I'll come with you." Juan pushed away from the table and stretched out his legs. I feel stiff myself. It's been a long day of sitting." They each took one hand of Juanito's and swung his up into the air while walking out the door to the field. After much running and dodging, swinging and tickling Juanito collapsed in a laughing heap on the dry grass.

"All right, little man, time to go to sleep. The sun has gone to bed, too." Juan pointed to the glowing horizon. "Goodnight, sun."

"Goo-nigh." Juanito pointed. Juan picked him up and put him on his shoulders legs straddling his neck. Sara followed them into the inn and spread out a blanket on the little cot. Sara sang a lullaby, as Juanito's eyelids got heavy. Soon he relaxed into sleep. They tiptoed to their bed.

"I hope there are no bugs," said Juan, inspecting the mattress cover, a coarsely woven fabric. "We'll be scratching though, because of this rough bedcover."

"Keep your clothes on as protection." Sara lay down and closed her eyes. "I'm so tired I don't have the energy to undress." When Juan planted a kiss on her cheek, she was already breathing deeply in sleep.

"Sleep well."

During the night, however, Sara awoke with strong cramps in her abdomen. "It's that stew! I knew there was something wrong with it." She got up to find a chamber pot and retched into the foul smelling container. Juanito stirred and woke with a howl and then a scream. Sara wiped her mouth and went to comfort her son. His body tightened even as she tried to soothe him. His cries woke Juan.

"I don't know! He seems all right, but he can't settle into sleep." Juanito's hands flailed the air and he pushed away from his mother. "I can't hold you when you do that, Juanito." Juan took his fretful child and walked around the room, patting his back. Juanito relaxed against his shoulder and closed his eyes. But, when he set him down, another howl and a roar.

"Quiet, little one." Juan put Juanito against his chest again and jostled and patted him. "I'll just keep walking until Juanito is deeply asleep, I guess. You, Sara, go back to bed." Sara gave a half smile and made no objection to the suggestion. She faded into sleep, occasionally hearing a protest from Juanito. Sara awoke to the new day and felt Juan next to her. She opened her eyes and saw Juanito asleep on her husband's chest and Juan sprawled on top of the blanket. *What a night for all of us!*

The second day of travel passed uneventfully. Sara never saw the black robes again. It might have been the same three friars they met on the road, but she never saw their faces. Juanito was fretful and whiny. Juan answered questions with clipped sentences and Sara covered her face from the sun. Her eyes didn't focus and her head ached. *Maybe I need water.* She reached for the water bag and took a long drink from the tepid stream flowing out. She wore her lightest weight dress, the linen one that should be cool. But, still she felt hot and sticky. *It's a very hot climate and it's August! I must endure it.*

They continued on the road another day. Juanito fussed all the time.

"Can't you settle down?" Sara said, and then felt guilty when Juanito got tears in his eyes. The second night went well. Juanito either was too tired or Juan was more expert in handling him. Sara didn't volunteer to help in the middle of the night. *Another thing to feel guilty about today.*

Finally, they came to Sevilla.

"We'll stop at the monastery to eat the midday meal," said the driver as he tethered his team at a hitching post under a lattice of grapevines. He took care to water his horses and loosen their harnesses a notch. "We're just outside the city walls. And if you look beyond that wall, you'll see the king's garden."

"Are we near the Alcázar, the royal residence?" said Sara. She turned her neck left and then right.

"Yes," said the driver. "Now, please get out of the cart. We'll eat and rest here."

The driver led them into the public area, where the hospitaller, the person responsible for seeing to the guests, greeted them. He motioned them to a table and set wooden plates and cutlery in front of them.

"Brother Mateo will serve you," he said, as a slender young monk brought in a tray of offerings. He set before them a bowl of steaming boiled turnips, a plate of chicken with onions and herbs and a pitcher of wine diluted with purified water.

"Thank you," said Juan, and the young monk looked up through his long tonsure. His eyes registered recognition. "I think we met you on the road, brother."

"Yes, sir, I remember. Welcome to our monastery, Santo Domingo Portacoeli."

"And your name?"

"Brother Mateo, there's no need to talk. Return to your duties." The monk in charge knit his eyebrows together. The young monk dipped his head and withdrew. "You may have extra to drink and bread, too," he whispered. "Just beckon me." Sara kept her eyes on her plate.

"We should push on, travelers." The driver herded them back to the cart. "If we travel till dark today we may arrive in Moguer tomorrow. Would you like that?" Sara's face shone like a mirror reflecting the sun's rays.

"Oh, yes. Do whatever it takes."

"As long as we have a place to stay tonight, and at the end of the journey." Juan slapped a hand on the driver's shoulder.

"*Bueno, hombre.*" The animals quickened their pace, no doubt dreaming of oats at the end of a tiring trek. Juanito, too, sat still most of the time, looking around to spot birds, rocks and an occasional parched tree. Juan and Sara held hands and looked at each other often, and whispered together. "What will you do first when we get to Moguer, Sara?"

"Take a bath."

"And after that?"

"Explore the town. We might settle here if we like it. What will you do?"

"Get re-acquainted with my wife." Color crept into Sara's cheeks.

"I hope you take a bath, though." She poked him in the ribs.

"Funny girl." He ran his hand through Sara's hair. Sara tossed her hair back, then reached for the water bag and shared it with her family.

The scenery rolled along and the fiery sun raced toward the western horizon. Shadows lengthened. The sun now shone directly in their eyes. Sara shaded her eyes with one hand and kept Juanito under part of the shawl. Sara sneezed, as dust swirled up with a gust of wind.

"We will stop for the night soon at Niebla, on the Rio Tinto," said the driver. "Then tomorrow, we will reach Moguer at mid-day. There you will feel the cooler air coming up the river valley from the sea."

* * * *

They arrived in Moguer at mid-day as promised. "Here we are at Santa Clara," said the driver.

A middle-aged nun greeted them and led them to their room, an unadorned whitewashed room with spare furniture: two narrow beds and a small cot. A plain but well-crafted table between the beds held one candle on a wooden candlestick. A crucifix was nailed to one wall and a basin and pitcher with soap and towel completed the furnishings.

"We have blankets for each of you, a chamber pot and a smaller blanket for the little one. Please rest now during siesta hours. Come to the *comedor* for your supper at sunset." Juan and Sara thanked her and Sara curtsied. The nun, an older woman with a peaceful face, tucked her hands in opposite sleeves of her brown homespun habit and glided out of the room.

"I don't think we'll get a bath here, Juan. Let's just clean up the best we can. Maybe we can ask in the morning." Sara spent some time cleaning her face and hands and fingernails, also. She brushed her hair while Juan splashed some clean water from the pitcher into the bowl. The soap smelled fresh and refreshed them. Supper was leftover stew from lunch, cooked vegetables and a loaf of bread. Their drink again was *tinto de verano*, a red wine mixed with pure mineral water. They gulped it down. It was welcome refreshment after a hot summer day of travel. Juanito went to bed after a good wash of hands and face.

"Tomorrow we'll look for Catalina de Torres, your brother's widow."

"I'm so curious to see what she's like. She sounded so gloomy in her letter. I hope we can cheer her." Sara pulled up the covers and leaned toward Juan. "I love you Juan." She gave him a kiss. He reached out to her, smiling, but she was already asleep.

Chapter 23

The morning meal consisted of day-old bread soaked in diluted red wine. Sara ate a moderate portion. *Will this be enough until the midday meal?* She imagined: *For lunch I'd like to have cold asparagus, fried cheese croquettes, roast chicken with onions and mushrooms, and for dessert, flan custard.* She sighed and returned to the bread. The nuns gave Juanito a slice of fragrant yellow cheese. "It's from sheep's milk and it's delicious," said the cellarer. Sara took a bite of the aged cheese. Juanito grabbed a piece and reached for more.

"Do you happen to know a woman named Catalina de Torres?" Juan said to the cellarer. The woman pursed her lips and creased her forehead.

"I can't say I do. Sorry. But ask the prioress." She returned to her duties.

"The church will have a registry of births, deaths and baptisms," said Sara.

"But which one? There are so many. And what if she's Jewish?" whispered Juan. Sara shrugged her shoulders.

"If she's a recent convert to the faith, there may be a baptism recorded here at the convent church. But I don't want to alert the clergy here at the convent that we are making inquiries."

Sara gave Juanito another piece of bread. "Let's just ask quietly. A nun who records data won't have much dialog with her superiors."

Juan scooped up Juanito, Sara her bag. After exiting the dining area, they left their bags at the guest lodgings and walked into the central patio area of the compound. Offices bordered the perimeter of the patio and most doors sat ajar. A well, a bubbling fountain and a bench complemented the pots of flowers and trailing vines.

"Let's try that door, Juan." They tapped and went in. "We're looking for a lost relative living in Moguer or nearby. Can you help us?" A bent-over figure in a rumpled tan habit looked up from a small desk and pushed spectacles up on the bridge of her nose.

"Yes, yes. It's most irregular, you know, to interrupt the recording of important documents. But you look like proper people, though a little untidy." She removed her spectacles and stroked her nose with two fingers, which left smudges of ink. She wiped a finger under her nostrils and left another spot of ink there. Her face and habit had other dots and spots of ink, as well. Sara put a hand up to her mouth to hold in the laugh ready to burst out.

"We're very sorry to bother you, sister. We're looking for my brother's widow. She neglected to give us her address. I think she didn't expect us to come, but here we are." Sara stopped and gave a little smile and a curtsy. The nun-registrar sat up a bit straighter and smoothed out her habit before standing and walking toward them.

"Do you have her name and birthdate or any other information?" Sara produced a scrap of rough paper with all the information they had. The long-nosed woman donned a pair of soft gloves, took the scrap and walked to a bookcase of dusty tomes bound and protected with leather coverings and straps. She selected one and came back. "Now, let's have a look." She talked more to herself than them, running her finger lightly down the pages. She flipped pages once or twice, and then flipped back. "I'm sorry. I don't see her name. She must be a new resident here. Have you tried any other churches?"

"Which one?"

"Could be any of them. Santa Clara is the oldest, of course." She twitched her nose. They thanked her and left.

"Let's walk to Moguer and through the square and see if anyone knows her. That may be more productive," said Juan. Sara adjusted Juanito to her other hip and strode out the door keeping up with Juan. They walked a short distance and picked their way over the uneven cobblestones. They saw several old men sitting on one bench and another bench containing two women conversing.

"I'll talk to the women," said Sara, and wandered off.

Juan headed for the old men sitting on a bench. Each was dressed neatly. One wore a floppy hat. The middle one tapped a cane on the ground to emphasize the words he was saying. The third nodded with his eyes closed. Juan approached politely and listened to their answers. He returned to the spot near the city hall and under an olive tree.

"I found out nothing," said Juan. "The old men have a lot of good stories, though, and told me the history of the town, but they didn't know anyone by the name of Catalina de Torres." He smiled. "Listen to this. The old man in the middle told me about someone who used to live out in the countryside. One day he found a burro wandering in a dry *arroyo* on his property. He slapped its rump to scare it away, but the burro started following him around. The man got a stick and swatted at the animal. Instead of going away, it backed up to the stick and scratched an itch on its hindquarters. What do you think happened next?"

"I have no idea!"

"Well, the burro followed the man back to his home. By this time, it was sunset. The man thought he should feed the poor thing and give it some water. The burro looked at him like he was falling love with the man—big, shining eyes. The man went into the house to get some food and then headed to his bed. As he lay there, he heard steps in the hall. Clopping sounds. Guess what? The lovesick burro plodded down the hall and came into the man's bedroom. He put his moist nose in the man's face and licked him with his rough tongue. If that wasn't enough, the burro walked around the bed, nosed under the blanket and rolled his frame onto the bed. He cuddled close to the man and soon started snoring. The man was so surprised. He didn't know how to move a heavy burro off a bed. So he gave up and let the burro sleep there all night.

"The next morning the burro got up early and clopped down the hall and out the door. He kept walking and the man never saw that burro again! So ends the story." Juan laughed. "Guess what the man said next? He said, 'This shows you that Andalusian men have great magnetism.' Have you heard a story to compare with that?" Juan lifted up his head to the sky and laughed long and loud.

"Nothing that silly," said Sara, "but I did find out something useful. The ladies belong to a growers' organization and Catalina is part of it! She grows almonds and just last year sold her first crop. Did well at it, too."

"They're sure?"

Sara nodded. "And besides that, they recognized her as the widow of Luis, now considered a hero of the fateful Columbus voyage."

"Why didn't the men suggest that—or the nun at Santa Clara church?" Juan scratched his stubbly beard.

"Not as aware as the young women, maybe."

"Where does Catalina live?"

"Out of town on the *Camino de Almendros*, Almond Tree Road. Let's go!"

Juan hugged her and searched for a cart and driver. Soon, they clopped across the city's tiled roads and then joined the dirt road leading to the countryside. At an ancient olive tree, they turned left at Sara's direction. The driver followed the narrow path through a plot of young almond trees. They came to a rock and mortar house. Trailing geraniums hung from clay pots, flaming parrots of color in an otherwise dusty yard. A young woman sat on the porch, eyes closed and face tanned.

"Hello, friends. Did you come to buy almonds?" She roused herself and opened blue eyes and tossed her sandy hair.

Hello, we're looking for Catalina de Torres."

"That's my name. What brings you here?"

"I can see why Luis fell in love with you," said Sara, climbing down from the cart. The woman froze.

"Are you Sara Elena? Oh!" Her voice raised an octave. She closed the gap between them with a few running steps. Catalina touched Sara's face with callused hands. "You're beautiful." She embraced Sara.

Sara kissed her on both cheeks. "Luis never told me about you, Catalina." Sara stepped back to get a better look of the young woman. "You're pretty, too."

"Oh, no. My face is like leather and I have farmer's hands since I started raising almonds." Catalina hid her hands under her apron. "Did someone tell you where to find me?"

"Yes, two young women in the square at Moguer. They belong to your growers' cooperative. One is short and plump with a musical laugh and the other is thin as a sapling and blinks her eyes a lot."

"Rosa and Lupe?"

Sara nodded. "That's right."

Catalina turned toward Juan. "Can this be your husband? I thought you perished at La Navidad, like my dear Luis." Juan took her hand and kissed it.

"I traveled with Luis on the expedition and we kept close throughout the ordeal of La Navidad. I did not die of my injuries. A Taino woman doctored me back to health."

"Could Luis possibly still be alive?" Catalina's blue eyes intensified and grew bigger. "Please say yes."

"I'm very sorry to say no. I saw your husband's body after I recovered somewhat. He had been dead a while. But I recognized his clothes and the bag he carried." Catalina brushed a tear back from her eye.

"And here is your son? She shut her mouth but looked at Sara.

"He's was conceived on our wedding night," said Sara, turning pink. Juanito waved his hands and legs. Juan held him a bit tighter.

"The same with me and Luis. Luis had to leave after only three days. The baby was born before its time and lived only an hour." Catalina covered her face.

"We're so sorry," murmured both Juan and Sara. Sara held her in an embrace while Catalina wiped tears from her eyes.

"You must tell us your whole story," said Sara, drawing back. "We want to know all about you and Luis."

"Come in, please, and we'll talk. It's cool inside and I have some cold almond soup and asparagus. Join me." Juan instructed the driver to stay, so he maneuvered his team under a trellis of grapevines made for shading animals. Catalina served the food and then launched into her story.

"I met Luis in Cádiz on holiday. It was about this time two years ago—high summer and hotter than a lizard in a fry pan. I was taking a walk along the causeway, Playa de la Caleta, down by the sea. The sea breezes cooled the air, but one gust pulled my scarf off my shoulders and it flew into the path of an oncoming carriage. Luis ran into the street and rescued it just before the carriage would run it over."

"How chivalrous," said Sara. "Then what happened?"

"I thanked him, of course, and we started talking. He had taken some time to get away and contemplate the enormity of the Columbus adventure before he was about to embark on it. We had much in common—an adventurous spirit, Jewish heritage, *converso* conversion and a certain affinity. We talked and walked all afternoon and had supper together. I knew right away I could tell him anything and everything about myself. We met the next day and the next, discovering we had fallen deeply in love."

"I can see where this is going. When did Luis propose marriage?" Juan smiled at Catalina and switched Juanito to his other arm.

"The very next day. Luis said 'Let's get married' and I readily agreed. We walked to the nearest cathedral and asked the priest to marry us. He gave us words of counsel, but we were so filled with desire we couldn't keep a thought in our heads."

"I hope you didn't regret it, getting married so quickly." Juan's brow creased.

Catalina shook her head. "Oh, no. After we married, Luis bought me flowers and we ate a large afternoon meal. We had three glorious days together, loving each other, walking on the beach, and marveling at our good fortune. Luis had to leave the next day for Palos. He promised to write as often as he could and said he'd be back in six months or so."

"Did you hear from him after that?" Sara smoothed back a stray curl.

"He did write from La Navidad and sent the letter with Columbus when he returned to Spain. I still hoped to see him again, because Columbus arranged a second voyage to rescue them."

"You said you got pregnant?" Sara said in a soft voice.

"The baby came unexpectedly and too early—in December instead of April. It was perfectly formed but it struggled to breathe and only lived an hour."

"How sad! Did you have anyone to help you?"

"Only a midwife. My parents are dead and all my brothers and sisters left during the expulsion. I was too weak physically."

"So tragic!" Sara wiped her eyes.

"I felt a heavy weight of grief and was fatigued from bearing the child—a boy. I called him Rafael." Catalina got control of her quivering lip and continued. "The news that Luis had stayed in the New World was a blow, but I expected him to return. I recovered and decided to become a laborer in this almond orchard. I began by learning all I could. My father had been a farmer, but almond growing was new. An old man named Señor Jorge Pardo lived in this house and asked me to stay and help with the housework, too."

"Did you have your strength back? Wasn't it strenuous?" Juan looked down his chin as if consulting a patient.

"Not completely, but I needed to work. So, I moved into an upper room. I pruned the trees and cultivated them as everyone told me. In between work times, I cooked and washed and swept the floors. The rains were good that year, spring and late summer rains. I joined the harvesters and we brought in a good amount. Señor Pardo got a good price for the almonds and gave each of his workers a share of the profits. The housework earned my room and board."

"Where is he now?" said Sara.

"That was his last harvest. He fell ill in the fall. He had a high fever and mental confusion. He declined rapidly and had me send for his children." A daughter in Córdoba came and then a son from Sevilla."

"Didn't one of them hope to inherit the orchard?"

"The son is a monk and sworn to poverty. He's a scholar-teacher in Sevilla. He didn't want the responsibility and couldn't keep the profits. And the daughter is married and has become a city-dweller."

"It could be sold and the money donated to the church or given to the daughter." Juan raised his voice as he expressed his opinion.

Catalina shrugged her shoulders. "In the end, Señor Pardo gave me the house and a few acres. He gave the rest of the land to his daughter and son-in-law to rent out to local farmers."

"When did he die?"

"Last December."

"I felt optimistic. Everything would be all right when Luis returned." Catalina crossed her arms. "Then, the bad news came: La Navidad had been burned to the ground and Columbus found no survivors! I was crushed, destroyed, at the end of any hope. I became hysterical, cried incessantly and sat for days in my darkened bedroom. I didn't eat or sleep much. I lost a lot of weight. I went into a dreamlike state, unable to think or converse with anyone. The only normal thing I did was cry and wail. Señor Pardo's daughter, Luisa, found me after several weeks, while making arrangements about the orchard. I was 'thin and pale, a shell of a woman,' she said."

"I'm stunned." Sara covered her mouth to keep from sobbing.

"They took me to the nuns—to their hospital. There I stayed for many days. I remember the nuns singing lullabies to me, patting my blazing forehead with cool washcloths, and spooning chicken broth into my mouth. Ever so slowly, I regained flesh and a balanced mind. I prayed constantly during that period: 'Bring Luis back," but God never granted that plea. Later, I changed my prayer to: 'Give me peace in my heart.' God answered that request, but I still have days when I collapse in weeping and dream of what could have been."

"You are a courageous woman," said Juan. "Much like my Sara."

"I had to work to support myself, and I have done that. The letter to you, Sara, I wrote deep in my desperate loneliness. However, after one harvest, I have hope. I may have enough to keep me from starving over the winter and spring. And I bought a few chickens and a pig, so I'll have meat and eggs."

"Señor Pardo gave me a few acres of my own, as I said, so I have all those profits for me. But I help harvest all the sections and get just a share of that. Maybe in a few years I can buy another section of my own."

"What an amazing story, Catalina. I hope you don't think we're asking too many questions." Sara gave Catalina a smile that included bright eyes.

"No, you feel like family already. When harvest comes, I'll be busier than a hen guarding her chicks. Say, could you help me now? Stay until after harvest. Live with me in this rambling house. Help me make repairs, pick almonds. At harvest time, and later - help me expand the orchard. Does that suit you both?" Catalina held out her hands to each side and smiled widely.

Chapter 24

Sara looked at Juan. "We hardly know what to say! We came here with the idea of cheering you, but you have surprised us with joy."

"We are looking for a home, a quiet place to raise our son, and," Juan looked at Sara, "to have more sons and daughters. I am a doctor, and hope to work in the area, but I would like to become an arborist, too. That's a pleasing occupation, to spend time outside tending trees and reaping a harvest."

"I'm pleased to hear you say that. Does that mean you accept?" Catalina looked from one to the other. Sara and Juan both nodded. "Do you know anything about cultivating almond trees, Juan?"

"My parents spent much time in the garden and I learned from them. But, as far as knowledge of trees—no. I am a novice in that area. So, perhaps I am not so useful to you?"

"Come. Let me show you your place and we can talk about details." Catalina jumped up and ushered them out the back to a smaller house built of rocks and plaster and sheltered by an ancient olive tree on one end and a lemon tree on the other. They stepped over a granite doorstep into a hall inlaid with ceramic painted tiles. The large rectangular windows let in the sunlight. It had shutters to close out the heat of the day and darken the rooms for siesta time. The whitewashed walls of the bedrooms held a wrought iron rail of hooks for cloaks and shawls. Large oaken wardrobes had more than enough room for their sparse array of clothes. A second bedroom held a small table and chairs as well as a narrow full-length bed.

"And the kitchen?" Sara looked to Catalina with eyes big.

"This way." They followed her into a spacious room full of shelves with pottery, pots and utensils hanging from large hooks. A hearth with a hanging pot and a work counter occupied another area.

"There's an outdoor cooking area where you can bake breads and roast meats, too. It gets hot here in Andalucía, you know, so we don't do much cooking in ovens."

"Could we see the garden, too?" Juan took Juanito and let Sara go first behind Catalina. The confusion of vines, thistles, grasses and young trees assaulted the senses. Jasmine vines twining up tree branches, thistles and grasses poking their stems through the mat of tangled vegetation like a man's two-day beard. It was hard to step through the tangle.

"I'm afraid it's a bit overgrown," said Catalina. "I haven't had the time to tame this area." Sara stepped through jumbled plants and noticed a small fountain and pond.

"See the fountain, Juan?" Her smile spread from cheek to cheek.

"We can do the weeding and get the pond cleaned up," said Juan. "I know Sara would like the sound of running water. It's a necessity for her." He winked at Sara and poked Juanito in the side. "I think your Mama has decided, Juanito."

"We accept your offer, Catalina. We'll do our best to help you and your business. We're not sure what's ahead for us, but we will work and hope." Sara took Juanito and twirled him around at arm's length. Juanito flapped his arms.

"You can move in today, if that suits you," said Catalina. "There's a cooperative meeting soon and we'll talk to old José Moreno. He's an expert orchardist. He's raised almonds for many years. I'm sure he'd love to train you. But, beware, he tells a lot of stories. He's had a wealth of experiences. Just keep him focused on the subject. Keep him focused." Catalina shook her head.

"Let's get our bags from the Santa Clara hostel," said Juan. "Do you want to come, Sara, or stay here with Catalina?"

"I need to buy a few things at the market in town so we can eat today and tomorrow. So, I'll go with you that far. Maybe you can pick me up on your return trip. And then Juanito will need to sleep." Sara and Juan thanked Catalina again and went out to the wagon waiting for them.

"Take us to the farmers' market in Moguer, driver, and then I'd like to go to Santa Clara. I'll need you to bring me back here, and then you're free to go with my thanks." The driver acknowledged the instructions and flicked the reins to turn the wagon toward town. Catalina waved from the doorway till they disappeared from sight. By wagon it was a short drive to the city center. The driver stopped at the edge of the open-air market and helped Sara descend the two stairs, Juanito balanced on one hip.

"Wait for us here, Sara. I'll return within half an hour, I expect." The wagon rolled away as Sara scanned the array of a dozen produce stands.

"This is a dilemma I love to face. Too many choices." Walking at a light step, Sara almost waltzed through the vegetable and herb stands. "It will be great to start cooking again." *I can't believe I said that! It's all so difficult with a baby to watch.* Sara selected onions, garlic and peas from one stand, and then bought salt, rosemary, thyme and parsley from the herbalist. She got a pinch of saffron, too, for a special dinner, and a bagful of rice. Then she purchased a plucked chicken and a piece of fish. Last of all, Sara found the bread vendor walking through the market with a basket of long loaves. "I'll take two of those, please." By the time she had made all her purchases, she saw the wagon returning. Juan waved and came to take her bundles.

"You've had good success." After stowing the bundles, he took Juanito while she climbed up to the wagon.

"Good food makes me happy."

"It makes me happy, too," said Juan. "Now, back to Catalina's orchard." The wagon rolled on out of town and along the road, turning at 'Catalina's Almonds.' Juan thanked and paid the driver and made arrangements to have him come the next day. "We need to purchase a cart and a horse," he told Sara.

"I agree. We need lots of things for this house, too." Sara had already started feeding Juanito some pieces of bread. Juan held up a bottle of red wine.

"I bought this from some monks. They have a vineyard and a small *bodega*."

"Good for drinking and cooking." Sara cleaned Juanito's face. "Juan, can you find the bag with diaper rags? We need a change here before the siesta."

Juan brought it and fetched out what was needed. Sara performed the job and Juan lifted his little boy into his arms. They walked down the hall and settled Juanito on the single bed in the second bedroom. Juanito fussed for a while, but dropped off to sleep an instant later.

Sara found a jar of olive oil and made a simple lunch of cooked vegetables with fried chicken. While she cleaned the dishes, a knock sounded on the door. Juan disappeared for a few minutes and then returned. "Sara, I have some bad news. Let's go to the living room *sala*." With little lines bunching at the corners of her eyes, Sara followed Juan to the living room and dusted off a wooden chair. Juan did the same. He took her hand, still damp from washing dishes. "Catalina just gave me a letter and I took the time to read it."

"What's happened" Is it your father or mother?"

"No. I'm afraid it's Rodrigo. He had another spell of a racing heart and then clutched his chest. He moaned that the pain felt like someone squeezing his heart. Unfortunately, then he fell to the floor, dead."

"No! How awful! How will Margarita cope?" Juan embraced Sara while she wept for their friends. Juan wiped at his eyes, too. "I wish we could go to her. I feel like she's my mother." Sara heaved a sigh.

"We can send a letter of condolence. Maybe this fall after the harvest we could go her." He patted Sara's back.

"I don't think she has family there."

"Surely Rodrigo's relatives will support her. We just can't leave now."

"I know it's harvest, but my heart is hurting."

"Come with me, Sara." Juan took her hand and drew her into the large bedroom. He settled her on the wide bed. "Sleep a while, dear Sara."

Sara awoke after a long siesta, rubbed her eyes and got up. She heard voices outside. A dozen workers, both men and women, walked along a path toward the almond groves. They carried sturdy poles and sang as they strolled. Sara wrapped a scarf around her hair and donned a work apron, so she'd look like the women. All the men wore hats with brims. *I'm curious. I think I'll watch.* Sara slipped out the door with Juanito on one hip. Juan had already mingled with the workers. She hurried to catch up to the group of harvesters. She stood in a nearby section of the almond orchard.

The group divided into groups of two. When they approached a tree, whack and whack! They shook the tree multiple times till the nuts let go and dropped to the ground. Then two signaled each other with a whistle and moved to the next tree, repeating the same process. Each team worked up a row of trees in a methodical manner. By the time they reached the far end of a row, the ground had hundreds of almond hulls.

Catalina walked up to Sara. "Why don't they gather up the nuts?"

"We leave the hulls on the ground for a week to get drier. Then, they will be easier to shell. Each process happens in a sequence. We finish one step before starting the next."

"Oh. I imagine the shelling process takes a while. Does it all happen by hand? Lots of women cracking shells?"

Catalina laughed. "Sometimes. We've tried different methods. We gather all the nuts and put them on a large cloth. Then many hands pick through the pile and remove hulls, shells and bits of rocks and twigs. That works best."

"Then you gather it all into a storage barn?"

"Yes, they go to storage."

"And then you sell the nuts."

"Yes, but some are sold raw and some we roast and salt."

"At the local market?"

"We have drivers who take them all over Spain—to Ronda, Sevilla and Málaga, for example." Juan joined them carrying Juanito with him.

"I came late to this discussion."

"Juan, I saw Sara out here watching and came to watch with her. I just explained all the steps to harvesting almonds. I'd be glad to tell you as well, but I expected to start tomorrow."

"That will be fine. I'm glad Sara's so interested." The workers moved to another section of the orchard. Catalina, Sara and Juan headed back to the house. The sun beat down on the earth with ferocious heat. Juanito wriggled himself out of Juan's arms and hit the dirt running. The next minute he tripped over a root. Juan set him on his feet. Off he went again. "Such an adventurer."

"Like you, Juan," said Sara.

"It's wonderful to hear the sounds of a child in my orchard and my house," said Catalina. "You enrich my life." She touched Sara's hand.

"I'm making a special meal tonight. Will you join us, Catalina?"

"I'd be delighted. See you at sunset. Till then, I must oversee the harvest."

"Tomorrow, we work, too," said Juan. "So, let's enjoy this evening." Sara kissed him and then went to the kitchen. She spent some time washing all the dusty pottery and dishes. Then she filled a basin with hot water and soap and wiped the shelves and counters. She looked through a cabinet and found some pans. She pulled them out and looked farther back. She grabbed a handle and—

"Here it is, a paella pan. That's just what I need." She scrubbed it with a stiff brush and added soap, till the shallow pan shone. Sara grinned.

* * * *

"The paella is heavenly, Sara. Such a dish is only for special occasions." Catalina wiped her mouth and push her plate away from her.

"It is a special occasion. We have found you, Catalina, the one Luis married. And we have a new life, thanks to you. A double blessing." Sara beamed brighter than the setting sun.

"We expect you to give us work assignments right away, starting tomorrow. We're ready to work." Juan leaned forward.

"As I said, we'll have you meet José Moreno, who can give you the best instruction. I learned everything from him. He'll tell me when you're ready to go out to the fields." Catalina stood up to leave.

"We have some melon for dessert, Catalina." Sara jumped up to get it.

"Thank you, no. I'm quite tired tonight. Think I'll retire early." She waved to them and walked out.

"I'll prepare Juanito for bed," said Juan. Sara set to cleaning up, humming.

Chapter 25

The following day, Catalina wanted to start early. The farming collective met on the other side of Moguer at José Moreno's *granja*, one of the largest homesteads in the region. Sara and Juan ate yesterday's bread dipped in olive oil. They grabbed Juanito and went out to find their driver had already shown up.

'Buenos dias' was said and returned by everyone. Catalina flicked the reins and her team of horses turned toward the road. Juan and Sara jumped into the cart and the driver followed along behind.

"Follow her," said Juan. "It's another hot day," he said to Sara. She smiled and bounced Juanito on her lap. They road along Almond Avenue under a canopy of leaves, made their way through the center of town and came out the other side on another dirt road. Other carts and wagons were already on the road.

"It's the first gathering of the collective since spring," yelled Catalina, from her wagon. "Be ready for a celebration."

"I wish I had known that," said Sara. "Is my dress good enough?"

"Sara, you're beautiful all the time. Don't worry." Juan kissed her cheek. Sara's mouth turned down and she looked away.

"I don't know—" They bumped along a rutted dirt road until they came around a bend. "Oh! Look at that." Sara covered her open mouth with her hand. A large estate house came into view. It was built of sandstone blocks and had a circular driveway in front. Almond trees spread out on both sides as far as a person could see, and wisteria clung to the oak railings that bordered the porch. A crowd of people stood around. Conversation buzzed through the air like bees bent on pollination.

"Look at all the wagons. There must be twenty!" said Juan as they drew near. "And I smell food cooking already. Lamb on a spit!" The driver pulled up under a trellis of vines and tied the cart to a post. He helped them down. They joined Catalina and walked toward the house.

"Welcome, Catalina," said a robust man with a head of wavy brown hair. He held out callused hands and kissed her on both cheeks. "And who are these people?" He turned toward Sara and Juan. Juanito squeaked. "And a little one?"

"Big, big," said Juanito. They all laughed.

"My mistake, young man. I'm José Moreno. And you are—?"

"Juan and Sara Sánchez and their boy Juanito," said Catalina. "They are staying to help me with the orchard. I brought them to listen and meet everyone today. And to learn, too."

"*Bienvenidos.* Welcome." He clapped Juan on the back and bowed over Sara's hand. She drew back.

"I'm not royalty," she said.

"You are as beautiful as a queen," he said with a flourish of his hand. "Please come meet all our friends and neighbors. They are all almond growers in this region. Juan, I hope we can talk more about growing trees. Ask me your questions. I've been a successful grower for twenty years." He smiled and then turned to speak to some of the other guests.

"What do you think?" said Catalina. She smoothed her hair.

"Impressive." Juan stroked his chin.

"Pretentious." Sara touched her glowing cheeks. Catalina took Sara's elbow.

"Come with me. I'll introduce you to the others. There will be a meeting after a while." They all moved through the group, stopping to speak to each man and his wife. Catalina asked about everyone's children and knew each person's concerns and particular situations. When they stepped over to the table to take a glass of wine and taste a sampling of almonds, Sara said,

"I had no idea there was such a successful community of almond growers here. When we drove into Moguer, I thought it was just a lazy town where nothing much happened."

"Actually," said Juan, "I hoped to find a place to live a quiet life—to become invisible." He frowned. Catalina looked at him.

"Why the need to disappear? Are you in trouble?"

"No. I don't think so. But, I'd rather not have people know I came back from La Navidad, Columbus' mistake. And if I write more about the experience, I don't want people to come searching for me."

"We want to live a quiet life and raise our son in peace."

"That's what we all want, but it's not always possible," said Catalina.

"*Sin embargo*—nevertheless, we'd appreciate it if you didn't tell anyone about our background. Just tell them we grew up in Andalucía."

"You have your reasons and I will honor them," said Catalina. "I hear José calling the people to meet in the grand *sala*. Let's go join them." They strolled into a wide room that had terracotta tiles on the floor with smaller ceramic tiles interspersed at regular intervals. It was a kind of covered patio, with vines twining overhead to shelter them from the hot sun. Potted geraniums flared their frilly dresses in every corner like flashy flamenco dancers. Painted ceramic plates lined the walls. Narrow carved tables lined one wall like swarthy male dancers in tight-fitting trousers. José raised his hands and clapped them.

"*Damas y caballeros*. Ladies and gentlemen, welcome. Our pre-harvest gathering is important for two reasons. We need to share any problems we've been having in growing our trees and share solutions. We all benefit when everyone has success. The second reason is we need to plan the harvest and share resources for taking the almonds to market. It looks to be a bountiful harvest this year, so we may need to hire extra wagons from nearby towns."

"Are there any new taxes this year?" asked someone, and the swirl of talk began. Sara listened for a while, but Juanito squirmed and tried to get down. She motioned to Juan she would take Juanito outside and he nodded, eyes locked on the current speaker. Sara took Juanito's hand and walked him through a few couples and out the door.

A breeze was blowing. The almond trees swished quietly and birds flitted through the rows and rows. The almond hulls had split open, revealing the inner shell of the nuts. The wind made them click together like castanets. Juanito turned his ear and pointed. "Yes, Juanito, click, click." She posed like a flamenco dancer and stamped her feet. Juanito clapped and grinned. Sara repeated the action, and Juanito did, too. Soon, they were dancing through the grove of trees under the shade of the spreading branches. She picked up her little boy and swirled him around and then perched him on one of her hips. "That was fun!"

"Fun, indeed. You're good dancers." Juan strode up to them and took Juanito. "The meeting was getting technical and I couldn't understand most of it, so I came to find you both."

"How long will it go on? I suppose we should try to understand it." Sara turned to go. Juan sighed.

"I guess you're right. Let's see if together we can learn something today."

They clasped hands and walked back to the grand house. A clamor of voices rose as they strode in. They slipped into a corner to listen. There was some argument about the best way to care for the trees in drought conditions. The argument quickly turned to who had rights to the limited water. Wives tried to calm their irate husbands.

"Gentlemen, before we have a fight, I remind you we have a council where you can air your grievances. Take your complaints to them. Ramón Ortega is the moderator. Raise your hand, Ramón." A hand shot up. "The council meets Monday. Talk to him." José raised his hands. "Everyone, it's time for our midday meal, *almuerzo*. There's plenty for everyone out in the back patio. Lamb and all the cold salads you could want. Follow me." He motioned for them to adjourn to the outdoor dining area, long tables laden with food and long tables for eating.

Catalina threaded her way through the throng and encouraged Sara and Juan to join her at one of the tables. Sara sat there with Juanito while Catalina and Juan went to get food. As people brought their food and sat down, servants poured wine and the tense atmosphere eased. Sara found herself chatting with a middle-aged woman next to her. She told about her five sons and tickled Juanito under his chin. Juan spoke with several men around him and Catalina smoothed over the curiosity everyone had about the newcomers. After an hour or two, Juanito wailed and stretched out his body stiffly.

"He's tired, Juan. Shouldn't we go?"

"It's up to Catalina." She turned to them and gave a nod. She rose and bade goodbye to all. She thanked José and they went to their wagons. Their driver woke up and readied the cart.

"I'll stop in town and purchase a cart and horse of our own," said Juan. "Would you like to take Juanito home now?" Sara nodded. Catalina motioned for Sara to join her.

"I'll take her home. Can you find your way back?" Juan nodded. Juanito leaned his head on Sara's shoulder and fell asleep before they reached Catalina's almond ranch. Sara carried him into the house and laid him on his bed. His body relaxed into the mattress. Sara tiptoed out. She went to the kitchen to check on her food situation and then lay down on her own bed. She opened her eyes later when she heard to clop of a horse and the squeak of wheels pulling up to the cottage.

"Sara, come and look." She jumped up, slipped into her shoes and ran out. There was Juan with a buff-colored horse with a dark mane pulling a large cart.

"The cart is polished and the horse is beautiful." Sara stroked the nose of the horse and it bobbed its head in reply.

"So you like it?"

"Of course, but wasn't it expensive?"

"An old woman needed to sell it. Her husband died and she's going to live with her daughter's family."

"That's our good fortune, then. Come inside and get cool." Sara brushed beads of sweat off of Juan's face. He took her hand and kissed it.

"This has depleted our money significantly, so we'll have to find ways to earn money as the harvest comes in. Anyway, I don't know how Catalina plans to pay us or how much." Sara nodded and made Juan sit down. She got him a glass of cool *limonada*.

"My bag of money is getting lighter, too."

"Maybe we can inquire at church tomorrow. Meet people and tell them—"

"Tell them you're a doctor and I can translate documents."

"Or make your good bread to sell."

"I could sell that at the weekly market on Thursday." She thought a while. "That might work. We have a workable brick oven and I only need a few things to make bread. But, it's so hot this time of year. I like to avoid using the oven. Guess I'll get up early to bake." Her face brightened. "And I'll add herbs to the dough, like the Italians." Juanito squawked just then so Sara went to get him.

* * * *

The next day, they went with Catalina to the main church in town. It was large and occupied a prominent place in the central square. Inside, the nave exuded a cool rush of air. Sara shivered and pulled her shawl higher on her neck. They sat on a hard rough-hewn bench with kneeling boards at their feet. They listened to the familiar mass. The priest gave a short homily and Sara listened intently. *You can always tell the heart of a priest by listening to his own remarks.*

"God commands us," droned the priest. "He commands us to submit to the higher authorities." *Yes, the Holy Scriptures say that.* "Not only that, we must obey the queen and king, the Catholic Monarchs. King Ferdinand has set a high standard for orthodoxy. Do not fear the Inquisition, but rather search your hearts. Bow to God and the Church fathers. Obey them in all things and you will be safe. Saved by your right living and right thinking. Amen." Sara shifted her position. *This pew is hard and so are his words.*

As the parishioners filed out, Sara kept her head covered and avoided the eyes of the priest. "Good morning, father," said Juan.

"Welcome. You're visitors, or do you plan to stay here in Moguer?"

"We'll stay for a while with Catalina and help with the harvest. We hope to find a home here."

"You'll find many helpful people here. Has your child been baptized?" Sara drew Juanito closer to herself.

"We haven't been able to do that until now." The priest frowned.

"Strange. You'll want to do that soon, I'm sure. All devout Catholics have their children baptized as infants. Contact me this week. What are your names?"

"Juan and Sara Sánchez, and our son Juanito."

"The Sánchez family, I'll remember that. And your job, señor?"

"I'm a doctor."

"And I'm a translator," Sara chimed in, and then snapped her mouth shut.

The priest raised an eyebrow and then turned his attention to the next family group. Catalina, Sara and Juan walked out into the sunshine.

"Father Diego is a bit stern." Catalina steered them around to meet a few people. Sara mentioned she'd be selling bread on the coming market day. As they climbed in the cart and turned toward Catalina's ranch, Father Diego greeted the last of the attenders and called to a novice standing by. He whispered in his ear. The young man's eyes widened. He covered his mouth, bowed to the priest and walked quickly toward the stable area, remembering at the last minute to tuck his hands into his wide homespun sleeves.

"I wonder what Father Diego told that young priest," said Sara.

"The young man's eyes almost popped out of his face," said Juan.

"Could it be something about us? He did it so quickly after meeting us." Sara and Juan stood outside the church a few minutes chatting with Catalina, as she pointed out people she knew. Not five minutes later, the wide-eyed novice led a donkey out to the main road and swung a leg over the creature's back.

"He's heading toward Sevilla, maybe. Hm, I wonder—" Sara pursed her lips and furrowed her forehead.

Chapter 26

"The drying process of harvest are in full operation now, so I have just a little time for learning the trade," said Juan. He put on his oldest clothes and some sturdy shoes. "I'm going to José's today to watch and listen. He said he'd take me out to his orchard and show his techniques."

"He's been successful, as his grand house shows, so maybe it's good. Here's some food for midday." Sara handed him some slices of bread and cheese and a small jug of lemon water. Juan kissed her and turned to go.

"Could you repair some of this furniture, Juan, when you return? The chairs are about to come apart." Juan nodded and waved.

"Guess I'll ask Catalina for a ride to Moguer. I need some things." Sara fed Juanito and dressed him for the day. They walked over to Catalina's and found out she was about to travel into town.

"I'll get my bag and be right back," said Sara. She put Juanito in the cart with Catalina and ran back to the guesthouse. She found her bag and some coins. She climbed in the cart. Catalina set out.

"The big market's not till Thursday," Catalina said. "But, there's always a few vendors on the streets." They arrived in Moguer and arranged to meet one hour later at the main fountain. "We can both get our errands completed."

The cobblestones in the main square radiated out from the fountain in concentric circles. Four streets intersected the circle in uneven slices. A cart entering from one street had to roll around the circle till it came to the street the driver wanted to travel. People on foot dodged the occasional cart. Sara took Juanito and strolled down the main street to the corner nearest the fountain. Sure enough, she saw a display of fabrics on a table and draped over a pole.

"Good morning. I need to have some play clothes made for my little boy."

"He looks like an active one," said the old woman. "Maybe some short pants and a loose shirt? Here's a strong homespun. It will not tear and can be washed many times." She held up a length of tan cloth and measured out the right amount. Sara nodded and accepted it. She gave her a few small coins, and bought some thread. She still had her needle and scissors carefully stored away.

Sara noticed a small vegetable stand across the plaza and walked straight for it. She purchased rosemary and sesame seeds and a large sack of flour, a small packet of salt and yeast. "This is more than a vegetable stand." She thanked the woman and turned to go. A novice priest with blotchy skin stood across the street near the fabric stall. *Is he watching me?* The young man took a few steps with his large sandaled feet. He tripped over a loose cobblestone and grabbed his toe. Sara stifled a laugh. *As inconspicuous as a charging bull!*

Just then, Sara saw Catalina and headed for the fountain. The novice ducked his head and rubbed his toe. Sara motioned to Catalina to head for the cart, which she did. "Drive away quickly. I think someone is following me." She hid herself behind Catalina and under a blanket as the cart headed out of town.

"That was interesting. Do you have an admirer?"

"A young priest. I hardly think so." Sara sat up and pulled a squirming Juanito out, as well. "It's a long story. Sometimes I think people are watching me. Did you get what you needed?" Catalina knew when to stop asking questions. She listened to Sara, and by the time they reached home, Sara had told her about her plans to make and sell bread. After some lunch, Sara put Juanito to bed.

Now I can tackle the yard. She found some large shears and a sickle. First, she used the shears to cut away the intertwining vines that matted the yard. *I hope some of this survives. I doubt I'm pruning at the right time.* Next, Sara swung the sickle and mowed down the thistles and tufts of dry grasses that had pushed through the vines. She stood back, wiping her brow with a forearm. *Much better.*

Sara moved inside. It was a hot day again. If you looked toward the horizon, you could see waves of heat rising off the parched ground. *It's an oven!*

I'm crazy to bake bread in this kind of weather. I thought I saw a brick oven in the yard, so I should test it out. Too busy to search the yard—that's loco! Tomorrow, before the sun's up, I'll practice. Sara sat down for a few minutes. When Juanito came walking toward her, she opened her eyes with alarm.

"Juanito, did you walk all the way from your bedroom?" Juanito grinned and headed for the doorway. Sara scooped him up. "Where are you going?" Juanito waved his arms and kicked his legs.

"Let's get you some lemonade." She poured him some and a cup for herself. "How long did I sleep?" She looked out the window to the sundial.

"Life is certainly busier now, with a boy who ambles everywhere." Sara poked Juanito in the tummy. He squealed. "Let's go outside and look at the garden, little one." Sara lifted Juanito to one hip and slipped outside. The sun shone in the western sky, still in control of the day. An eagle soared and dipped in the blue expanse, its brown speckled feathers a sweeping arch.

"See, Juanito, an eagle—way up there." She pointed. But Juanito heard something behind him. "Oh, a shrike. See its white belly and rusty head? And look, Juanito it has a beetle in its beak."

"Bee—" Juanito looked and pointed.

"Very good." Sara put Juanito down and let him run around on the dried grass. She sat and watched him take pleasure in the smallest things, each weed a rose, each pebble a ruby. Juan found them there when he got home.

"Goodness, I didn't know it was so late." Sara got Juanito and followed Juan into the shade of the house.

"Here, let me play with Juanito while you do what you need to." Juan reached out and received his little boy.

Sara brought in clothes she'd laid out on bushes outside. They dried quickly in the summer sun and now were stiff. She folded them quickly. Next, Sara went inside to start dinner. The sun skimmed the tall trees to the west. It was time to warm the stew and set out the cold salads she had waiting. They ate less at supper. The majority of their food Sara served at lunch, before the day became too hot. It was intolerable to cook over a hot stove in the evening. So hot! When Juan couldn't be home for the midday meal and siesta, she sent something substantial with him to his job.

"Come outside, Juan, and see what I have been working on. I'm trying to revive the garden for Catalina." They left the table and stepped outside. Sara showed Juan her work in the garden. He looked at the fountain and pond that were now uncovered.

"I can repair this easily," he said. "The spigots are clogged with dirt and bits of rock." He flushed water through it till it flowed easily. "There. Now, if the workings of the fountain draw water, we'll have the sound of flowing water, as you like it."

"Good!" said Sara.

Juanito jumped up to chase a skittering lizard.

The next day, Sunday, they followed Catalina's cart to the church. They parked in an area near the church and under a row of poplar trees. Juan yanked at his shirt opening and Juanito pulled at his shirt.

"It's hot today, isn't it, Juanito? I feel it, too." Sara wiped his forehead and got out a fan. They all filed into church and out of the stifling heat. Sara found it hard to keep her eyes open. They greeted Father Diego as they filed out after the service.

"Señora Sánchez, did you plan to have your son baptized? I didn't hear from you this week." Father Diego gazed at her with brown eyes.

Sara caught her breath. "Oh, I'm sorry. I forgot. We will come in this week to do that." She looked at Juan, who gave a slight nod.

"Fine. Set a time with my assistant. Now, I have a translation job for you, or at least, a copying job, señora. Please stop by the parish office tomorrow if you wish to do it. There is a small commission upon completion." He turned to Juan. "And your name is being circulated around town as the new doctor." They bowed their heads slightly and passed out of the church.

Juan and Sara looked at each other but didn't say a thing as they walked to the cart and climbed in.

"Father Diego is a good man," said Juan.

"I don't trust him," said Sara. But she did treasure the chance to get back into copying and translating. She had Juan drive her into town the next day. Tapping on the parish hall door, she entered to get her instructions.

"We have a small copying job. The church wants to honor a generous patron with a portion of the Psalms, the first Psalm, in fact. Do you know it?"

"Yes, I think so. It's about the righteous man." She wrung her hands.

"Indeed, and also the ungodly man. 'The way of the ungodly shall perish', it says. Do you believe that?" Sara looked away from the priest, her face hot. "Another psalm says 'His mercy is eternal.' I put my hope in that."

Father Diego folded his hands and examined his fingernails. "Yes. Well, let's give you instructions and send you off with your project."

Sara returned to a waiting Juan.

"I need to get ink and some quills," said Sara. "I saw a shop in town."

"I've just been summoned to José's house. A messenger, Felipe, came. Seems he has great pains in his belly. Can you go to the shop and get home yourself?"

"It's a good thing Catalina has Juanito. I'll do it." Sara hopped down and watched him urge the horses toward the Moreno mansion. Shopping for ink, quills and paints became a pleasant diversion. She priced the gold leaf but didn't take it. Sara walked along Almond Street, but nobody drove by. She kept on walking and finally reached Catalina's driveway. She heard a horse and cart behind her.

"Are you just getting home?" Juan climbed down from the seat. Sara nodded. "I had a curious appointment with José. I tried to find out the nature of his problem, but instead of answering questions, he asked them. Probing and disturbing."

"Father Diego asked pointed questions, too. What are they looking for?" Sara gazed into Juan's eyes. "People wandering from the true faith?" Sara winced.

"We must be careful. We're being observed." Juan took Sara's hand.

"I'm frightened," said Sara. Juan kissed her hand, and then he drove the cart up to the house. Sara walked over to Catalina's and got Juanito.

"I have all the makings for chicken and rice, Catalina," said Sara. "Why don't you come over at supper time?"

"Don't make a lot. I don't eat too much in the evening."

"All right." But Catalina filled her plate when the time came.

"*Delicioso.*" She stayed a while to talk, but then yawned and said goodbye. Juanito made no opposition to being put to bed. Sara and Juan flopped on the sofa and heard a cracking noise. Bang! They landed on the floor. Juan's laugh shot out like an *arquebus* blast. "Ha! Too much supper. I'll repair it tomorrow. But now, I'm tired." He held out his hand to Sara.

"Oh, Juan, I need to work for a while on this copying job. Just an hour."

"Sara." Sara dropped the quill and accepted Juan's hand. "Tomorrow is another day."

Chapter 27

✻

Sara worked on the copying project every day and had it completed in one week. She put the quill away and admired her work. She had painted a miniature tree for the illumination. A tree of ripe pears by a flowing stream. A symbol of a righteous man or woman. She wrapped the parchment carefully and had Juan drive her to the church. She tapped on Father Diego's door and entered as bidden.

"The parchment copy of Psalm One with illumination, Father," Sara said. "I hope it is pleasing." She glanced up and saw a number of men crowded into the priest's modest office. She froze.

"Señora Sánchez, perhaps you know some of these men."

"No." None of them looked directly at her. Father Diego continued.

"Fathers Aguilar, Bautista and Castillo are here to convene an investigation. They stopped here to pay me a courtesy call."

"Whose investigation?" Sara looked up. Her hands trembled.

Father Aguilar stepped forward and called a guard. "We arrest you, Sara Sánchez, in the name of the Grand Inquisitor and of King Ferdinand. You will be detained here until a proper court can be arranged."

Sara let the parchment drop to the floor. The guard fastened chains around her wrists. "Please, I need to tell my husband. He is outside waiting." She swayed and closed her eyes.

"Father Castillo, you may deliver the message." Father Diego dismissed him with a nod.

"What am I accused of?" said Sara, her voice strengthening.

"We're looking into the death of Don Antonio Morales and hear you played a part in it."

"She's done nothing wrong!" Juan came running in.

"Control yourself, sir, or you'll be detained, too." Fathers Aguilar, Bautista and Castillo blocked his path to Sara. "Your wife will be detained in the city jail with a trial to be arranged soon." Father Castillo motioned to the guard. "Take her away." Fathers Aguilar and Castillo followed them to the jail.

Juan crumpled against a wall and slid to the floor, hands covering his eyes.

"No!" Then, "Sara, I'll be there tomorrow *Te amo.*"

Father Diego crossed the floor and picked up the parchment. "Exquisite." Juan reached out and grabbed his ankle.

"You will pay me for the work Sara did for you. Now." Juan stood up, crossed his arms and stood very close to the friar. Father Diego shrank back and retreated to his desk. He opened a metal box and took out some coins. Slipping them into a small cloth pouch, he handed it to Juan.

"Pity. Her work is careful and accurate," said Father Diego, his lips a thin line. "Would she consider another project?"

"What do you think?" Juan curled his upper lip and bared his teeth.

"No, I suppose not." Father Diego let out a sigh.

* * * *

Juan left for home, shaken. His shoulders sagged. He slumped in the cart.

At the edge of town he saw a tavern, old and sun-bleached. Etched on the weathered sign it said, "The Painted Rooster."

Do have time to stop for something? thought Juan. He thought of Juanito waiting for him. He flicked the reins and went on. *I better get home to my little son. He'll wonder where his mama is. How will I explain it?*

"Sara's been arrested by the Inquisition," he told Catalina. "It's about something that's been building for a long time."

"I'd like to know about it. How can I help?" Catalina's smooth forehead wrinkled with concern. "Since Juanito is sleeping, we have a little time to talk."

"It's a long story. And I hope you won't think worse of Sara. She's suffered a lot these last few years."

"I think I know Sara's character already. Whatever it is, I'm sure she is innocent." Catalina sat down at the table and folded her hands.

Juan paced the floor as he shared the saga of Father Morales' obsession with Sara, and the priest's many devious ways of following, abducting and even beating her.

"Stop! Is this all true?" Juan nodded. "The man's a monster!" shouted Catalina. "Where does this all end?"

"Unfortunately, the last time, he had his servants take Sara forcibly off the streets of Naples by drugging her, and when she awoke he declared she was now his possession. They had a skirmish and Sara blew out the candles. During the scuffle, Sara lifted the giant candlestick and swung it around to keep Morales away. But, the heavy thing hit the unholy father in the head, and dealt a fatal blow. Sara got away and heard later the servants would bury him and go home,

223

without reporting the circumstances. He was consumptive, you see, and already his death was approaching."

"But, someone must have reported it, am I right? And, now the issue is opened again." Catalina wrung her hands.

"That's right. All I can imagine is the two servants of Morales were persuaded by the Inquisition to tell a different story—and you know they can be persistent. So, here we are, facing a murder trial, which I thought was only for the civil authorities to administer. But, the Inquisition wants to insinuate that Sara bewitched the poor Father Morales, I think. Such a travesty." Juan stomped around and kicked the wall. Juanito let out a wail.

"I'm so sorry, but perhaps it's not as dire as you think. Let's try to keep hopeful. Let me help with caring for Juanito for a few days." She heard a wail. Catalina ran to get him. "Go now, and take care of yourself. I'll give you back your little boy tomorrow." She shooed him away and Juan nodded his approval of the plan. He slipped out the door and went to the guesthouse, his and Sara's residence that was beginning to feel like home. *But not without Sara.*

Juan sat thinking of strategies and defenses for his beloved wife until the sun sank over the hills and the trees gathered up darkness like a cloak. Juan got up, stretched and found some leftover Spanish tortilla, that egg and potato pie he loved so much. *Now, I'm thirsty. Maybe I'll go back to that place I saw.*

Juan got the cart and horse ready and headed back through town and out the other side. He let the horse take him on a path he'd never traveled much. At the edge of town he saw The Painted Rooster, old and sun-bleached. He climbed down and tethered the horse and cart. The smell of sweat, garlic and beer greeted him at the door. The men at the tables looked up with narrowed eyes. *Who are these men?*

thought Juan. *Strange creatures—garish clothes, painted eyes and lips, and hollow faces. They look—*Juan turned his face toward the bartender.

Juan ordered a beer and the onlookers returned to their conversations. Juan sat at a table that faced a side door, partially open. A breeze let in cool air. He took a great gulp of beer. A movement caught his eye. Someone passing by the door paused to look in. Two men were dressed in work clothes, woolen hats jammed on their heads. And one had brilliant blue eyes. *Hats in this heat? And they have the same look as the others. I wonder—are they men who use men for their evil desires?*

The bartender nodded at the two men. And then they disappeared to the back of the tavern.

Juan dismissed the scene as they passed by. He finished the beer. *I'm getting out of here.* Juan went back home and fell into the empty bed. He slept fitfully. A reddish glow from the moon filtered into the window.

Chapter 28

Sara opened her eyes and sat up. Her back ached from lying on the hard pallet with its greasy blanket. Morning light streamed through the small barred window and was already heating the sandstone block cubicle. She sat up and made an attempt to straighten her hair. Her face felt greasy where it had touched the blanket. She rubbed it off. *What hope do I have here? How will I ever escape punishment by the Inquisition now?*

A key turned in the lock and the door creaked open.

"Food for you, señora." A monk with hood hiding his face brought in a bowl of food—a watery stew and a crust of bread. He closed the door and waited while she chewed the stringy meat and mushy turnips. "Can I help you in some way?" The slender monk spoke so softly she wasn't sure she heard right.

"What did you say?"

"Brother Mateo from the monastery in Sevilla. Do you remember?"

"What are you doing here? Isn't it dangerous?"

"I came with the three judges. I can't stay long. Is there something I can do to help you? A message? A bit of evidence that should come to light? Quickly!" His hand twitched and his eye darted toward the door.

"I was followed by Father Morales from Granada to Naples. He tried to capture me several times. He hired evil men to help him. Finally, he captured me and intended to possess me as his paramour. A priest did this! I fought him off and in the struggle I struck him with a candlestick. He fell to the floor, dead. I did not intend that to happen, but it did. I was fearful for my life. A few months before, he beat me with a broom handle when I was with child. He thought I was unfaithful to him. I always resisted him! He would have violated me—and his sacred vows. I was properly married to Juan."

"Finish eating!" Brother Mateo said with a too-loud voice. He grabbed the bowl and spoon. "I hear someone coming. I'll be at the trial. Look for me." He turned to go.

"Ask my husband what happened. He knows everything." Sara whispered, as the door clicked shut and the key scratched in the lock. His soft shoes padded down the hall. *Can I trust you?*

* * * *

The door opened once more that day, to Juan. A jailer stood in the room and locked the door behind him.

"Leave us alone, man," said Juan. "Can't you see I need to talk to my wife?"

"I have orders to watch you. She's a dangerous one. Will you be slipping her a knife or such?"

"You have it all wrong. She'd never hurt anyone. She's gentle. She's a mother." Juan turned his back on the man and reached out to embrace her.

"Can't get any closer, Sánchez. I'm serious."

Juan stepped forward and gave Sara a quick kiss. "I'll kiss my own wife!" But, he stepped back two paces and looked Sara in the eyes. "How are you?"

"A little shaky and much dirtier. This place is filthy."

"Guard, could she get some warm water and a cloth to wash her face and hands?" Juan got up close to the jailer's face.

"Can't promise anything." He touched his sword hilt.

"Sara." Juan looked at her again. "I've hired an expert in the law to help you. He's already gathering information. He may come visit you. Santana—"

"Time to go, Sánchez—" The jailer pulled out his sword and stepped forward.

"Wait. Just one more thing—" The jailer nodded assent and stepped back. "Catalina and I are finding witnesses. I sent a message to Margarita." He whispered.

"How's Juanito? Give him a hug for me." Sara's face was still as a painted portrait.

"He wants his Mama. Have courage, *mi amor*. Truth will triumph." Juan leaned in for one more kiss. The jailer prodded him with his sword point and they swirled out the door. Click. Sara lay back on the bed, careful to cradle her head in her hands. The chamber pot dispersed its stink throughout the tiny room.

A few minutes later, a bowl of hot water appeared with a towel and soap. Sara accepted it with a face she hoped looked grateful. After washing, she put the bowl on the floor by the door and lay back down. *I just want to close my eyes and make this all go away. This never-ending nightmare.*

* * * *

No other visitors came the rest of the day. Someone with another bowl of bread and watered-down wine. She soaked the dry bread in the wine and sucked the wine out of it before downing it. *So thirsty!*

I haven't let myself think about my situation. Just numb, I guess. Who wins when the Inquisition rises against you? Not many! But, I must arm myself with more courage than I feel. If an unintentional act can be excused, I will go free. I would even be grateful if I received a milder punishment for this accident I carried out. Wearing those humiliating costumes to magnify my shame. Or taking a pilgrimage, say to Santiago de Compostela. That could take months if I had to walk or ride a burro. But it's better than death by fire. There are many tools of torture I could endure.

Sara shuddered.

I don't see how a defense lawyer can help. The accused don't even know what charges are made against them usually. Give me wisdom and courage. I need it. Help my righteousness to 'shine like the sun,' as it says in the psalms. Sara clasped her hands tight, closed her eyes and turned toward the wall. Her breathing steadied and she slept.

A few days later, Brother Mateo entered her cubicle. He wore a robe of rough woven homespun. Sweat beaded on his beardless face.

"I can't stay, but I brought something from your lawyer. He wrote down a few thoughts about your case. He said use it to help yourself through the coming tribunal. Since he's not allowed to present your case."

"What's his name?"

"Santana. Miguel Santana. Your husband hired him. Here, take this scroll and hide it. Conceal it so nobody takes it from you. It's a gift from your husband. His attempt to save you. Sara put the scroll in a pocket of her dress. " Brother Mateo bowed and asked for the jailer to let him out. He gave a quick nod and departed. Sara sat down to consider what he said.

How can anyone help me?

* * * *

The harvest was in full force. Juan joined the workers. *I need this activity—something to do besides brood.* Catalina was busy from sunrise to sunset, seeing that the extra hired workers shook the almonds off the flourishing trees. The trees staggered with abundance and many branches had been propped up to keep them from breaking off the tree too soon.

Juan joined the shakers, at first watching their technique and then putting more force into the process. Piles of nuts grew under each tree until all were shaken. Catalina dismissed the extra workers.

"Come back in one week and help gather up all the nuts. We'll need people to sort out the hulls and bits of twigs and pebbles, also. The rest goes into the wagons and then to the storage barn. From then on, we'll roast some in the oven with oil and herbs. If you're an experienced almond cooker, see me for a special job next week. When the almonds are sold, see my orchard manager for your pay. *Gracias.*"

* * * *

Juan made another visit to Sara in the Moguer jail.

"Thank you for helping me prepare for the tribunal. I have it close to my heart." Sara touched her pocket to show she possessed the scroll, and then gave him a kiss. Juan put his arms around her. The guard cleared his throat and shifted his feet.

"None of that, Sánchez." Sara took his hands instead.

"Blisters already. You're a laborer now."

"Yes. Anything to earn money for us." Sara touched the blisters.

"How is Juanito?"

"Still asking for Mama. How are you?"

"Sleeping a bit more. Praying and thinking make up my day."

"Time's up, Sánchez."

"Never lose hope, Sara. Be strong. Be humble when questioned." The jailer jingled his keys.

"I'm not afraid." Sara lifted her chin. Her face lit up with turned up lips and a spark in her eyes. Juan exited the door followed by the jailer, who locked the door again. Sara slept until the door creaked again and Fathers Aguilar, Bautista and Castillo entered.

"We've come to get your confession and hear your story."

"I understand." Sara straightened her back and lifted her chin. She waited. Her hands trembled and her neck was sweaty.

"When did you first meet Father Morales?"

"Did you encourage him? You must have!"

The questions came fast from all three priests, without a pause. Sara looked at one priest and then another.

"Why did you move to Naples?"

"Did you plan to meet him there, away from your country and family?"

"Did you have any other meetings with him?"

"And the night Don Antonio died—you wore a gown he gave you. Doesn't that show you cooperated with his requests and, in fact, acted as his mistress?"

"Did you strike him with a candlestick that night?"

"So, aren't you responsible for his death?"

"Didn't you bewitch him, so he was not responsible for his actions?"

"You are a murderer!"

"No! I'm not a murderer!" said Sara panting, voice rising. Her heart raced.

"He attacked me and I defended myself. I could hardly lift the candlestick; it was heavy. So, when I swung it, I couldn't support its weight long. The next moment the candlestick came down and his head cracked."

"Isn't it true you intended to kill him?"

"No." Sara lifted her chin and spoke into that silent moment.

"Did you hear a voice telling you to do this?"

"No, it was a reaction. He could have killed me or violated me."

"You claim he was morally depraved—a beast. Really? A trusted priest and examiner for the Inquisition?"

"Yes. It's true."

"I call that a lie. Perhaps we can find the truth after water torture."

"I've told you the whole truth."

"We'll see. Prepare for it, Castillo." The three friars escorted Sara, her wrists shackled, to another room in the jail. It was a place of shadows and foul smells. A wiry shirtless man with well-muscled arms secured her to a slanted board and placed a cloth over her face. He poured water from a pitcher at a slow rate, till the cloth became dampened and then soggy with liquid. Sara braced herself, but it brought back the nightmares. Though she couldn't move and she was gagged, Sara felt the water cover her face and wash past her nose. *I'm dying! I'm choking! Stop this! Help me*! She strained against her bonds.

"St-stop!" Her voice croaked out the word. *Did they hear me?* "Stop, stop!" The pouring halted and the cloth was removed. Sara gulped in air, lots of air. She made retching noises. One of the friars let out a strangled scream.

"The *toca* worked again. Do you confess your sins and make confession of your guilt?" Aguilar leaned over her to hear.

"Y-yes. Anything. Just stop." Aguilar narrowed his eyes and formed a tight-lipped smile.

"Untie her, *hombre*. We'll walk her back to her cell." They pulled her up off the board and prodded her ahead. Strands of hair hung down over her shoulders, dripping onto her clothes. Back in her cell they unshackled her and left her without a word. She found a scrap of toweling and rubbed face and hair. Next, she blotted as much water as she could from her clothes. *It should dry fast today, anyway.* She flopped on the bed. Tears streamed down her cheeks. *Did I do something wrong to be tested like this? What does my confession mean? I was desperate. I meant to endure much longer than I did. I must be weak, without faith.*

Sara covered her face with her hands and rocked. The rhythmic motion soothed her and tears slowed. *Oh, to be cradled in my mother's arms, safe from all danger! But there's no safety here and now. Or even in the future. Who can escape the reaching claws of the Inquisition? Protect me, God, like a hen covers her chicks. I will focus on that picture.*

Sara's involuntary trembling subsided. *I'll picture myself in your loving arms—in your arms—* She drew the dirty blanket up to her chin and relaxed into sleep. When she awoke, shadows had crossed the wall and a flaming sunset greeted her.

Oh, Juan! Will we ever be free?

Chapter 29

※

Sara's trial came quickly. A heavy knot tightened in her belly. Any action by the Inquisition drew more people than vultures to a carcass. Sometimes she felt like she was almost dead—accused, tried and convicted—and the curious would circle around till the final gasp of defeat.

Juan came early, bringing news. "When I hired Miguel Santana, I hoped he could present evidence and witnesses for you. It seems the Inquisition has all the power in this matter." He sighed. "Señor Santana will be your advisor until I can find a way to persuade them. Till then, he's not allowed to speak in court." Juan clenched his teeth. "I must find a way."

"Thank you, Juan. What will he do, then? Can he visit me here?"

"He will tell you what to say when answering the inquisitors' questions. He'll look for weaknesses in their arguments and dig into their lives for holes in their armor. I hope he can come today."

"A religious man should be blameless."

"They are human. They have vulnerabilities."

"Maybe. Has Margarita come yet? Has she written?"

"Not yet. I brought a clean dress for you, so you can look your best, and a hairbrush." He took her hand and squeezed it. "Be brave." He stood up and cracked his knuckles. "By the way, the almond harvest is over and loaded into large vats in several storage barns. It's a record harvest this year. Good news for all the growers."

"I don't understand why the jailer let you in. We're talking privately, too."

"I'm right here," said the jailer, opening the door. "It's time to go, Sánchez. I can't bend the rules too far."

Juan whispered to Sara—"He favors you."

"This could be the last time we are free to talk together."

"No, I'll see you again, free and acquitted."

"That's not what usually . . ." Juan put his fingers up to her mouth.

"Don't say anything negative. I'll be at the tribunal tomorrow and however long it takes." He kissed her and let the jailer usher him out. A turn of the key and they were gone.

Juan's efforts to be strong and encouraging had drained him completely. He was a dead man, arms hanging at his sides, his eyes empty wells. He mounted the cart and flicked the reins. He directed the horse toward the far edge of town. The uncared-for exterior of the tavern, like a bereft beggar, appealed to him. *I can go here. It's a place nobody will bother me or question my motives.* Juan made his way through the door, ordered a beer and dropped onto a wooden bench at a corner table. He leaned over his cup a long time until a waiter approached him.

"*Señor*, do you want another?"

"Sorry?"

"*Cerveza*?" Juan looked at him. The man's eyes were outlined with kohl and his hair was fluffed up high on his head.

"Might as well. Say, *hombre*, what goes on in the back room?"

"Why do you ask?" His jaw tightened and a muscle around one eye twitched.

"Last time I was here, I saw two men go by heading for the back of the tavern, that's all. Blue eyes on one. Dressed oddly—woolen hats in summer—like they were hiding something. Do you know them?"

"I might have seen them before. Can't say." The waiter left to fill Juan's order. Juan rested an elbow on the table, knuckles supporting his chin. *Each time I come here I have more questions, and that waiter answered none of them. But his looks betray him.*

* * * *

The day of the trial promised to be hot. Heat waves spiraled up from the cobbled streets. The white-chested shrikes and many-colored goldfinches retreated to leafy trees. Animals gathered in the shadows. A parched stillness settled like dust over the town. People had streamed into Moguer seeking lodging at the few inns operating. During the hottest time of year, many families flew to the hills or the seaside to seek relief from the cruel rays of the sun. Sara sighed and waited. *I wish I could be any place but here.*

The church bell tolled its deep voice. People milled about in the morning sun. Three inquisitors walked with measured steps around the square. Their finery made the ladies murmur. Black satin collars atop finely woven dark wool and leather shoes! Sevilla had sent its finest specimens in these religious men.

Aguilar's long nose came to a point like an eagle's. Piercing eyes and sunken cheeks completed the raptor-like effect. Father Bautista's wild brown hair fluffed around his face, a nest for the bald, egg-shaped head in the middle. He held his pale hands limp, folded one over the other. Father Castillo had a jutting chin and cold, blue eyes. The crowd fell silent at the spectacle. Juan's eyes followed the three judges.

Aguilar strutted in front of the procession. *I'd like to knock that leering smile off his face.*

Then, the jailer and his guard guided Sara around the square, to be seen by everyone. Juan gazed at Sara, but she didn't look up. The jailer had bound her hands but unbound her hair. Auburn waves cascaded around her shoulders in bold display. The sun made her hair glisten like a warm halo. Whispers buzzed when people saw her.

"A pretty woman. Doesn't she know married women conceal their hair?"

"What do you expect? She's a murderer."

"If the inquisitors are telling the truth."

"Poor thing. Chased by that old goat."

"Shh."

The three priests filed into the room. Brother Mateo followed. He was the scribe. Tribunals happened infrequently, but always promised grim entertainment. The accused rarely got a reprieve. After all, truth resided with the righteous, the sons of the church. People made the sign of the cross as Sara walked by. Sara stood in the prisoner's box, a raised rectangle enclosed by wooden balusters and handrails. Once in the courtroom, the three judges took their seats.

"The charge of murder is brought against Sara Elena Sánchez," said Aguilar. "She willfully provoked Don Antonio Morales to the sin of lust and while living in Naples, she accepted his invitation to become his lover. On the night they came together, they argued and she struck him with a large candlestick. He fell to the ground. She ran out of his residence, not even rendering assistance to wipe the blood off his brow or see if he was alive." Aguilar's voice cut through the stale air of the courtroom. Sara frowned and wrung her hands. Gasps and murmurs skittered through the room like mice seeking a place to hide.

"Because of the complex nature of the proceedings, I will ask Father Bautista to delve into the nature of the shameless behavior of Señora Sánchez. Father Castillo will set out in detail the sequence of the events that led up to the death of Don Antonio, including the night of the murder. I, Father Aguilar, will ask Señora Sánchez to elaborate her confession and I will summarize all the proceedings at the end." He turned to face Sara. "Please begin. Tell us what you confessed to the three of us judges a few days ago." He nodded to her.

Sara gripped the handrail and took a deep breath. Her voice wavered at first, but grew stronger and louder as she went on. "I admitted I killed Morales with a silver candlestick, at least I guess I did. Father Morales kept following me and watching me. I thought he wanted to find a reason to bring my family and me before the Inquisition. But, after a while I realized he wanted to possess me—and he's a monk, an officer of the Inquisition!"

"Keep to your confession," yelled Aguilar.

"Well, I left Spain at the time of the great expulsion and thought surely I would be rid of his prying. But no, when the ship reached Tangier, a hired man tried to abduct me and take me to Morales. And he would have succeeded, except the local police saw him."

"How did this happen?"

"I was knocked on the head and rolled in a large rug. I woke up and struggled to free myself. They dropped me. The police came by and ordered them to stop. Father Morales was brought before the local authorities. I think it embarrassed him." She looked around, "My friend Margarita was there, too."

"Your personal opinions are not needed. Continue."

"The ship continued on to Naples and I thought I would not be followed anymore. But, somewhat later, Father

Morales came into the restaurant I owned and beat me with a broomstick. I was great with child then, and the baby came before its time because of the blows to my abdomen." Gasps exploded in the room and the women shrieked and cradled their stomachs.

"Yes?"

"Morales received injuries when I fought back and he disappeared. A body was found in the bay. I was a suspect, but the investigation stalled. Then, while I walked one day in the streets of Naples, two of his servants knocked me on the head and took me to the residence of Morales. And he was there—not dead at all. He told me I was now his lover. He gave me a gown to wear and had an elegant dinner served. I said I never wanted to be his paramour and blew the candles out. He followed me, using his hearing to guide him." Sara licked her lips.

"He's crippled, you know, and not well. He coughed occasionally and I tried to evade him. But he seized me at the great table in the dining area and tried to kiss me. I did the first thing I could think of to defend myself. I grabbed the candlestick—it was heavy—and I swung it around to make him step back. But, instead, it hit him in the skull and he fell backward, stunned, I think, but not dead. I wanted to get away from this prison, so I ran down the hall and out the front door, until I made my way home."

"What about the servants? Where were they?" Aguilar paced in front of the witness box.

"He instructed them not to bother us. It was to be a lover's tryst." Sara blushed and hid her face.

"And did you mean to kill Morales?"

"No, of course not. It was an accident." Aguilar scowled.

"Father Bautista, you may proceed." Aguilar nodded to Bautista, who stood up and took mincing steps toward Sara.

"You are a woman of loose morals, Señora Sánchez. Isn't that true?" The question hit Sara like an arrow piercing a melon. Her arms flew up across her chest.

"No! I live by the highest Christian moral standards, sir."

"Then how do you explain your visit to Father Morales' residence in Naples?"

"I was forced to go there." Sara frowned at him.

"That's what you say, but what we all see is that you put on a gown that he gave you, arranged your hair and powdered your face. You ate a rich meal with him, including wine. All the while, you conversed with him, possibly flirting with this respected member of the Church and then tantalized him by pretending to resist his romantic advances." Bautista spit out the words, aiming them like darts.

"No, no, no!" Sara's voice rose. "You have it wrong. He was the aggressor. He wanted to possess me. He held me prisoner—Is was to be forever, he said." She waved her shackled hands up and down.

"Very emotional," said Bautista, tucking pale wrists into their opposite sleeves. He leaned forward on the balls of his feet. "In reality, you drove him to a special kind of madness by promising and retreating, agreeing and refusing."

"No, I never did that!"

"But he followed you from Spain to Tangier and to Naples with the hope of winning your companionship."

"Is that how a man of the Church should act?" Sara's clear voice rang bell-like throughout the silent room and hung in the air.

"The point is your actions, Señora Sánchez. You— tempted a priest, a respected citizen, to commit grave sins. And then you raised a candlestick and shattered his skull. What do you say to that?" Bautista looked down his nose, eyes ablaze like embers in a fire. Sara caught his glare and looked away.

"I can tell you only that I never meant to tempt him." She pinched back the tears rolling down her cheeks and onto her chin. She brushed them away with a swipe of her manacled hands and raised her chin.

"That's not what your actions show. You are a depraved woman, guilty of indecent behavior, and then to hide it you killed Don Antonio Morales." Sara wept, unable to stop. Father Bautista returned to his seat at the judges' table.

"Hrmph." Father Aguilar cleared his throat. "Father Castillo, will you please lead us through the events that led up to the killing of Don Antonio." Castillo's tonsured head glowed with beads of sweat. He carried extra flesh on his body, although still a young man. His eyebrows knit together in a furry shelf above ice blue eyes. He approached Sara.

"Just a few questions about the order of events, Señora Sánchez." Sara nodded. "You lured Don Antonio step by step, didn't you? First, you said you would be his lover, then you took back that promise."

"It wasn't really a promise."

"Oh? He followed you across Spain, because of that promise. And then you boarded a ship leaving Spain?"

"Because of the Expulsion."

"Or to confuse a simple religious man? He trusted your words."

"He should have realized it was impossible. I was much too young. He could have been my grandfather. Not to mention his religious vows!"

"Hope is powerful, Señora Sánchez. And then, in Tangier, you slipped away from him."

"He abducted me. That shows I was opposed to the idea. And I was married."

"A man old enough to be your grandfather?"

"Montenegro helped him."

"Are you changing your story?"

"Montenegro was his hired henchman."

"And why does he not appear in these proceedings?"

Sara didn't answer.

"I asked why?"

"You know."

"Because this is not true?"

"No. Because witnesses are afraid to testify."

"Or maybe your account simply is not true." Castillo smirked and looked down his nose. Sara shuddered and gripped the railing of the witness box.

"Let's continue," said Castillo. "You traveled on to Naples, I understand."

"How do you know all this about me?"

"Yes or no?"

"Yes. I knew my brother settled there."

"And where was your husband?"

"On the voyage of discovery with Admiral Columbus."

"Did you marry in Granada?"

"No, in Palos. The day before we were expelled."

"Are you of the Jewish faith?"

"I was, but I am not now."

"Answer! It appears you are still."

"My family and I are *conversos*. We adopted the Catholic faith as required." Sara paused. "And now, I believe the Holy Writings with all my heart." A murmur surged through the room. Sara clasped her hands and bowed her head.

"Touching, but let's continue."

"I left Spain because I feared Don Antonio. And we were expelled."

"And so, you lived and worked in Naples."

"Yes."

"But Father Morales found you."

"He followed me, and Montenegro helped him."

"What happened next?"

"Morales came to the restaurant I worked at, and confronted me."

"Confronted?"

"Yes. He saw I was with child and called me 'unfaithful."

"With child, but not married?"

"No, never! I was married, I told you."

"But not in a church."

"By a priest aboard Columbus' ship."

"Lies. What happened during this argument?"

"Morales began to hit me—with a broom."

"Righteous indignation at being rejected and replaced."

"No! He was a lunatic crazy with madness. He wouldn't stop!" Sara gripped the rail.

"But, you injured him. You bewitched him."

"He tripped over a cobblestone, chasing me up the street. I only wanted to get away. He was striking my stomach—my baby!" Sara's face dripped with sweat and tears. "He almost killed us." She panted. The news caused a sensation. Whisperers spread the news to the crowd outside. Sara's legs wobbled.

"Father Castillo, we must cease the proceedings for today. The accused has taken this trial in the wrong direction. We must restore order." Father Aguilar stood up and banged a gavel on the table. Juan ran to her and stroked her face.

"Sir, get away from the witness."

"She's my wife. She needs attention. She's tired."

"We'll get her to her cell again." The guard pushed him back.

"Proceedings adjourned till tomorrow," Castillo's voice boomed over the chaos. Juan looked at the three priests standing there together. He understood.

"Hey, *padre*, didn't I see you at The Painted Rooster?" Juan spat out. The stony faces cracked. Blue sparks flashed from Father Castillo's eyes. Bautista's neck rose with color. Aguilar maintained tight lips and shuffled to the door. The other two followed. Guards forced Juan out a side door with a rough shove. He slipped away.

Chapter 30

✳

Guards returned Sara to her cell cubicle. She flopped onto the hard bed and turned her face to the wall. Tears rolled down flaming cheeks. *What hurts most—the insults or the insinuations?* Sara rolled on her back and dried her face with part of her sleeve. *I must be ready to defend myself tomorrow. I'd better plan what I'll say and do. I must not give way. I need help. Who will fight for me?*

Juan waited till the crush of people cleared the central plaza area. He walked, scanning on both sides of him as he ambled across the square. He untied the reins and noticed a scrap of a scroll tied to his horse's mane. The horse snorted and bobbed its head twice. Juan gave him a pat and stepped up into his wagon. He unrolled the parchment piece and read the words:

What do you want? Meet at the *bodega* at sunset tonight.

Juan got there as the orange sun dropped into the dark bowl of night. He ordered a beer and sauntered among the rough tables and benches. He saw what he expected: a hooded figure sitting in a dark corner. A nod signaled he should approach.

"I have two demands of you," said Juan. "The first is to let Miguel Santana, the lawyer, defend Sara."

"Absolutely not! You dare threaten a member of the Inquisition? A holy father and your superior?" The shadowed man puffed out his cheeks and squared his shoulders. He clenched his teeth and let out a hiss.

Juan leaned back from this reaper of death figure. "You will not intimidate me. Remember, I have nothing to lose now. If Sara my wife loses her fight, my life is over." He narrowed his eyes to slits and lowered his eyelids half way.

"What is your second demand, Señor Sánchez?" The hiss stretched out his name to a snake's warning: S-s-s-s-s.

"The second is just as important: acquit Sara. If you do both, I will not reveal your dark secret." Juan leaned forward in order to talk in quiet tones. The hooded figure inclined his head and brushed a part of the hood back from one ear. The hooded man's blue eyes fixed on him a blank stare.

* * * *

The next day, the three judges, Aguilar, Bautista and Castillo, glided into the crowded courtroom. The red of their sashes shone in the bright sunlight. All the windows were thrown open to let in any cool breeze that might pass by. Sara moved to the witness box. A guard opened and closed it around her. She looked for Juan and lifted the corners of her mouth when she saw him. He gave a faint nod. Sara steadied herself by holding the handrail.

"Let everyone know," intoned Aguilar, "the proceedings are now in session. I have decided to let a lawyer assist Señora Sánchez. This is a complex case. Señor Santana, you may proceed." Amid the gasps, including one from Sara, a short, stout man stood and walked toward the accused. He whispered to her, "Courage." Sara smiled, a light momentarily flickering in her eyes.

"Thank you, sir. I am indebted to you." The lawyer clicked his heels together and gave a small bow to Sara. Then, he held up a parchment and eyed it.

"Distinguished judges, I intend to prove that *Señora* Sánchez is innocent of any wrongdoing. She had to endure years of Don Antonio Morales' unwanted attentions. He followed her like a predator. He tried to abduct her twice, succeeding the last time. He forced her to accept his wishes, desires that were contrary to the vows he took to become a monk. In a fight to protect her virtue, she struck Father Morales accidentally, causing an injury that led to his death. I beg you to consider her tragic circumstances with an open heart and declare her not guilty." Santana returned to his seat.

"Do you have witnesses?" Santana shifted his weight. The chair creaked.

"We were informed last night to prepare for the trial. You know it is difficult to get witnesses to speak for the accused. We hope that Margarita Galvan will arrive soon. She has been summoned."

"But she's not here?"

"Not at this time, but we reserve the right to question her if she comes."

Aguilar raised his eyebrows. "Very well. We will proceed. We have two witnesses, Alexo and Paco, servants of Don Antonio." The two men filed in. They did not raise their gaze from the floor.

"Alexo and Paco, don't be afraid. Just answer the questions." Aguilar's smile was a tight-lipped smear across his sallow face. "Did you observe the behavior of Sara Sánchez at any time during your service to Don Antonio?" They both nodded.

"Yes."

"And what was that behavior?"

"She flirted with him."

"She tossed her long hair."

"She stood close to him."

"She came to his house just before his death."

Sara looked at them, her mouth open and forehead creased.

"No. It's not true."

"Silence." Alexo and Paco shifted their feet and looked at their shoes.

"Would you say she encouraged Don Antonio and made him feverish with desire?"

"Yes, sir." Paco sighed.

"Yes, sir." Alexo's shoulders slumped. Sara's kept shaking her head.

"Never!"

Santana pushed himself up out of his chair. "I'd like to question them, Your Eminence." Aguilar nodded.

"Why did Morales beat Señora Sánchez?"

"He was angry with her," said Alexo. "She was with child. It was not his."

"So, if she was pregnant with another man's baby, how could she have been enticing Father Morales? She was a married woman." Sara darted a look at Juan. His knuckles glowed white from across the room as his fists tightened.

"I don't know, *señor.*"

"She was a bad woman, maybe," said Paco.

"On the night of Father Morales' death, did you serve them dinner?"

"Yes."

Were you at the door to attend to Don Antonio's commands?"

"Yes."

"So, why were you away—out of hearing when he was injured?"

"We were . . . He told us to go away," Alexo and Paco said together.

"He wanted privacy, right?" Santana kept probing.

"I don't know, sir," said Alexo.

"You don't believe that, neither of you. And didn't you knock her on the head, Alexo, to get her to Don Antonio's?" Alexo shrugged his shoulders.

"I can see that someone has threatened you. Maybe it's one of the judges?" Santana scrutinized each one. Alexo and Paco looked down and shuffled their feet.

"I warn you, Santana," boomed Aguilar. "You are venturing into dangerous territory."

"No further questions," said Santana and sat down heavily. The chair cracked and collapsed, drawing the attention of everyone in the room. Whispers multiplied and spread while Santana took his time to stand upright. Someone leaned out the window and murmured to someone outside. The murmuring spread through the outdoor crowd like a contagious disease. Aguilar banged a gavel on the table. Santana smiled.

"If there are no other witnesses—" Aguilar looked toward the door. A scuffling and parting of the spectators revealed a breathless, middle-aged woman.

"Your honor, I wish to testify."

"Margarita!" Sara clapped her hands and let out a shriek. Margarita looked her way and blew a kiss.

"Come forward, *señora*." Santana struggled to his feet, pushing his belly before him. Margarita walked like a queen into the room. All eyes followed her. She stood before the judges' bench. Santana joined her there.

"What is your name, for the record?"

"Margarita Galvan, from Córdoba."

"And how do you know the accused?"

"She is a good friend. She is like the daughter I never had."

"Are you aware of Sara Sánchez' dealings with Don Antonio Morales?"

"I am. He watched her and her family, to begin with. Then he just followed her. He wanted her." Aguilar interrupted.

"And why did he follow the family? Did they offend the dictates of the Church?"

"No, sir. They are Christians and adhere to the rules of the church."

"New Christians, perhaps? *Conversos*, recently converted?"

"I'm told they've been Christian for three generations."

"So, he followed to verify their orthodoxy to the faith."

"I suppose."

Santana reasserted himself. "Did Sara Sánchez in any way encourage Don Antonio to think she would be his lover?" Margarita shuddered.

"No. She always rebuffed his advances." Aguilar asked the next question.

"Why are you so loyal to her? Surely she has some flaws."

"We are all sinners, sir. I'm loyal to her because of her unfailing friendship and support. Why she even promised Morales—" Margarita clamped her mouth shut.

"What's that? Go on. Promised Morales what?"

"Well, she promised Morales she would be his companion if he would release me from jail back in Granada."

"Are you under suspicion by the Inquisition?"

"That matter was dismissed."

"What was it? You must tell the truth."

"I gave aid to people in jail, awaiting trial. Food and blankets, that's all."

"So, you have a doubtful reputation. And now, we see *Señora* Sánchez did encourage Father Morales." Aguilar's eyes shone.

"Lies. She never meant it. She did it to get me set free. It shows the intensity of Morales' obsession, though," Margarita added.

"She never meant it. A likely excuse." Aguilar smiled.

Santana wiped his brow. Juan held his head with both hands. Sara sobbed.

"Margarita, how should we take your testimony?" said Santana. "Can you prove she never meant this promise?"

"Let me see." Margarita paused to consider. "After she made this false promise, she immediately joined a caravan and fled to the western coast, to Palos, to get away from Morales."

"That's a strong bit of evidence. Anything else?"

"She disguised herself and always tried to hide from him and his thugs."

"Oh, so he hired men to do Sara harm?"

"Yes. A man named Montenegro pursued her from Tangier to Naples. He was paid by Morales." Gasps and murmuring.

"Perhaps they were hired to protect Father Morales from her."

Aguilar's voice boomed out once more. "This line of questioning is impertinent, Santana. Stop it."

"No, he captured Sara, and me, in Tangier. I call that harm."

"Finish your arguments, Santana. The day draws toward luncheon. We'll adjourn until after siesta, about half past four. Then we'll deliberate and render a verdict, Bautista, Castillo and I."

"After lunch, I wish to interview two men seen at The Painted Rooster recently," said Santana. "One is named

Nando." A choking sound came from Bautista. He quickly suppressed it. Castillo frowned.

"Mid-day adjournment. We'll resume at half past four." Aguilar banged the gavel. The room exploded with a dozen conversations. Juan nodded at Santana. The judges had already gone to their food.

Juan whispered to Sara "Take courage," before four guards pushed him away. Juan slipped out. They waited till the outside square cleared and then the four guards escorted her to her cell. Sara's *luncheon*, usually the largest meal of the day, included a thin stew with vegetables and a chunk of bread. She drank from a mug of weak ale, also, wiped her mouth and leaned back on her pallet.

I have no idea what will happen this afternoon. But, Señor Santana has helped my cause. He's pointed out inconsistencies in the judges' arguments. Margarita gave me strong support, too. Bless her!

Santana mentioned it during the trial, but what is The Painted Rooster? Why does it make the priests freeze in place, especially that one with the wild hair? I don't dare to hope. This day could easily bring my death sentence. Sara closed her eyes. *Whatever happens, God, my hope is in you.*

Sara lay down, a heavy feeling in her stomach. *The tension of the trial has made knots in my insides. Unless it's tainted food.* Because of the pain, she slept poorly all afternoon until the key turned in the lock and a guard shook her.

"Get up, it's time to go back to the tribunal." Sara put out her wrists to receive the manacles and moved forward with the guards, one on each side. The people lining the square stared at her, as if seeing a curiosity. *They think it's the last time they'll see me. Conviction is certain.*

Father Aguilar stood at the judges' table. The other two seats were empty. He banged the gavel. "The tribunal is in session. Fathers Bautista and Castillo have been summoned urgently to Sevilla on important church business this afternoon. They will not be present." Murmurs rippled through the room. "I have discussed the whole situation with them and will now render a verdict." He paused as murmurs turned to loud conversations.

"I wish to interview Nando," yelled Santana. "I believe him to be a rogue priest who frequented The Painted Rooster, and who may have ill-used another priest at the same establishment." Shouting broke out in the room, cutting through the stale air.

"Silence!" Aguilar waited. "As I was saying, the other two judges and I have reviewed the case against Sara Sánchez. We have probed with questions and even taken the unusual step of permitting a defense for the accused. This is unprecedented! But Fathers Bautista and Castillo urged me to permit it. This woman—" he pointed to Sara—"willfully enticed and tempted a respected member of the clergy to contemplate and carry through on his lustful imaginings. He followed Señora Sánchez because she bewitched him with desire and did little to dissuade him from this course." Sara suppressed a sob and covered her face.

"Of the night when Don Antonio Morales died, we have only Señora Sánchez' testimony. Nobody else saw what happened. The servants Alexo and Paco said they heard noises and a scuffle, but they didn't witness the killing. Is Sara Sánchez deserving of death?" Aguilar paused and took a breath. The silence in the room weighed heavily on Sara's shoulders. She sought Juan's eyes and caught his raised eyebrows and upturned lips.

"Is Sara Sánchez deserving of death?" Aguilar paused as if measuring his next words. "We don't know. We don't have enough evidence of the actual event either way.

Therefore, we cannot render a death sentence." A whoop of joy, handclapping and slaps on the back burst forth like Mt. Vesuvius. This continued for several minutes, until at last Father Aguilar banged the gavel. "That is the first part of our rendered judgment. But, I would like to remind you of the depth of this woman's fall."

"The accused's behavior was wanton and so contrary to our faith's basic teachings that we believe she needs to suffer a significant punishment. Therefore, for the next six months she is commanded to wear a conical hat and a sign stating her sins. You are to shun her company. Do not speak to her. Do not trade with her. Amid the growing din of yelled objections, Aguilar added, "If she shows sufficient proof of humility and repentance, the punishment may be lifted." Aguilar banged the gavel one last time. "Release her. This matter is closed."

"Wait!" Margarita stood up and approached the judge. "Didn't you receive a message from the Queen? She promised to send something."

"Nothing." He gestured to the guards who supported Sara's sagging frame. Sara let out a moan and grabbed her abdomen.

"Aagh! Something's wrong!" A bright blot of crimson landed on the floor by her feet. Juan ran to her and took over holding her up. "Quickly, Juan, I need to lie down. Please, take me away from here!" Juan picked her up in his arms.

Aguilar banged the gavel till the handle broke.

"Clear the courtroom!" Juan threw a dark look at the judge.

"My wife is ill! Let me through." Juan pushed through the room. Knots of chatting people stepped aside and then closed ranks behind them. Juan helped Sara up the two steps of their cart and smoothed out a blanket for her in back. She lay down clutching her middle and moaning.

"I'll drive as carefully as I can, dear Sarita." Juan's brow furrowed with a fresh worry. He unhitched the reins and guided the cart through the crowds still filling the town square. They looked up to scold, but stepped back when they saw Juan's face. "Let me pass. Let me pass. Emergency." Sara moaned with each bump in the road. "It's taking an eternity to get you home. "Juan. Help me!" Juan pulled off the dirt road just out of town and drove to a shady grove of almond trees. He tied up the horse and turned to assist his stricken wife.

"I'll do all that I can." Sara's body convulsed then relaxed. "You're overcome. Take a few drops of lemon balm. Juan dripped the liquid onto Sara's tongue. "Now, let me rub some lavender oil on you. Inhale it and let it relax you." He patted her hand. "Take some deep breaths and relax. That's it." Sara took one gasping breath and let it out. She took another steadier breath and let her body go limp. "Is it time for your courses? Any more blood?"

"I don't know. No." Sara's eyelids fluttered.

"Let yourself sleep. Good." Juan stroked her forehead, brushing tendrils of hair off her hot forehead. "Sleep. Sleep." The medicines took their effect. The muscles spasms eased and Sara fell asleep. Juan sat watching her. Sara still slept.

Juan picked up the reins and coaxed the horse to a gentle walk.

Chapter 31

❀

Juan eased back onto the road and drove at a slow pace till they reached the drive leading to Catalina's almond orchard. Juan drove in and tied up the cart and horse just outside the door. He stepped surely down to the ground and carefully lifted Sara in his arms. Entering the warm guesthouse, Juan walked on tiptoe and placed Sara in their wide bed. Juan unlaced the linen gown, eased her arms out and slipped the whole thing off. He saw another spot of blood. Juan roused her enough to place three more drops of the tincture on her tongue. Sara turned and curled up shielding her stomach.

She looks shrunken, unwell. I am afraid for her.

He encountered Catalina in the hall. Juanito came running.

"Papa!" Juan swung him up in the air and down.

"What's the news? Are you celebrating?" Catalina wiped hands on her apron as she approached father and son.

"There's no death sentence, but six months of penance. Sara heard the verdict and collapsed."

"Oh, no!"

"Do you know if she's been feeling unwell, Catalina?"

"I haven't talked to her since she was arrested two or three weeks ago. Before then, she wasn't complaining, though. What's wrong?"

"Not sure, but she's convulsing and bleeding."

"I hope it's not—"

"That, or a number of other ailments. I don't know." He raked a trembling hand through his untidy hair.

"How can I help?"

"I need to stay with her—watch her. Could you feed Juanito his supper. I'll get him to bed."

"I'll do that, and bring some chicken broth." Catalina patted his shoulder. "You go back to Sara. I'll say a prayer." She picked up Juanito and took him to her house.

"Thanks." Juan heard Sara calling and dashed back into the bedroom.

"Juan, help." She was convulsing again.

"Take a deep breath. More drops of lemon balm." *What else, man?*

"I'm so thirsty, Juan. Water, wine—please!"

"I'll get the sweetened lemon water. Just a minute." He brought the pitcher and a cup. Lifting Sara's head up, he helped her drink two cups of the cool liquid.

"So good. Better." She licked her lips and lay back.

"Rest again, dear one." Juan rubbed more lavender oil on her neck. She took a deep breath and sniffed the air.

"Sweet. The air is sweet."

Juan paced the floor while Sara slept.

* * * *

Father Aguilar returned to the local monastery. He looked in Bautista's and Castillo's rooms, but they were gone, as he knew they would be. Aguilar tapped on Father Diego's door next.

"The trial is over and I'll be leaving." Father Diego touched all his fingers together in the shape of a steeple.

"Go with God." Father Diego made the sign of the cross. "There is a man waiting to see you. A *Señor* Santana."

257

"What does he want?" Father Diego shrugged his shoulders but led Father Aguilar to the library.

"Here he is." He bowed and left.

"Santana, what do you want? The trial is over."

"Yes, but I still seek justice. Why didn't you let me interview the persons I saw at The Painted Rooster?"

"It's a separate issue and should not come out in a public hearing. Men using each other in a shameful way." Aguilar cleared his throat several times. "I will deal with that." The two men heard a disturbance in the hall. A rap on the door came next.

"Who is it?"

"Messenger Felipe, sir. From the Queen." Father Aguilar stepped quickly to open the door.

"Come in."

A young man in a tabard bearing the castles and lions of the royal crest crossed the threshold and clicked his heels together. Blemishes pocked his cheeks.

"A message for Father Aguilar from Her Majesty Isabella, sir." He held out a scroll fixed with a red wax seal and the impression of the royal insignia. Father Aguilar took it and broke the seal. He read the contents carefully.

"Can this be?" Father Aguilar raised his eyebrows. "The trial is over."

"What is it?" asked Santana.

"The Queen was indisposed," announced Felipe, "and uncertain what to do when *Señora* Margarita Galvan came to her. But you can act on her instructions now. It is not too late." The young man lifted his chin and touched his sword hilt.

"What is it?" said Santana again.

"Look. Isn't that amazing!" The two men perused the scroll.

"Aguilar, you must publicize this immediately," said Santana. "Call an assembly in the town square for tomorrow. But first, let Juan and Sara Sánchez know."

"There is hardly need of that, sir. I also have a scroll for Juan and Sara Sánchez," said Queen Isabella's messenger. "Could you direct me to their residence?" The young man touched his leather message pouch.

"Along Almond Tree Road just out of town. Take a left at the first driveway you see. They're staying with Catalina de Torres." *Señor* Santana gave the directions quickly. The young man saluted with a fist to his chest and then pivoted and strode out of the library.

Father Aguilar held the scroll in his upturned hand. "This is extraordinary, most unusual." His mouth slid open.

"I've learned that nothing is ordinary with Sara Sánchez," said Santana. "She is a woman of the highest moral standards. She lives life with urgency and she takes risks to help her friends." Santana shook his head. "Amazing woman."

"It seems you have won the day, Santana," said Aguilar. "I'll post a notice quickly. You'll hear about it shortly."

"I'll be waiting and will surely expect your prompt action." Santana grabbed his hat and cloak and exited the room.

"You will drop the other matter, won't you?" said Aguilar to Santana's retreating figure.

"Done." Santana turned and gave a nod, before continuing out.

Aguilar called for a scribe and dictated a suitable announcement to be posted on the door of city hall. Santana checked after lunch. *Finally, it's ended.*

* * * *

The young priest, Brother Mateo, stopped the Queen's messenger in the cloister.

"Messenger Felipe, permit me to go with you. I can direct you, and I'd like to visit and give comfort, anyway."

"Not needed. What is your purpose?" His facial blemishes reddened.

"I have herbs and potions for the *señora*. She fell ill earlier today, upon hearing the outcome of the trial." Brother Mateo gestured with his hand.

The messenger gave a cursory nod and pivoted to go. "Then, come."

"One moment, I'll meet you in the courtyard. Must get the medicines." The young monk veered off to a passageway leading into the cloister's interior. The messenger adjusted his cap and strode to his horse.

Brother Mateo searched for a certain bottle and several packets of herbs. His sandals slapped a staccato in the passageway. An older monk peered out of a doorway. Brother Mateo slowed to a gliding pace and inserted opposite arms into his voluminous sleeves. Messenger Felipe's horse pawed the ground and circled around as Brother Mateo saddled a donkey and straddled it at last.

"Let's go." The messenger kicked the sides of his black horse and rode out of the courtyard. Brother Mateo kicked his donkey into action, as well, and it trotted at a brisk pace after the retreating horse. Brother Mateo caught up in the central square of Moguer, when the messenger slowed for the tangle of carts and pedestrians. It was market day.

"Follow me this way," motioned Brother Mateo. They took Almond Tree Road out of town and turned at the first driveway. The black horse cantered ahead and pulled up to the rustic farmhouse. Brother Mateo tied up his donkey, just as the messenger rapped on the door. The trees rested now after shedding their abundance. Hulls and fallen leaves had been cleared away. The afternoon began rustling the trees. They swayed their branches like a woman stretching on a couch. Brother Mateo paused to listen to the sighing—and the peace.

The loud nose of rapping broke through his reverie. Juan Sánchez made a quick response, opening the door with sword in hand.

"What is it, *hombre*?"

"*Señor* Sánchez?"

"Yes?"

"The Queen commanded me to bring this to Sara Sánchez. Is she here?" The Messenger Felipe bowed and held out a large scroll.

"My wife is resting. The Inquisition tribunal exhausted her. I pray her health is not ruined." Juan scowled. 'I hope this is not bad news."

"I was instructed to give it into her hands only."

"She is my wife." Juan grabbed the scroll from the messenger's hand.

"Then read it, sir. I have further instructions after that." He stepped back and straightened up.

"Sir." Brother Mateo interrupted. "If I may. I've brought herbs and a sleeping potion for your wife. I'm Brother Mateo, if you remember."

"Yes. Hm. Let me read this first, if you please." Juan's eyes studied every word of the scroll slowly. His furrowed brow gradually eased. His stony face softened. He drew in a quick breath.

"If this is true it's amazing." Juan's eyes scanned Felipe's tabard, and then looked once more at the red wax seal. He dropped down on the hall bench.

"It is completely true. I brought it directly from the Queen. You may rely on its authenticity. I have delivered a letter to Father Aguilar, stating the same thing. Perhaps I should deliver it directly to your wife's hands." Felipe reached for the scroll and grabbed it back.

"I'm here," said a soft voice. Sara appeared in the doorway, a large shawl draped over her shoulders. "What's all this, Juan?" She stood next to Juan.

"Sara, you're not well." Juan put his arm around her shoulder and felt her forehead.

"I heard the noise and the conversation. I was curious." Sara laid her head against Juan's shoulder.

"I'm trying to sort it out myself. Tell us, Messenger Felipe," said Juan.

Felipe cleared his throat and spoke. "Señor and Señora Sánchez, I bring a message from Queen Isabella." He bowed and his cap fell to the floor. He retrieved the hat and his dignity while turning to Sara. "The Queen grants you clemency. She remembers your service to her with fondness. She also remembers she never gave you the reward she promised. So, this proclamation is for you." He handed Sara the scroll. "A declaration of clemency for you. The Inquisition will never again prosecute you. That is Queen Isabella's solemn promise." The messenger bowed and took a step back.

He turned to Juan and held out a pouch. "Senor Sanchez, for your service to the Queen in writing an account of the historic first contact in the Indies, the Queen grants you one thousand *maravedis*, with the hope it will help you re-settle in our fair country." The Messenger Felipe saluted with one fist to his chest. He turned and mounted his ebony horse, trotted down the shaded driveway and disappeared.

"Oh, Juan!" Sara covered her mouth with both hands to muffle the sobs welling inside her.

"Don't give way to emotion, Sara, or you will return to convulsing." Juan turned to the smooth-cheeked priest. "Look, Brother Mateo has come to give you medicines and a sleeping potion."

Sara nodded her head, but tears cascaded down her pink cheeks. She reached her hand out.

"Brother Mateo, once again you are kind to me. I do appreciate it." Sara stood and motioned for the novice priest to enter. Sara took Juan's hand and led them to the living room *sala*. "I feel I will soon recover from my present fatigue with your help and that of my doctor husband."

"Oh, I didn't know." Brother Mateo's neck colored.

"I'm very grateful," said Sara. "May God bless you for your kind actions."

"Juan." She turned to her husband. "Could we celebrate by offering Brother Mateo some sherry? I think is would revive me, too."

Juan smiled, gave Sara a peck and went to fetch it. Catalina came in behind him when Juan returned. She brought a bowl of seasoned almonds and a decanter.

"Taste a bit of our harvest, Brother."

"And a toast to Sara and to all our friends who helped us." Juan gave a tumbler of sherry to each person in the room. "I found an old bottle of sherry in the pantry. Catalina said we should use it."

"*Salud*. To your health, Sara." They all raised their tumblers.

"*Salud* and many years of health and happiness." They drained their cups. Brother Mateo bowed out and left at a trot, late for vespers.

"Come back sometime, Brother Mateo," said Juan, "and we will speak of what I learned of medicine in the New World."

Brother Mateo waved a hand and kept trotting.

Sara returned to bed.

Chapter 32

"Sara, how do you feel?" Juan entered the bedroom, bearing a tray. He gazed at his wife, chestnut hair spread across a snowy pillow. The filtered light softened her face to the color of rich cream.

"Mm? What time is it?" Sara covered a yawn with one hand and moved her head from side to side. She sat up and rubbed her middle.

"Any spasms or pain? Any clots of blood?" Juan set the tray down and brought a filled wooden tumbler to her. "Drink this sweetened lemon water." Sara took it and sipped.

"Just what I needed. I'm thirsty and I feel hungry."

"Any symptoms?" Juan felt her forehead.

"I don't think so. Maybe just a touch of indigestion." She looked into the corner shadows. "Time?"

"Nine in the morning. Do you feel like getting up?" Juan took her elbow and supported her as she stood.

"I'd love to get a bath and put on fresh clothes. I want to wash away all the bad memories of the last few weeks." She rubbed her hands over her arms and gave them a shake.

"I'll bring some hot water and a basin. Let's start with that. You still need to recover some. One more day of rest."

"I'll look for a fresh gown if you'll bring the water." She reached up to kiss Juan. He left on his errand after returning the kiss with warm lips and a tender embrace. Sara touched her lips, then walked to her wardrobe and looked at the meager offerings. *Life has been difficult lately. Maybe now I can buy a few proper gowns, when Juan has established his practice, of course.* She chose an everyday gown of fine homespun.

Juan brought hot water, towel and a bar of rosemary soap. Sara lathered herself with the fragrant foam and then rinsed with clean water. She dried her skin and then slipped into the summery gown. Juan stepped forward to lace the back ties that held the gown closed.

"You look lovely, Sarita. Much improved." He touched her shoulder. "Let's go eat now. Juanito is already devouring bread." They chuckled.

"It feels wonderful to laugh again—with no cares but what to eat." Sara and Juan smiled and walked down the hall toward the smells of food cooking.

"I have fresh squeezed orange juice and boiled eggs, as well as fresh bread. We need to feed the patient a hearty breakfast." Catalina placed two small kisses, one near each of Sara's cheeks. "Sit down."

"Mama," said Juanito. He waved his hands and wiggled his feet.

"How's my sweet boy?" Sara chucked him under the chin. "Big!"

"You are big! Look at all you're eating." Sara pushed a crust of bread toward him. She accepted all the food Catalina offered her and began to peel an egg. She gulped and rubbed her middle. "I think I'll just have juice and bread."

"Hm," said Catalina. "If you have a list of things you need, I'll go into town and get them. You should stay here and relax."

"Of course. It will be nice to do ordinary things again. I expect to get back to domestic duties tomorrow." Juan glanced at her.

"You should guard your health, especially in your condition." He stifled a smile.

"I'm going to be fine, Juan. Just a touch of bad jail food, I think."

"Think back over the last few months. Has anything changed physically for you?"

"What?" Sara looked at her fingernails as if the answer might be written there. She folded her hands. "Hm. A lot of travel, tiredness often."

"Are you bilious? Tender anywhere?"

"Why all the questions?"

"I don't know without an examination, but I think you may be—"

"With child! Yes, that explains it. Congratulations, Sara." Catalina beamed. "What a joy for you. You deserve it."

Sara caught her breath. Juan put his arm around Sara's shoulder and drew her close. Juanito banged on the table with a spoon.

"We'll need to move to our own place, with two babies," said Juan. "Even though the guest house is cozy. Thank you, Catalina, for letting us live here."

"You can stay until you've found something, but that will ease the situation." Catalina grinned. "I asked Margarita to come stay with me. We'll be two happy widows."

"Where is she now?" Sara looked around.

"She's already left for Córdoba. She'll pack her few things and return in a week or two." Sara clapped her hands.

"Can I leave you and go into town today, Sara? Said Juan. "I want to start looking at properties. It might be good to have a larger place for my growing family. Sara nodded and gave Catalina her list of groceries.

"Thanks, Catalina. Another reason I should stay home is because I could attract attention. The trial is still fresh in people's memories."

"You might be overrun with people wishing you well," said Catalina.

"Or the reverse, I suppose. Some may think I should have been punished." She turned to Juan. "When you find something, I'll move in without fanfare, maybe some evening—until Moguer gets back to its normal patterns."

"If you're sure," said Juan "It's wise to relax and rest. You've been through so much." Juan kissed her on the cheek and jumped into the cart.

"In that case, can I go with you, Juan, and buy the food we need?" Juan nodded. Catalina went in to get her money and a bag while Juan readied the horse and cart.

"I'll stay and give Juanito a nap—and me, too." Sara yawned and turned toward the house. She waved to the two as they rode down the drive. They soon arrived in the center of town.

"I'll meet you in an hour at the fountain. Is that enough time for you?" said Juan. "Who handles properties in town?"

"An hour is fine. Talk to *Señor* Díaz. His office is down the street. He owns a lot of property in and around Moguer. And he knows what is available." Catalina waved and moved toward the produce stands clustered around the central fountain. Juan tied up the horse and cart and strode down the street. A warm wind ruffled his hair. Rounded cobblestones jabbed the soles of his feet through his soft leather boots.

"Where's this *Señor* Díaz?" Juan noticed a sandstone block building up ahead, with a window containing real glass. A man stood in the open doorway.

"Looking for someone, señor? Can I assist you?" Juan reached the door and noticed a small sign: 'A. Díaz.'

"Are you a land broker? I'm looking for Señor Díaz." Juan raked his hair back. The man smiled widely.

"That's me. What are you looking for? Come in and sit down." He ushered Juan into the small office. He took the chair behind a large table with peeling varnish. Juan sat in the other chair facing him.

"I am a doctor looking for an office to examine and treat patients."

"Don't you make calls to people's homes?"

"My family and I are new in town. We need to find a place that has two or three bedrooms and a garden, and—oh, sorry—this office for patients that I mentioned should be in our home. My wife wants a Moorish style garden with a fountain and spouting water."

"Are you *Señor* Sánchez?" He narrowed his eyes.

"Yes, the very same."

"Your wife has suffered unjustly." Díaz clenched his hands together.

"Thank you for your kind words." Juan rubbed his hands together.

"I have two properties in mind that would combine those elements you mentioned. We can go there now, to one of them. It's nearby."

"I have to be back in less than an hour."

"That is easily done. We'll take my carriage." Señor Díaz extended his hand and gripped Juan's. "My name's Alberto."

"Juan." They settled into an open carriage of polished wood. A fine Arabian horse held its head high and cantered at the command of Señor Díaz.

"The first property is located away from town just a mile, on Olive Way. The Guadalquivir touches it on one edge, and in the spring and fall you can expect a rush of water. There are some olive trees on the land and you can hire a tenant farmer to tend the trees. It's a small side income."

"What about the house?"

"Three bedrooms, a good-sized kitchen and a covered porch that could double as a treatment room. Just needs a curtain. We're almost there." Díaz turned right onto Olive Way. The Arabian strained at the oiled bridle and reins. The road slid over a hill and around a curve. They came to a brushy grove of olive trees. Beyond it sat a house made of sandstone blocks with wide breezeways.

"Come and see." Díaz jumped down and adjusted his blue doublet. He picked his way through the strewn rocks and thistles. A few grasshoppers leaped at the sound of footsteps.

"When was this place last occupied?" said Juan. "There's a lot of work needed to restore the property alone."

"Five years ago a man died suddenly, and his wife left to live with family in Sevilla. Nothing has happened since then. It never has been bought by anyone since then."

"I wonder why. What's wrong with it?"

"It's vulnerable to attack, they say. Out on an isolated road."

"Was the old man murdered?"

"Yes, but come look at the house. It has many rooms." The two men walked through marble and granite floors, now coated with gritty silt and a few tumbleweeds. Juan turned away.

"Sorry, this won't do for my family. I know Sara wouldn't like it." He started back to the carriage. "What about the other property? Where is it?"

"It's on Laurel Lane, just three miles from here. And less isolated."

"If it's on the way back, I'll see it now."

"Let's go." Díaz slapped the reins. The horse picked its way over the stones and onto the road. It set a quick pace, at Díaz' direction. Sunlight leapt through breaks in the leaves above. The clopping of the horses' feet lulled Juan into a reverie. *I hope I can find that place Sara's been dreaming of for so long.* Finally, Díaz took a turn through a grove of poplars. "Here we are."

Díaz gestured toward the house. Juan jumped down and crunched over the small gravel on the drive. A lizard skittered across his shoe. He kicked it away.

"What is this?" Juan approached a compact house of carved sandstone. A Moorish arch led to a central patio. At the center sat a neglected fountain, green and clogged with poplar leaves. The patio's interlocking bricks lay in disarray, many broken or dislodged from their place. Small buildings spread out on all four sides, all needing fresh stucco. Juan walked toward one. "A living room *sala* with ceramic tiles on the floors. Some are broken." He raced to the next module. "A dusty kitchen with lots of shelves and cracked pottery."

"The other two outbuildings have two bedrooms each," said Díaz. "Of course, one could be used for a treatment room for you, doctor."

"There's one thing this house must have—doves. Sara talks about that so often—the sound of doves and moving water."

"Ah, my friend, I can solve that problem. I know just what to do. If you buy the place, I'll see to it you have doves."

Juan smiled. "This has possibilities, but I must get back. Can you bring me here again tomorrow?"

"Of course. We can take a longer look and then discuss the price."

"Now, back to Moguer. I have an appointment," said Juan.

"We'll talk about the doves on the way back to town," said Díaz. He urged the fine horse to go faster. The dust flew from its feet, but the breeze blew it away from their eyes. Díaz told him his plan for the doves. Soon, he tied up in front of his office. Juan leaped down.

"I'll call on you tomorrow." He was gone. Juan trotted to the fountain and saw Catalina was already there.

"Sorry to keep you waiting."

"I only arrived here five minutes ago." Juan took her elbow and assisted her into the cart. He slapped the reins and his horse headed back through town and along Almond Tree Road.

"Here we are. I'll help you with your parcels." Juan and Catalina divided the packages and walked into the kitchen. Sara looked up from the bench.

"I just got up. Was sit a fruitful journey?"

"Lots of vegetables and some fish for dinner," said Catalina.

"And you, Juan?" Sara looked at her husband with wide eyes.

"Hm," said Juan. "I have a lot to think about." He exited the room and went toward Juanito's room. "Is he awake yet?"

"Soon. You'll hear him soon." Juanito let out a yell. Juan laughed.

"You know your son well."

Chapter 33

✵

March 1495

Sara found her second pregnancy more taxing than the first. She woke most days with a sick feeling in her belly. Food made her run outside and retch. The only things that agreed with her were bread and *limonada*, that honey-sweetened lemon drink she had concocted in Naples.

"If I ever own a restaurant again, I'll offer *limonada*. It's so refreshing on a warm day. I always boil the mixture to dissolve the honey. It never once has made me sick." She looked at Margarita, who was sitting on the repaired couch in the guesthouse. "Would you like some more?"

"No, I've had two tumblers full already."

"How are you settling in with Catalina?"

"We get along well, I think. We're just working out where to put all my things. I brought a couple of chests and a bed."

"She has a generous heart. I see why Luis fell in love with her," said Sara.

"Yes, but I want to respect her as the owner of the house."

"Of course."

"What has Juan been doing lately?"

"He's busy all the time visiting sick people in Moguer and around the countryside, he tells me."

"Did he ever find a house for you?"

"He went that first day, but then he's said nothing about it since then. I've asked him over and over. He just clamps his mouth shut and puts on a silly face."

"What does that mean? Did he change his mind? Is he still looking?"

"I don't know, and it's making me crazy." Sara struggled out of the low couch. "Oh, my belly is getting in the way already." She got to her feet and picked up Juanito, who was chasing a spider across the tile floor.

"Bug," he said.

"Yes, another bug. Do you catch them all?" Sara laughed.

"How do you spend your time, Sara? I know you don't feel well most mornings."

"I've been reading, Margarita, when not chasing after Juanito. A book of Andalusian poetry."

"Oh?"

"It was my father's. The poems are lovely. So descriptive and full of longing. I just read one that talks about doves. I've decided doves are my favorite bird. They remind me so much of this area. Southern Spain is home to me." "I've heard some of that type of poetry long ago."

"Listen to this poem I've written. It's in the same spirit of these poems, I hope." Sara stood and began:

> "The vines twine over tree and iron gate,
> Their purple majesty a cloak of splendor.
> Doves laugh for joy and coo to their mates
> As I await the splash of stars on the skirt
> of night."

"It is romantic," said Margarita. She sighed.

"Something wrong?" Sara returned to her place on the couch.

"I miss Rodrigo sometimes."

"I miss my mother, my father and my brother Luis, but to lose your love—that's different." She reached over and squeezed Margarita's hand. "I'm glad you came here. You're a second mother to me."

"Call on me anytime, Sara. You're the daughter I never had." She smiled. "Well, I should go back next door and help Catalina with the noon meal. Why don't you join us? There's plenty."

"Thank you, but I think I'll just eat something here with Juanito."

"He's growing. A lively little boy." Margarita got up and left. Sara sat a while and dozed. The sunshine had fallen on her where she sat.

"Hello, Sara." Juan kissed her on the cheek "My sleeping princess."

"All I do is sleep. Sorry." Sara stirred and got up. "How's your practice going?" She followed him into the kitchen area. "Would you like some *limonada*? I made a big pitcher of it."

"Sure." He poured a tumbler full and took a big gulp.

"How's your practice developing, Juan? Are you happy about how it's going?" Sara cut some cheese for herself and munched on a piece.

"Everyone knows about us and the tribulation you went through, Sara."

"We went through," said Sara.

"Yes, and it seems to have put most people in a favorable disposition toward us. I'm getting many clients because of you, I think."

"That's amazing. I thought everyone would shun us, even though the Queen sent a reprieve."

"*Señora* García, my last patient, spent a lot of time telling me how much she sympathizes with us. My ear is still hot from her many words." Juan pulled on his ear and smiled. "You don't need to hide yourself, Sara. Most people side with you. Your suffering has touched many."

Sara's face turned rosy red. "Maybe I'll start going into town. It would be nice to choose our own food and other necessary items again."

"Just be careful about getting in and out of carts."

"I will. Now, my joy would be complete if we could find a home and settle in it before the baby is born." She looked with large eyes at Juan. He fidgeted. He thought a minute, and then made a decision. He turned to her.

"I have a surprise for you, Sara." Juan rocked back and forth on the bench and let Juanito down. Sara held her expanded middle and listened.

"You've been secretive lately. I'm curious."

"I want to show you something. Could you go with me now?"

"We need to take Juanito." She reached for her toddling son and got a snack of cheese and bread for him. Juanito stuffed the bread in his mouth. "Is it a *big* surprise? You come home dusty or with sawdust in your hair every day."

"I've been seeing many new patients all over the countryside," said Juan.

"I have my suspicions."

"So many questions! Just come and see." Juan gathered up Juanito and took Sara's hand. She swayed back and forth.

"I'm so awkward now, with this growing baby. No graceful steps." She grinned and toddled with exaggerated movements.

"You're beautiful, Sara. An auburn-haired Madonna." Juan stroked her hair. They made their way to the cart.

"Hi, Estela." Sara stroked the horse's soft muzzle. It pawed the ground and tossed its head. Juan helped Sara get into the cart, then he handed Juanito up to her. Taking the reins, Juan coaxed their horse in a new direction. They drove through town, around the fountain. A breeze blew spray from the fountain onto their faces. Sara lifted her face to receive the cooling water. Juan turned onto a poplar-lined road. The tall, narrow trees held their branches up as if reaching for the clouds above.

"Laurel Way? I've never been here before. Hm." She sat up straighter and looked around. "Where are the laurels?"

"We're almost there. Be patient and close your eyes."

Juan found the clump of poplars by the road that signaled where to turn in. He directed the horse to follow the path. As the cart bumped along, Sara's eyelids fluttered. Juanito made noises and waved his hands. Sara gripped him tightly.

"I smell laurels, Juan."

"Don't look! Almost there, Sara," said Juan. He drew up the reins and tied the horse and cart to a shading tree, as was his habit.

"The March sun invites us to explore," said Juan. "No need to hide in the shade. Come, you can look now."

Sara's eyes popped open. She clapped her hands and Juanito's together.

"Juan, how wonderful. Is it our home?"

"Yes, my love. Let me show you what I've been working on the last few months." He lifted Sara with Juanito still in her grasp. Down to the sprouting green grass of spring. Sara let Juanito down and leaped forward up a cobbled footpath. At the end, it led to a central patio surrounded by four white stucco outbuildings. Several workmen were worked at tasks. Sara ran ahead of Juan.

"Oh, a big kitchen. The floor tiles are lovely! And there's more on the counter and walls. Made by local artisans, perhaps?" Juan nodded as he caught up to her. "Oh, and you bought a lot of pots and crockery for me!" She swirled around the room, touching this, sliding her hand along a counter, looking up at a wrought iron chandelier for candles. Each new discovery merited another exclamation of approval.

"The next building has a living room *sala* and dining area, near to the kitchen but away from cooking smells. The prevailing winds will blow them away from the house." Juan gestured and Sara followed his lead.

"Couches with plush pillows and a Berber rug from Moorish times. Do you like the candle chandelier in here, also? It's a high ceiling. We can lower the chandelier to light candles and then hoist it up for lots of light." Juan showed her the way to lower it.

"It will be magnificent for special occasions," said Sara. "Then back to candlesticks on tables for most days." Juan grinned and nodded. Sara took off to the next building in the quadrangle.

"Two bedrooms in each of the next buildings. One will have our bedroom and until the children are bigger, the nursery. The next module, for visitors who stay with us."

Sara ran to Juan and hugged him.

"It's perfect. So beautifully restored. I can see your handiwork in many thoughtful details. I'm so happy." She kissed him with abandon. Juan gasped and drew back.

"Have I made you happy? Is this the home you always dreamed of?"

"Yes, oh yes. And now with Margarita living near us, I feel I have a mother figure to lean on, too." Juan drew Sara to the patio and held her hand.

"This part of the house isn't done yet. But soon, the eight-sided pond will spout streams of water, fed by a water tube coming from the hills over there." He pointed to a distant, rocky outcropping.

"How clever of you, Juan." She hugged him.

"The piping was there. The workers discovered it," said Juan. "They'll be planting vines and flowers in the garden beds by each section of the house. Then they will set up an arch for the vines to tangle onto."

"There's only one thing missing," said Sara. "I hate to complain."

"What is it?" He looked around. "Oh, I know. Senor Díaz brought a pair of doves for the garden." Juan looked around the patio. "You know, I learned something about doves lately, from a wise woman named Margarita."

"Doves?"

"If you build a garden full of water and vines—that's not enough. A dove will only come if she senses tranquility here. That's why doves are considered a sign of peace. Remember, in the Holy Writings Noah sent out a dove that brought back an olive branch."

"And the second time, the dove didn't return. She had found a quiet place to nest. That's what I want our home to be—and our garden." Sara turned her head. She and Juan kept still as statues.

"Look." Sara's eyes went to the tile roof nearby. Two white doves looked down, tentative and ready to fly off. When nobody moved, one flew to the eight-sided pond and then the other followed.

"Hear that?" One bird called to the other, a gentle calling sound. They jumped to the fine gravel in the patio and started pecking around. Their coos alternated between pecking for specks of food.

"It does! It sounds like laughter. Or at least, glee."

"I hear it, although I never believed it before."

"Now, I know this is home. A place of peace, everything made right again by our loving God, and doves who have taken residence in our garden." Sara took a deep breath and brushed away a tear.

"May it ever be so, my dear Sara." Juan held her close. *Shalom.*

A Few Parting Words:

Proverbs 13:12 says, "Hope deferred makes the heart sick, but a longing fulfilled is a tree of life." Langston Hughes, the African American poet, wrote eloquently in "Harlem" about the results of a dream deferred. But here, we have come to the end of Sara's story where she experiences a longing fulfilled.

Certainly there is satisfaction in reaching a long-awaited goal. We hope and dream, despair at any setback, re-focus our energies and persevere. But, the results are seldom under our control.

The 200,000 Jews expelled from Spain in 1492 had little control over their lives. They left their assets and fled, many paying huge sums of money for passage, eventually landing in a hostile country. Only the Ottoman Empire received them with welcome.

Sara faced her fear of the Inquisition and returned to her homeland. Juan returned from the New World against great odds and found his wife and child. They still struggled and faced the Inquisition once more as they sought to rebuild their lives and home. (The historical Juan Sanchez wasn't so fortunate.)

What is it about going home? People say you can't go home again, but many still try. That ideal spot of paradise is often changed, ruined to the mind's eye. A longing fulfilled, whether flawed or not, feeds our desire that all may be made right and good and secure.

We satisfy that hunger with possessions and often work very hard to create a perfect setting. Note the abundance of home renovation shows currently available. But, an ideal environment fails if people can't find harmony with one another.

True fulfillment comes as we reunite with loved ones and seek reconciliation when some injustice mars our existence.

Facing difficulty and conquering fears gives rise to a new sprout on that tree of life. May you find the courage to bring your hopes to fulfillment.

Home also makes me think of food. Have you noticed I take great delight in describing meals throughout Sara's saga? Home is a place of hospitality and an abundant table promotes a wonderful sense of deep satisfaction and joy. I've noticed that in Psalm 23:5 it says, "You prepare a table before me in the presence of my enemies." In Zephaniah 3:17 it says, "He leads me to his banqueting table."

When I first saw *Babette's Feast*, that foreign film depicting the pinched existence of a Danish religious community, I was swept away with the power of one meal, a banquet prepared by a servant (formerly a Parisian chef) who won the lottery and wanted to help heal strife within the community. A meal prepared with love and abundance, led long-broken relationships to heal and laughter to be restored. It felt sacramental.

Sara's story is complete, but new adventures wait. What happens to Juanito when he grows up? And, what about Brother Mateo? Will he embrace a new cause in his mature years? Look for new stories to come—

By the way, Juan Sanchez and Luis Torres, two actual names of people on the *Santa Maria* ship's roster, presumably perished at the burning of the fort at La Navidad in the New World. Luis Torres is celebrated now as the first person of Jewish descent to die in the New World. Juan Sanchez' body may have never been found, giving me license to bring him back to his true love, Sara Elena. With incomplete journals of Columbus and a voyage cloaked in mystery, I have freedom. After all, we needed a happy ending!

Love to all my readers—

Beryl Carpenter, August 2017

Words and Foreign Phrases

Abuelo—grandfather (Spanish)

Andare con Dio—go with God (Italian)

Arquebus—an early rifle, using a ball and loading ram. When the trigger was squeezed, a curved arm known as the serpentine was lowered, plunging a slow-burning match into the flash pan and firing the weapon. (Alternate spelling: harquebus)

Basil—used to relieve headache

Buona fortuna—good fortune (Italian)

Capisco—I understand (Italian)

Capsaicin—crushed red hot peppers, used to heal muscle and joint pain

Cerveza—beer (Spanish)

Che rimedio—what remedy (Italian)

Cinnamon—bark of a tree, which is used to control indigestion and regulate cholesterol

Crenelated—regular indentations along the top of a tower or castle for defense

Crujiente—crunchy (Spanish)

Epasote—Caribbean and Mexican herb for indigestion

Guapo—handsome (Spanish)

Mal di testa e liquido nei polmoni—headache and liquid in the lungs (Italian)

Molte grazie—many thanks (Italian)

Mozo—orderly, cabin boy, waiter (Spanish)

Niño—male infant or small child (Spanish)

Non bene—not good (Italian)

Neem—plant grown in Caribbean; leaves are made into tea; calms rapid heartbeat

Noni juice—juice of this Caribbean fruit treats fatigue

Olio di menta piperita—oil of peppermint, used to aid breathing (Italian)

Paseo—a walk (Spanish)

Pomade—a preparation to make the hair shiny, made of wax or lard and fragrance

Salmorejo—a cold soup of pureed vegetables served in the summer months in Spain

Tinto de verano—"summer wine," usually a diluted red wine with spices

Toca—waterboarding; torture device used by the Inquisition

Turmeric—bitter yellow powder used in curries, and to heal inflammation

Printed in the United States
By Bookmasters